THE LEGACY SERIES

Maximum Speed
Kevin Clouther

Reach Her in This Light
Jane Curtis

The Spirit in My Shoes
John Michael Cummings

*The Effects of Urban Renewal on Mid-Century America and
Other Crime Stories*
Jeff Esterholm

What Makes You Think You're Supposed to Feel Better
Jody Hobbs Hesler

Fugitive Daydreams
Leah McCormack

Hoist House: A Novella & Stories
Jenny Robertson

Finding the Bones: Stories & A Novella
Nikki Kallio

Self-Defense
Corey Mertes

Where Are Your People From?
James B. De Monte

Sometimes Creek
Steve Fox

The Plagues
Joe Baumann

The Clayfields
Elise Gregory

Kind of Blue
Christopher Chambers

Evangelina Everyday
Dawn Burns

Township
Jamie Lyn Smith

Responsible Adults
Patricia Ann McNair

Great Escapes from Detroit
Joseph O'Malley

Nothing to Lose
Kim Suhr

The Appointed Hour
Susanne Davis

WELCOME BACK TO THE WORLD

"Life can get serious fast. Across six stories and one novella, Davidson follows characters learning to live in a world not as they want it to be, but as it is. An impressive set of stories from a skilled observer of the human animal."

—*KIRKUS REVIEWS*

"Davidson's gorgeous prose never overshadows story. It all works together beautifully: characters well-drawn and surprising, stories with suspense and satisfying endings, places that ring true with the felt life Davidson has observed. He takes to heart the advice of Henry James—be the kind of person on whom nothing is lost. With authority and authenticity, Davidson has become a truth teller and purveyor of hope, a master of the short form. Bravo!"

—PATRICIA HENLEY
author of *Hummingbird House*
National Book Award Finalist

"These striking, deeply moving stories took me in and held me. Their generous range and tender vision—in prose irradiated with compassion, sensuousness, a gentle yet lively attunement to absurdity, and always a great, thoughtful love—won my heart. Each superbly imagined story welcomes us into a palpable world, and Rob Davidson's diverse ensemble struggles passionately to love that world. We lucky readers dwell within them every step—and in each story's wake, feel an aura of revitalized wonder."

—JOAN FRANK
author of *Where You're All Going, Late Work,* and *Juniper Street*

"Rob Davidson's stories are adventurous, accessible and moving. He is a master craftsman at home in the heart of his greatest subject in this collection—love. I love these stories, too. They give me hope, most honestly and resolutely. I'm in the hands of a major American storyteller."

—STEPHEN D. GUTIERREZ
author of *Captain Chicano Draws a Line
in the American Sand*

"Rob Davidson's *Welcome Back to the World* is an invitation to linger in the goodness that lives beneath despair, that shines through loneliness and the shadows of mistakes made. Primarily told in the flickering glow of Covid and the darkness of Trump-time, these stories somehow emit beauty and yearn toward a collective understanding. Davidson's characters, despite their misguided choices, their bad behaviors, ache for compassion and forgiveness, and we, Davidson's readers, allow them these things. In prose well-made and places stunningly rendered, *Welcome Back to the World* is a reminder that brightness, despite the odds, is possible."

—PATRICIA ANN MCNAIR
author of *Responsible Adults*

"The novella and stories in Rob Davidson's *Welcome Back to the World* are possessed by his best writing. His lyrical, detailed, and precise language makes these fictions vivid and sensual, compelling and mysterious, and the reading experience is a delight. Davidson captures the complexity of characters struggling with sadness, fear, shame, grief—a broken world. Davidson masterfully creates places where characters experience the wonder of transformation—no matter how hard they try to fight it."

—FRED ARROYO
author of *Sown in Earth: Essays of Memory and Belonging*

WELCOME

BACK

ROB DAVIDSON

TO THE

WORLD

CORNERSTONE PRESS
UNIVERSITY OF WISCONSIN-STEVENS POINT

Cornerstone Press, Stevens Point, Wisconsin 54481
Copyright © 2024 Rob Davidson
www.uwsp.edu/cornerstone

Printed in the United States of America by
Point Print and Design Studio, Stevens Point, Wisconsin

Library of Congress Control Number: 2024942406
ISBN: 978-1-960329-48-6

This is a work of fiction. Names, characters, businesses, places, events, and incidents are either the products of the author's imagination or used in a fictitious manner. Any resemblance to actual persons, living or dead, or actual events is purely coincidental.

Cornerstone Press titles are produced in courses and internships offered by the Department of English at the University of Wisconsin–Stevens Point.

DIRECTOR & PUBLISHER
Dr. Ross K. Tangedal

EXECUTIVE EDITORS
Jeff Snowbarger, Freesia McKee

EDITORIAL DIRECTOR
Ellie Atkinson

SENIOR EDITORS
Brett Hill, Grace Dahl

PRESS STAFF
Paige Beiver, Sam Bjork, Chloe Cieszynski, Gwen Goetter, Sophie McPherson, Eva Nielsen, Holly White, Ava Willett

For my parents, Don and Mary Davidson

ALSO BY ROB DAVIDSON:

Fiction

What Some Would Call Lies

Spectators

The Farther Shore

Field Observations

Criticism

The Master and the Dean: The Literary Criticism of Henry James and William Dean Howells

Contents

Unfinished Business

1

Claire dropped by Mark's Midtown gallery one morning, visibly upset. "I just got the worst phone call from Mom's roommate."

Apparently, Solange had gone for a walk in Golden Gate Park and had gotten lost. She found the roommate's number in her cell and texted her. The roomie walked down to the park, found Solange, and brought her home. Solange was perfectly sweet about the whole thing, but the roommate told Claire: Your mother misses work shifts. She can't remember where she works. Some days she's fine, has it all together, but on the bad days she just seems lost.

"I don't mean to pry," the woman said, "but I think there's something, you know, way wrong."

The lapses had started years ago, when Solange still lived in Sacramento. Missed lunch dates. Misplaced keys and wallets. Forgetting where she'd parked her car. She laughed it off, making quips about middle age. Mark didn't think much of it. Solange had always been absent-minded, caught-up in herself, the star of her own absurd cabaret.

Now his daughter stood before him, insisting that it was time to do something. Her mother needed tests. She needed help, their help.

Mark closed his eyes. Claire might be right, but damn if it didn't touch a nerve. It seemed he would never, ever get past this woman's place in his life. Just hearing her name sometimes felt like being stabbed in the side.

One good thing to come out of the divorce, he'd decided, was the freedom from obligation. And Solange, bless her fickle heart, never asked for anything. She had at least that much dignity—that and a truckload of pride.

He rose from his chair and hugged his daughter. "I'm sorry, sweetheart. I can't."

"Dad!"

Claire might not understand, but Solange would. Not that she'd ever ask. Anyway, that was enough.

AND SO MARK STOOD IDLY BY as Claire made several trips into San Francisco to visit her mother, getting her signed up for health insurance, scheduling appointments and escorting her to them. Finally, after rounds of referrals, the Memory and Aging Center at UCSF delivered a diagnosis: early-onset Alzheimer's. Solange spoke of putting up a fight, defying the odds, but there were no odds. This wasn't a bet on chance. She would eventually need an assisted living arrangement, the doctors counseled. It was hard to say just when; EOA develops at different rates. But every time Claire tried to talk to her mother about it, Solange became angry and defensive. She had no plan and seemed unwilling to formulate one.

All of this angered Mark. Solange was colossally irresponsible, self-centered, naïve—oh, the thousand complaints he'd harbored in the years since the split. And Claire, poor Claire, always willing to step in, to try again, to speak reason to this, this, this...

Who was he, criticizing a woman diagnosed with Alzheimer's?

Mark and Claire spoke about it often. Solange's diagnosis meant Claire had a fifty-fifty chance of inheriting the condition, an entirely frightening thought. More immediately, there was the question of what to do about Solange. Claire wanted her mother to return to Sacramento. She and Mark discussed it one morning in the living room.

"She hates Sac," Mark reminded her. "And anyway, where would she live? Rents are getting nearly as bad here."

Claire said nothing, only smiled. Mark felt his ears burning. He hadn't seen this coming, but he should have.

"Out of the question," he said.

"Why?"

A long, fiery reply flashed through his head, but he held back. His tirades against Solange upset Claire, and now, with the diagnosis, they could only be cruel.

"She'll never agree," he said.

"I think we can persuade her."

Mark tapped a finger against his coffee cup. "What if I don't agree?"

She sat forward, elbows on knees. "We'll set her up in the second bedroom."

Mark smiled. There was no second bedroom. Claire meant his study.

"It's just temporary," she explained. "A year, maybe two. Then we transition her into a home."

"You really think your mother will agree to assisted living?"

"At a certain point she won't have a choice."

True enough. But he didn't see how any of this could work. Solange still had a few of her wits about her, and she would never agree to any of it.

"I can talk her into it."

"Solange has never been talked into anything," he quipped. "She does all the talking."

"This is different."

"How?"

Claire drew in her lip. "She's scared."

Morning sunlight illuminated a golden slice of polished wood floor, revealing dust and dog hair. Everything needed a good sweeping. Mark suddenly resented the sunlight.

"We're the only people she can rely on," Claire added, breaking the silence.

This was basically true. There was an older sister in Maryland, estranged. Mark hadn't spoken to her since the divorce. He doubted Solange had, either.

This was all a bad idea, a crazy idea. Solange would never agree, and if she did she'd drive him nuts. It'd taken him years to get over the divorce, to make his peace with it. Selling the house in Land Park, downsizing into the Tower District bungalow, completely re-orienting his life as a single parent, a divorced dad. Alone.

Yet not alone. Claire had lived with him through that long and painful time, returning to Sacramento after one difficult year at UC-San Diego. Unlike her mother, Claire didn't suffer from wanderlust. Coming home had been good for her. She was doing reasonably well at Sac State, not stellar, but holding it together. She'd finish her degree in another year or two—it was looking like the six-year plan for Claire—and then test the job market.

When Claire was young, Mark used to joke that he'd change the locks the day she left for college. But the truth was he was happy having her around. If she were to leave, and one day she would, he would not cherish the isolation. He liked having someone to talk to; he liked cooking dinner for two, splitting a bottle of wine.

In the end, Mark agreed to think it over. Claire deserved as much. But Solange? He had a few ideas about what she deserved. She was, he supposed, just being herself: guileless, defiant, profane. But so what? No one could fault him for turning away. No one but Claire, and that truly meant something to him. More like everything at this point. For her sake, the situation required a certain, specific delicacy.

He did not have the words—not yet, anyway—to reject her plan. Of course it would never, ever happen. Which meant that some other thing must happen. Solange's failure to plan for herself was his chief obstacle at this point.

He needed to see Solange, to talk to her, to sound her out. But he must be careful. Any direct inquiry would be rebuffed. If he were to approach, he'd need a pretense. Something compelling, irrefusable. They exchanged a quick round of text messages. He had something important to discuss about Claire, he said. Nothing dire. He would be in the City next week on business. Could they meet? It was agreed.

On the day, he drove around the San Pablo Bay, coming into San Francisco via the Golden Gate to Solange's place in the Outer Richmond. A little early, he walked over to Sutro Heights and stood overlooking the ruins of the old bath house. He remembered a visit years ago with Solange, scouring the site for bits of blue and green glass which she collected and later arranged into a collage. She presented it to him for his birthday. He remembered being pleasantly surprised by the gesture, and the collage wasn't bad, either. One of her better pieces. It was early in their marriage. She still thought of herself as an artist.

And then it was time. Solange met him at the door, blinking her eyes and smiling. "Mark! What on earth are you doing here?" She looked thinner, with cheap plastic bracelets on her wrists and a fuchsia headband.

"We agreed to meet."

"We did?"

He showed her their text exchanges. Her eyes narrowed as she read them. "Oh, yes. Yes, of course. Silly me." She smiled.

"May I come in?"

He followed her up a narrow, dark staircase to apartment 2A, which opened into a spacious living room with windows facing the avenue, filling the room with natural light. Billowy couches with bedspreads draped over them bookended a low coffee table. There were paperback books piled here and there, a ceramic tea mug, somebody's Apple laptop with stickers plastered all over the back. Exactly like a college apartment.

He followed her into the kitchen. "What on earth ever made you come and see me?"

He didn't feel like spinning yarns. He muttered something about being in town on business and Claire urging him to drop by.

"Did she leave something here?"

"She thought it might be good to touch base in light of the diagnosis."

"Oh that!" she said brightly. "It'll be years before it kicks in. I'm not about to let it slow me down. Now let me fix you a cup of tea, and you tell me how the gallery is doing."

He rattled on about the gallery. He could tell she didn't know any of the names he was dropping, though they were good names, names to know, names on many people's lips, in fact the gallery was doing well. But she wasn't really listening, so he stopped.

On every kitchen cabinet were colored sticky notes: bowls, mugs, plates. On the fridge a big fluorescent note: "Solange: rent due on the 5th!" He asked what she'd been up to that morning.

"I did yoga with this teacher I've been following. In her forties but so fit. And the most amazing tattoos. Did you ever get one?"

"A tattoo? No. You?"

"Two on my back. This afternoon I'm job hunting." She regaled him with the tale of her last job, waitressing at a fondue place in the Mission. She'd been let go after a decline in business.

"I thought you were temping," he said. "A lawyer's office?"

"Oh, that. You know lawyers. They want you there at nine o'clock on the dot. And I try, I really do, but it doesn't always happen." She placed a mug before him. Behind her, the tea kettle began its gentle rattle on the stovetop.

"Why not?" Mark asked. "Lots of people in San Francisco have be at work on time, or they'll be fired."

"But you know me. I'm not a slave to…." She tapped her wristwatch. A puzzled look crossed her face. "This, this… hand-clock."

"Most people call it a watch."

Her chin trembled. "I know that."

The kettle whistled. Solange turned off the gas. Then she began opening and closing the cabinets. "I can never find the tea. My roommates keep moving things."

Mark reached over and pulled open a drawer with a sticky note on it that read "TEA" in Claire's handwriting.

"Oh, thank you."

She sat across from him. He watched as she bobbed her tea bag up and down in a precise, sinuous rhythm. Even the way she pulled her tea bag out, wrapping the string around it and squeezing the remaining liquid, was graceful, even mesmerizing. He missed simply watching her. She was pleasant to observe.

"Are you seeing anyone?" she asked.

He shook his head. "You?"

"A couple of guys off and on. I keep it light. But they can be so demanding. You'd think at our age they'd have gotten over the commitment thing."

He frowned. "Yes, you would think that."

She gave him a hard stare. "Why did you come?"

"I told you. I thought I should check in after the diagnosis."

"I'm fine. Can't you see that?"

He drummed his fingers on the table. "Do you have any sort of plan for what happens next?"

"Do any of us?"

"Come on, be serious."

She rolled her eyes. "Oh, here it comes."

He reviewed what he knew. Claire had signed her up for Healthy San Francisco, the city health plan, but it didn't cover long-term care or hospice. He'd been researching her options.

Solange raised an eyebrow. "Whatever on earth for?"

"Because you need a plan."

"Eventually," she conceded, blowing on her tea. "I'm years away from that."

"But by the time things take a turn, when you're…. Now's the time to plan, is what I'm saying."

Solange gave him a patronizing smile. "Mark, darling, it's really none of your business."

So far, he'd planned for this. Almost line-for-line. He knew where he had to go.

"Claire is concerned. It's eating her up. That makes it my business." He sipped his tea, which tasted bitter. He reached for the milk. "I trust you understand what's happening. Within a year or two… I mean, worst case."

She picked up a spoon from the table and turned it around in her hand. She shook her head.

"You will need help," he said. "You just admitted it."

"I did not."

"Just a minute ago, when I said you needed a plan. You said 'eventually.'"

She sat back and folded her arms. "You're beginning to annoy me."

"And you're making this difficult."

Her eyes flared at him, jaw set tight. "How am I making it difficult? You show up, unannounced, and start making demands on me. For no reason at all."

Mark pressed a finger to the tabletop. "We agreed to discuss this because our daughter, Claire, is worried. Very worried."

"She worries too much," Solange said.

"If you won't do something for yourself, can't you do it for her?"

"You know what she needs? She needs to finish school. Finish, or just quit."

Mark gave a little laugh. "Sure, quit and walk away. Just start over, isn't that the next step? Great advice."

"She's wasting the best years of her life."

"Is that what you call it? A husband, a daughter, a home. Wasting your life?"

Solange threw up a hand. "What do you want from me?"

"I want you to acknowledge this condition, how serious it is. You have no plan, and you're worrying our daughter sick about it. Claire is concerned—more concerned than you, apparently!"

"Yes," she said, sitting back in her chair. "She's like her father, meddlesome and predictable. And in that regard a disappointment."

Mark seethed quietly, letting the sting throb. He could accept the jab at him, but Claire?

"How dare you," he hissed.

Solange rubbed the bridge of her nose. "Please don't tell her I said that."

They sat quietly, each stewing. Mark found himself studying a corner of the kitchen floorboard, a dark line of mildew along its seam.

"It's just life, Mark. Things happen. And when they do, people find solutions. New things happen. You can't control every little thing. That's always been your problem. You don't know how to let a person just be."

He leaned forward, over the table. "This isn't about me, Solange. It's about you. This diagnosis is real. And guess what? You don't get to hit reset on this one. The usual drop and run, it ain't gonna work!"

She slammed a fist on the table. "You're not my doctor! Or my shrink! Stay out of it!"

"I'm trying to help you!"

"How are you helping? You came here to insult me. You came to pick open old wounds, your wounds. You're like a child."

A nasty comeback rose to his lips, but he squelched it. He knew where all this was headed. He'd been there too many times already.

He stormed out of the apartment, stomping down the hallway, letting the heavy security door slam shut with a resounding thud. He walked for a while in a blind rage, his mind a red-hot tangle. He made his way to a bar stool on Geary Boulevard, where he ordered a double whiskey and began to collect his thoughts. He didn't know what angered him more: Solange's stubborn rudeness, or his willingness, once again, to step into her field of fire. It had been a mistake to see her, a mistake even to reach out to her, to initiate contact. It violated a cardinal rule he'd set for himself after the split. Damn it, he knew better! He wouldn't make the same mistake again. If Claire wanted to help, Claire could find a way. He was through.

2

Mark and Solange each had their own version of what went wrong and who was to blame. For him, Solange's choices amounted to a protracted midlife crisis. (She hated when he called it that, but what else was he going to call it?) There had been the unfinished business of living, things that, according to Solange, could not be accomplished within the strictures of marriage. These had included the predictable sexual escapades, none of which Mark would have objected to, had he been asked. (He hadn't been asked.) They included the requisite drifting around: to a spirituality center in Vermont; to a meditation retreat in British Columbia; to an arts co-op in Marfa, Texas. When she returned to Sacramento, she wasn't ready for anything permanent, not even a lease. She rented rooms in people's houses, or flopped on couches. She spent a few weeks living in a yurt in Grass Valley. Each situation was deliberately tentative, with as few ties as possible. She had become, she announced, "resistant to commitment."

"Not exactly news," Mark quipped.

"I mean in new ways."

"You mean in all ways."

Mark believed she was experiencing a second childhood. Raised by a brilliant but distant father, a professor of classics, and a mother more attuned to marching on the state capitol than parenting, Solange had enjoyed maximum freedom and she'd done, in her own words, exactly nothing with it. She'd been adrift all her life, searching for the missing puzzle piece. But every time she thought she'd found it, it failed to fit. And so she ran to the next thing. Eternal window shopping, Mark had once explained to Claire. The tumbling tumbleweed, that's your mother in a—

"Don't say 'in a nutshell,'" Claire groaned. "Mom could never be contained in a nutshell. Her life is too big, too expansive for that."

"Yes, like an oil spill. Messy and toxic."

Claire rolled her eyes, a curt dismissal she'd mastered at the age of ten. "The only person interested in reducing anything to a nutshell is you. You like compact meanings, small truths."

"You make me sound narrow-minded."

She smiled and put a hand on his forearm. "You are narrow-minded, Dad. But in the most adorable way."

Claire loved and respected her mother, which was her right, but she couldn't live with her, either. The two quarreled endlessly, the mother incapable of imposing rules on a daughter who openly asked for guidance, for boundaries. And that's why, in those years of rambling and drifting, Solange left the day-to-day business of parenting to Mark.

He gave Claire curfews, balanced meals, limited screen time. When she turned sixteen she got a job sacking groceries. ("Safeway!" Solange protested. "Don't you know they're in bed with Monsanto? It's unconscionable.") Claire learned to balance her checkbook, paid for her own gas and a share of the car insurance. She willingly accepted it all, keen to learn how "adult stuff" was done.

Claire had never been happy about the divorce. Twelve at the time of the split, she was old enough to comprehend that her parents were unhappy. Solange, always a little too eager to share, explained her reasons for leaving. It was not well received. Mark could do little to help. He understood Solange's yearnings, perhaps even the need to act on them, but not at the expense of their marriage. Privately, he suggested she be free to roam for a time, to do whatever she needed to do, but to stay married. Solange would not have it. It was she who insisted on the divorce, a final, irreconcilable parting.

What she wanted, Mark finally decided, she wanted for herself. It was not mutual, it was not a good idea, it was not anything other than a wife and mother walking away from her family by choice. Through it all, father and daughter drew closer, united in their suffering, both of them bewildered by Solange's decision. What can a twelve-year-old know of wanderlust or weltschmerz? Her mother had walked away and left her. What was there to say? There might be reasons, but those reasons wouldn't make sense to a kid. After one of her many breakdowns, a teenaged Claire confessed to Mark that she had one wish, one desperate dream: for her parents to reconcile, for someone to wave a magic wand and put it all back together again, the way it had been.

Mark tried to explain, in the gentlest way possible, that it couldn't happen.

"Why?"

Her mother had other plans. He couldn't explain it, exactly. That wasn't his job.

"But what if she did come back?"

The look on her face, so frank and vulnerable, too earnest to be anything other than heartbreaking—ah, what could he do?

"I don't know."

"So… maybe?"

"Oh, sweetheart," he murmured, pulling her close.

After many moments like that, all handled by him alone, Mark's hurt turned into bitterness and resentment. Solange was weak and selfish. She missed the best years of Claire's childhood, the ultimate cut and run. People like that—they don't deserve your sympathy, generosity, or tolerance.

3

Mark sat in his Midtown Sacramento gallery on a March morning, the back windows open to the warm spring air. He loved best the quiet, peaceful hours before the gallery opened at eleven. It was then he could focus on queries, make plans, and see all the possibilities.

He was interrupted by a phone call. A sergeant from the San Francisco police department, looking for Mr. Mark Stroud. Concerning Ms. Solange Stroud. The officer reported that Ms. Stroud had been found beaten, possibly raped, in Golden Gate Park. Likely she'd been there for several hours. There were injuries. Ms. Stroud had mentioned him and a Claire Stroud by name.

As Mark listened, an icy wave washed over him.

"Claire, yes, our daughter," Mark said. "Have you called her?"

"We have no contact information. The victim has no ID or paperwork on her. I'm working off an internet search at this point. Found you at your place of business."

Thank god for that website, which he'd paid through the nose to develop. "Where is she now?"

Zuckerberg SF General, the safety net hospital for homeless in the city. Mark winced at the word. Had she been? Claire would have told him. Or he should have known.

SOLANGE LAY IN BED, all bandages and IV lines and a cast on one arm, in an open ward. No privacy. She was pretty doped up from the pain meds and slept a lot. When she was awake, tears glistened her cheeks. Mark dabbed at them with a tissue, whispering comforting words. The nurses came by often, assuring both of them that Solange would be all right. She was in the clear now, and safe. The worst was behind them.

Mark took comfort in their words, and hoped Solange did, too. In all the years he'd known her, he'd never seen her so broken. Even at her lowest moments, she'd always had spunk and zeal. It was what he'd loved most about her. He'd always been attracted to intelligent women, outspoken women, assertive women. Even now, when their love had dissipated and been transformed into other energies, he respected this about her. Maybe that is what shook him so terribly when he saw her in that hospital bed. To see a strong person broken, dispirited, weeping and incoherent with pain… it frightened him.

When visiting hours ended, he assured Solange that he'd be back the next day. An attendant pointed the way out. He walked in a kind of daze. The hallways of the trauma ward were lit with buzzing fluorescent lights. The floors were dull and streaked from the rubber tires of gurneys speeding through, the knicked walls yellow like rancid butter. Emergencies all the time, bodies hurtling down hallways in crisis. The smell, a grim mix of sickness and bleach, the stench of injury and death.

From far down a hallway, a solitary voice screamed, desperate and hoarse. "No one's helping me! Why won't anyone help me!"

OVER THE NEXT TWO DAYS, they pieced together what they could. Solange had been evicted from her apartment in February after falling behind on the rent. No known current address. She'd been flopping on friends' couches. Then things took a turn. She couldn't remember exactly what had happened, how she'd ended up sleeping in the park. She had no address book. Her phone had been stolen or lost. Then the attack, of which she had no memory. Probably a blessing, the doctors said. The rape kit confirmed there had been a sexual assault.

Mark returned to Sacramento. He had a show opening in two weeks for which he was behind schedule. Claire stayed on in San Francisco, sitting with Solange for every available visiting hour, holding her hand. She called home each night to update Mark and discuss options. They agreed that Solange could no longer care for herself. The days of independent living were over. The question was where she would go. Mark insisted they research every option.

The next Sunday, when the gallery was closed and Mark had a little time, he drove back into the City to see Solange, who looked much better. He took Claire to Delfina in the Mission for lunch. Then they walked over to Mission Dolores Park. They sat on a bench at the top of the hill, overlooking the downtown skyline. Kids took turns riding skateboards down the long, curving sidewalk that ran the length of the park, rushing at breakneck speed, spilling out onto Eighteenth Street.

Claire reviewed what she'd learned. The city health plan did not cover long-term care. There were assisted care facilities for the homeless, but with limited space and availability. The same held true for hospice, when it came to that. "But I will never allow her to—"

"—Of course not," Mark agreed. "We'll upgrade her insurance. What's she got in the bank?"

"You know the answer to that."

"She must be eligible for assistance through Medi-Cal or something." He'd do the homework, research their options. He could pay some of it. Hell, he'd pay all of it—though even as he said it, he knew that might be impossible. God bless America, land of cheap guns and overpriced healthcare.

"The consultant says Mom is one of the lucky ones," Claire said, softly. "She still has family who care. There's a lot who don't."

A skateboarder came screaming down the sidewalk, crouched low, arms spread, sweeping back and forth in wide arcs until his board flew out from under him, spilling him into the grass. A shaved ice vendor pushing his cart up the steep hill stopped and shook his head. "Tonto estúpido."

Mark laughed, he wasn't sure why.

"Dad," Claire said, "it's time."

"Yes, we should get back."

She put a hand on his arm. "To take her home."

Mark looked into Claire's gray eyes, strikingly identical to her mother's—one of their closest shared features. The urgency of the moment had settled on her, he saw that. A resolve emanated from her, something cool and focused. She was a woman now, twenty-two years of age. She knew what she wanted. She wanted to care for her destitute, broken mother. This meant taking Solange into their home, an impossible and yet somehow inescapable conundrum. The look in her eyes, a fierceness that demanded consent.

4

They set Solange up in the home office with a cot. She had no belongings. She couldn't recall where her things had gone, with whom she'd left anything. She entered the house physically feeble, seemingly having aged ten years. She wept frequently. She didn't want to be left alone. She spent long hours sitting in front of the television watching nature shows or travel documentaries. The old Solange had never owned a television, scoffing at the drones wasting their lives glued to it.

She was not herself, not exactly. And though neither Mark nor Claire said as much, he knew they both were worried: when was that point where the identity slips away, like dissipating smoke? When are you no longer you?

Claire tracked down the remaining friends she could find. A few of them had some of Solange's things—books, photos, vinyl LPs. A roommate from the apartment had graciously tossed a few items in a box when the landlord evicted Solange in absentia. The rest of it was just gone: Solange's art pieces; her photo albums; her clothes, jewelry, and books. Even her passport. A life in things, vanished.

Something about all of this—its seeming suddenness, its irrevocability—startled Mark. He'd never told Claire how, after Solange left, he kept smelling her all over the house, the earthy, raw human scent of her. In towels and bedsheets, in the linen closet, in his car. How she left various pieces of herself behind: a bracelet dropped behind a chest of drawers; a pair of panties inside a pillowcase; a pair of her reading glasses in the pocket of his shirt (she was eternally misplacing them). He never told her of finding strands of Solange's hair, graying and kinky with curls, on his shirts and sweaters, each strand pulling at his heart.

SOLANGE GRADUALLY IMPROVED, and when she could get up and walk on her own, things took a turn for the better. Physically, her appetite returned. Mark enjoyed cooking for all three of them, big meals that required a bit of planning, especially if he and Claire wanted to eat meat. (Solange was still vegan. She hadn't forgotten that.) But her spirit was slow to recover. She didn't want to leave the house. She puttered around in the back yard, tending Mark's flower beds. She wanted to start a small garden. Mark knocked together a few planting boxes, raised beds for tomatoes, peppers, and lettuce. Solange spent entire mornings out there, patiently tending each bed. They were immaculate, not a single weed to be seen.

During that summer, Solange seemed physically healthy, recovering from the bulk of her injuries. But she moved slower, and her mind continued to slip gears. There were good days when she could hold a conversation, when the memories came bubbling back up to the surface. She was lucid then, but it was never long before the sparkle died out of those eyes and the glassy, half-vacant gaze returned.

Claire and Solange went out a lot together. Shopping (Solange still liked to buy scarves), coffee, the movies. When Mark asked if it wasn't nerve-wracking, having to keep an eye on her mother all the time, Claire just smiled and said they held hands or linked arms and that made it easy. Mark rarely took Solange anywhere by himself. He saw the hours he spent alone with her as a kind of sentence, only he was in jail, too. Hell, they might as well still be married.

Only they were not married. They were divorced. He had no formal obligation to this woman. All of this was, he privately reminded himself, because of Claire. Claire's choice, Claire's wish, and Claire's authority, for it was she who held power of attorney. When the time came, she would be the one to move Solange into assisted housing.

As summer moved slowly into autumn, Mark asked Claire about returning to school. She said she was taking the next year off.

"You mean the fall term," he said. She'd withdrawn from last spring's classes to be with her mother. Taking fall off would make it an entire academic year.

"I know that."

"But by spring don't you think…." He looked to Solange, sitting at the kitchen table, flipping through a travel magazine.

"I don't know. That's why I'm planning to take the whole year off. I don't want to rush anything."

"I don't want to rush either," he said, "but don't you think sooner might be better, in a sense? It'll be hard later, for her."

"We'll move her when it's the right time. This isn't the right time."

"Your life is on hold."

Claire looked into the kitchen, smiling. "This is my life."

ONE AFTERNOON CLAIRE WAS GONE. Mark arranged for an employee to cover his shift at the gallery, but she canceled at the last minute, meaning the gallery was now closed on a Saturday during peak hours. Mark knew it was not a catastrophe in the grand scheme of things, but it needled him. Somehow, by some strange twist of fate, he'd been saddled not merely with receiving his ex-wife into his house, but babysitting her. The cosmic injustice of it seemed like a personal slight.

Solange was moody and restless, moving between the kitchen and the living room. She couldn't sit still. She said several times to Mark, "I don't know why I'm here. Why am I here?"

He explained, again, that she was living with them now. They were taking care of her.

"Who is?"

"Claire and I."

"Where is Claire?"

"She's out with a friend. She'll be back in a couple of hours."

Solange shook her head and frowned. "I don't know why I'm here." She walked into the front hall and started arranging a scarf around her neck. "I'm going for a walk," she announced.

"You want to go for a walk? All right, give me five minutes."

"I'm fine by myself."

"No, you are not."

She narrowed her eyes. "I'm not a baby!"

Pretty damn close, he thought. He looked at the clock. "You need to take your pills."

"I already took those!"

"Not today, you haven't." He showed her the little chart they kept, which she initialed every time so they could all keep track.

"Oh, shove them up your ass."

It was outrageous, what he was putting up with. From her, of all people. The nurse who visited every two weeks told him that people with dementia often lash out. "They're frustrated because they don't understand what's happening to them. They'll say things you wouldn't believe. But you have to remember why it's happening. You can't let it get to you."

Mark's phone rang from somewhere in the house. He remembered he'd agreed to take a business call, and as he darted off to find his phone he barked at Solange to stay put and wait for him. He took the call in his bedroom/study—an artist Mark would be showing in a few weeks. The guy was bickering about his contract, angry about shipping costs—all things they'd already gone over. It took Mark several minutes to calm the guy down and close the deal for a second time.

He returned to the living room and Solange was gone. He searched the bungalow quickly, every room, then the back and side yards. Nowhere.

A sharp stab of panic struck, followed by a flush of anger. He dialed her phone. Straight to voice mail. He got in his car and began driving around the neighborhood, muttering to himself all the while about this fucking bullshit disease and the ex-wife he'd somehow been burdened with… again. What version of hell was this?

He found her ten minutes later, thank Christ, clinging to a stop sign on a quiet side street, utterly lost. She was trembling.

"Solange!" he exploded out of the driver's seat. He grabbed her by the arm and dragged her into the car, aggressively fastening her seatbelt. "What in the hell were you doing?"

"I didn't know where anyone was. I thought you'd left me."

The irony of this did not escape him. "I was on the phone. I told you to just stay put. But you can't do that. You can't remember what I told you. You can't remember any damn thing at all!"

Tears streamed down her cheeks. She buried her face in her hands. "Don't be angry with me." Those words stabbed at him, quelling his fury.

He got her back to the house, calmed her down with a cup of tea and a nature documentary on the Roku, then sat with himself at the kitchen table. In twenty minutes—hell, in five—she wouldn't remember any of it. But he surely would. Now he was the one trembling, startled by his own carelessness, his impatience, his pettiness, and his rage.

Don't be angry with me.

He poured himself a stiff whiskey, sipping it as he stared out the kitchen window at Solange's garden beds, so orderly and clean. Now he wasn't even allowed to feel spite. Bitterness, hereby banished. All that anger, years of it banked up, the very thing that had sustained him in those dark years, useless now. Beside the point.

He chuckled miserably. The real problem was what to grow in its stead.

5

One evening, Solange and Mark sat watching a romantic comedy on Netflix, something recent. A couple sat at a picnic bench on the coast, sipping white wine and talking. The movie was innocuous and saccharine. Mark was only half-interested. Solange turned to him and said,

"It reminds me of that summer we spent in Half Moon Bay. You remember."

Mark sat up, startled. He paused the film. "Yes, of course."

It was the summer before they'd married. Solange was painting; Mark was working at a local gallery. They house-sat for a big shot art dealer, a summer of long evenings drinking jug wine, watching the sun sink into the Pacific. They were young and hungry, making love in every corner of the house. There was nothing more important to Mark than to keep Solange laughing, this girl with the incandescent eyes.

When Solange unexpectedly became pregnant, neither knew what to do. There was talk of termination, or giving the baby up for adoption. Solange insisted it was her decision, her responsibility, Mark shouldn't feel beholden in any way. Even if she had the child, he needn't be involved if he didn't want to. She would never demand that. Oh, the sweet fool! She didn't know what she wanted.

Mark's spontaneous marriage proposal surprised them both, but as the words left his mouth he felt absolutely sure that it was the right thing. He didn't expect her to agree, but she said yes. She said yes! Life, in that moment, felt radiant.

"You remember that little Italian place on Highway One," Solange said, smiling. "The one with the funny old guy with that big moustache? What did we call him?"

The accuracy of her memory in that moment astonished him. "Il Brontolone," he said, smiling. The Grouch.

"He was always surly."

"But who cared. His eggplant parmesan was out of this world."

"And the wine," Solange added, "whatever that house red was, served in those nicked carafes. And the tablecloths, spattered with candle wax." She pulled the blanket up close to her chin. "I don't suppose any of that is still there."

"It was ages ago," Mark said. "Probably all condos and Starbucks now."

They were quiet for a moment. In a soft, sleepy voice, Solange said, "It was good, wasn't it?"

Tears swam along the lower lids of his eyes. He reached out for her. She let him put his hand atop hers, resting it there. "Yes," he said, "it was good." Gazing into her eyes, he saw the old sparkle, the merry, dancing energy. And then, gradually, like an ice cube dissolving in a warm drink, her gaze turned glassy and unfocused.

She withdrew her hand from his. She asked if he wanted to watch television.

Mark resumed the movie, though he couldn't focus. He felt awash in many things—memory, affection, but also a deep sadness. For what they'd had, for what they'd shared, for what they could have had. It'd taken him years to recover, years to cauterize the wounds. How strange that she could pierce all of that so quickly, so cleanly, in just a minute.

Such moments were rare, a trick of memory. Tomorrow, she wouldn't remember what film they'd watched the night before, let alone what they'd talked about. But it meant something to him to know that in the catacombs of her mind she—they—remembered it all. It was locked up there in some vault, inaccessible for the most part. Memories of the good times, when they were happy and in love. Just the two of them, with everything spread out before them. The future was nothing but a bright and breezy promise, and the possibilities of tomorrow shone like a thousand diamonds.

The Photograph

It was a mild autumn afternoon, the temperature in the mid-fifties. We'd had a couple of days of rain. The ground was soft and slightly muddy, sticking to the soles of my shoes. I sat on a low brick wall outside the auditorium, grateful for the fresh air. As a campus budget analyst, I spent far too many hours in a climate-controlled office wearing a mask and maintaining social distance. Sometimes I needed to get outside, stretch my legs, and remind myself I was awake and alive on this climate-threatened cinder hurtling through space.

That's when I noticed a man photographing me. He wore a baggy, gray pantsuit and held a camera, a real camera. He darted about like an agitated insect, sneaking around columns, looming over planter boxes, even perching opposite me on a bench across the courtyard. Searching for the right angle, I supposed.

It didn't bother me at first. But after a dozen shots, each marked by that distinctive, mechanical click, I became annoyed. I crossed and uncrossed my legs. I turned my face away. None of it worked. He kept at it.

I stood. "Do you mind telling me why you're taking my photo?"

The man paused to meet my gaze. He didn't seem startled or defensive.

"Excuse me," I said. "I asked you a question."

He snapped another picture, then turned and walked away, his unbuttoned coat flapping at his side. I pondered pursuing him—his coldness offended me more than his camera—but told myself to ignore it. What were a few photos?

My mind drifted back to the data set I'd taken a break from. Fall enrollments were down for the second straight year. The first-year students who'd held off during the lockdown weren't showing up. It was my job to predict the numbers for next year, and the budget forecast to match. Usually I had a clue, but this was a pandemic.

Budget analysts prefer stability and predictability. Change, if it must come, is best delivered slowly. The pandemic wasn't slow; its rapid, destabilizing upheaval was frightening. All you could do was wait for things to calm down, though no one knew when that would happen. Even if you were vaxxed and boosted—as I am—you could still contract the virus. Always, you had to be careful. Always vigilant. Anxiety hung over me like a bad tule fog. My job, my life—amid this seemingly unending pandemic—I felt stuck in bizarro land.

My smartwatch beeped; break was over. As I stood from the wall and stretched, the man in the baggy pantsuit popped out from behind a shrub, camera in hand. *Click-click.*

I wasted no time. "Hey you! Stop what you're doing!"

The camera clicked again. I darted across the plaza. "Stop taking photos of me!"

The man dashed across the courtyard. A small, black canister fell from his jacket pocket. I scooped it up. This guy was shooting film! In 2021! Who did he think he was, Weegee?

He trotted toward the arts building. I quickly donned my mask and caught up with him just inside the door, in a wide, white hallway. The man wedged himself in alongside a water fountain, panting for breath.

"Do you mean to harm me?" The accent sounded Slavic.

"I want to know why you're taking photos of me."

He fumbled with a paper mask, looping it over one ear. "I have a right to shoot as I please."

"You're invading my privacy."

"You're in a public space."

"I asked you to stop."

He took a step away from the wall, walking slowly backwards, keeping his eye on me. We stood like that, facing off against one another, for a long moment. Then, with a practiced gesture, his thumb pulled a lever, advancing the film. He raised the camera slowly to his eye.

"Don't even think about it!" I hissed. Lunging forward, I stripped the camera from his hands, sending it to the floor. How was I to know it was a vintage Leica, worth hundreds of dollars? Maybe he shouldn't have been shoving it in my face.

The man shouted for help. A woman in trendy black slacks and a matching mask stepped into the hall. It was the gallery curator, Ms. Elise Holland. She'd already called campus police. Now would I mind stepping away from Mr. Zepilov?

Zepilov scrambled after his camera, muttering a curse.

I pointed a finger at him. "That man invaded my privacy!"

"He was shooting photos of you?" Ms. Holland asked.

"Yes! Even after I asked him to stop."

She lifted an eyebrow. "You should be flattered."

She informed me that Dimitri Zepilov was an invited guest of the university, the Rogers Visiting Artist. He was a distinguished street photographer and, she added, he had every right to take photos in public of whatever or whomever he liked.

I pleaded my case, citing common decency and civility. Somehow Zepilov had gotten under my skin. This isn't usual for me, I insisted. I'm a budget analyst, cool and objective. Since returning to campus after a year of telecommuting, I'd been a little tense.

Ms. Holland proved to be an unsympathetic audience. We ended up at the campus police station. An officer cited me for a public disturbance. It was up to the aggrieved to decide whether to press charges for assault and battery. The statute of limitations was two years.

I walked back to my office in a daze, dumbfounded by this turn. I'd been accused of assault! I couldn't have that hanging over my head. I would apologize to Zepilov and offer to pay for camera repairs. Surely he'd be reasonable about it.

AS A CAMPUS BUDGET FORECASTER, I prepare the future for the untamable now. My job is pure foresight, the divination of data. From a budget planning perspective—which, incidentally, is a practice that affects, and to some extent controls, every part of the institution for which I work— most scenarios can be anticipated. It's not uncommon to be wrong. But, with surprising frequency, I am close. And, on a handful of occasions, I am precisely correct.

Such moments, when they come, are fleeting. How long can the numbers align? Like stars, they keep moving. Eventually, we exit the projected period and, inevitably, in the next one the numbers are off. But that's all right. There is always another future to predict.

Once, I had two consecutive quarters pan out. Fiscal 16-17, my greatest year. From July to December, I lived each day in a special glow. It's a rare sensation, to be living in the past's future, occupying a moment that, back then, I dreamt of inhabiting with such exactitude (that is, statistical accuracy). Trapped in the transient now, I yearn for a past I can never reclaim, but only hope to forecast on future occasions. I set about my day's work, rooted in the predictive statistical present, envisaging another time, a year away, when I hope to feel then what I feel today about last year. Time becomes tri-layered, the present being but a moment of pure anticipation for a future which, if my predictions prove accurate, will sanctify the present as a moment of past accuracy. Anticipatory nostalgia: the rarest, the sweetest drug.

THE FACT THAT I KNEW NOTHING about Zepilov irked me, so I looked him up. He was indeed well-known. He'd had noteworthy shows in Europe and the States. He'd won big awards. An art historian had written a book arguing that Zepilov, along with a handful of other artists, had had something to do with the fall of the Berlin Wall, staging a famous gallery show that incited an uprising.

Online, I gazed at his images. Dirty children sit on stoops in run-down urban neighborhoods, garbage at their feet. Anonymous, drab tower blocks loom over them. A weary soldier directs traffic somewhere in Eastern Europe, standing before a tangle of barbed wire. And a series of sharp black-and-white images of rough looking kids vandalizing the Berlin Wall, spray painting it, or attacking it with sledge-hammers. There was something violent and menacing in those images, but that was ages ago. Anyway, Zepilov was on the right side of history. The Wall fell. People were liberated. Budget analysts in a reunited Germany were awash in new data sets.

I had a more immediate, pressing issue. Would Zepilov file charges? As a mid-level analyst with an eye on a future management slot, and a state pension to follow, I couldn't afford to take chances.

I decided to visit the art gallery. Elise was just locking the door, en route to a meeting. I begged a minute of her time. In a cool tone, she asked what she could do for me.

"I want to apologize for the other day," I said.

"It's not me you need to apologize to."

"Is Mr. Zepilov around?"

"He rarely comes to the gallery."

"But he's your visiting artist. What's he do, if I might ask?"

He was teaching a class and would deliver a public lecture, she explained. At the end of the semester, the gallery would host a show of his new work. They were very excited.

"You should be," I said. "Your funding has increased six percent every year for the last three years."

It's amazing how, when someone is masked, their upper face becomes more intensely expressive. For instance, a narrowed eye looks like a blade.

"Where did you say you worked?" Elise asked.

"The campus budget office. I'm a forecaster."

"I love how there's four administrators for every decision that gets made around here. Now if you'll excuse me, I'm running late."

I cleared my throat. "About Mr. Zepilov."

"Look him up in the directory. He has an email, like everyone else." Then she walked briskly away.

MY EMAIL WAS SHORT AND TO THE POINT. I apologized and offered to pay for any camera repair. I gave him my personal cell number. A few nights later, my phone rang.

"We should talk," Zepilov said.

"About the incident."

"Not that."

What else did we have to talk about? But I asked him to proceed.

He'd been looking at the photos he took of me, he said. There was something there.

Somehow, hearing that made me uneasy, but also intrigued. I asked what he meant.

"Meet me Saturday morning at the mall. Ten o'clock. I will be in the food court."

"My running group meets on Saturday mornings."

"Take a day off," he rasped. He'd cased out his location. He had some ideas about shooting me in that milieu. That was the word he used.

I wondered how many people would be at the mall. Since the restrictions had been lifted, people were crowding into restaurants, bars, and sports arenas. But we were in the thick of the Delta variant. Hospital beds were filled with the unvaccinated. The mall was essentially a giant germ exchange.

"You are vaccinated," Zepilov blurted. "Wear a mask."

"Why Saturday?" I replied. "I'd rather do it on a weekday. Less crowded."

He rattled off data concerning pedestrian density, age distribution, and the quality of light at noon. The weather forecast was for an absolutely clear day, no cloud cover.

I admired his data set, but something about it struck me as odd. What was he up to? What possible purpose could I serve? I never went to the mall, even before the pandemic. Never!

But this guy had the goods on me. He could press charges, making my life more complicated, or he could drop them. Given that choice—and Zepilov had said nothing on the matter—I preferred the latter. I told him I'd be there.

"One final thing," he said.

"Yes?"

"Wear what you wore on the day of our altercation."

I asked him to describe it: dark denim jeans, brogans, and a striped dress shirt under a burgundy cardigan. I recalled the specific combination. Business casual, as befits my station and occupation. I try to look good, and I keep up with fashion, especially footwear. I don't call attention to myself. On a campus filled with bright, energetic young people and highly educated faculty, I am content to fade into the background. No reason to call attention to me.

I FOUND ZEPILOV IN THE FOOD COURT, sucking on an Orange Julius. Does anything scream "mall" in America more than an Orange Julius? Maybe acid-washed jeans and off-brand walking shoes.

"These are delicious," he said, sipping on the straw.

No one in the food court was wearing a mask except the workers. Just walking into the mall, I'd felt unease. The vax rate in my conservative Northern California county was among the lowest in the state. You want to talk numbers? The States has just four percent of the world's population, and we invented these incredible vaccines, yet we suffered the highest number of Covid deaths of any nation. Why?

The truth is we're dumb enough to do ourselves in.

I turned to Zepilov. "Why did you ask me to come?"

"You are an interesting subject."

"I'm a pencil pusher at a state institution. I have a degree in business accounting. I'm the most boring person in this town."

Zepilov tapped a finger on the plastic lid of his drink cup. "You have read Kafka?"

"Maybe in college, I don't know."

"You should. He was the poet of the bureaucracy. What he did in his fiction, I try to do with my lens. That is why I came to America. Yours is a very rich country, very innovative in some areas, but very uninspired in others. Things here can be fast and slow at the same time. I want to capture that complexity."

I looked around the shabby, half-empty food court. A mother fed her toddler a French fry. A cluster of old guys nursed coffees in Styrofoam cups. Everyone else was on a screen. None of it struck me as complex.

"What do I have to do with any of it?"

Zepilov leaned forward. "The images I shot of you. There is something there. What I see in you. What I can make of you."

"I thought street photography was spontaneous."

"I no longer define myself as such. My new work is a departure."

He explained his plan. He'd mapped a route for me, certain choreographed moves near store entrances, a visit to the food court, a scene before the color-coded map, and so on. At no point should I engage with anyone or touch any objects. I was to convey an air of indifference, as if on a journey of higher purpose. Apart from that, he said, I was free to invent. Free to add a little touch here or there, a gesture or an allusion.

"I want you to wander as if in a dream," he told me. "Absurd and surreal, yet, because it is a dream, somehow normal."

"I'm acting? This is a role?"

"Yes and no. Be yourself. But be the other, too."

I cocked my head. "The other what?"

Zepilov smiled.

As we walked to the starting point for my trek, Zepilov stopped before a cluster of trees standing in an elevated planter, under a skylight.

"There is something of the sublime even in the most pedestrian of simulacra. Not the grandeur of the forest," he said, gesturing to the trees, "but the suggestion of grandeur. Do you understand?"

"Nostalgia."

He clapped his hands. "Precisely! Your country is drunk with it."

"I prefer to focus on the future, not the past."

He turned to me, stroking his beard. "Yes, I see that in the images."

"What's so great about those pictures?"

"Nothing," he admitted. "Rather, it is the potential I see in you."

We walked to one of the anchor stores on the north end of the mall, a name with a long and storied history in American commerce. In the age of online shopping—which mushroomed during the pandemic—its status had plunged. It had failed to adapt, and its viability was in question. It was from such a position, Zepilov explained, that his hero's journey was to begin.

"Hero?" I laughed.

"Every story must have a hero."

I'd never been the hero of anything, but I resolved to try. In doing so, I hoped that Zepilov would forget our tiff.

At the maestro's command, I traversed the zig-zag course he'd mapped out, moving between storefronts, pausing in some of the smaller courtyards to strike various poses. Some were scripted ideas he'd given me; some were my contribution. As we cycled through the rehearsals he annotated my moves, letting me know which to keep and which to discard. It was a slow, at times maddening process. Gradually, I got a feel for what he wanted, and what I might add to it, but it was work.

We moved to the food court, where I stood in line at the pizza place. Zepilov wanted me to look up at the menu items in a state of rapture, capturing "the anticipation of the order," but not the order itself. I was to step out of line the moment the clerk asked if they could help me.

Okay, sure. But as we undertook a second and then a third round of rehearsals, and as the lunch hour approached, the food court was beginning to smell pretty good. Your hero stands in line for pizza and guess what? Pretty soon your hero wants a pizza.

After three rounds of it, I felt exasperated. "You chose the wrong person for this project."

Zepilov frowned. "Forget everything I told you and just be natural."

Having learned the route, we walked it several more times. Zepilov circled me, snapping from every conceivable angle, dropping to a knee or hopping up on a bench for an elevated view. For a heavyset guy, he moved with admirable dexterity. Always, I was to act as if none of this were happening, ignoring the stares of shoppers, the wondering eyes of children, the scoffs of tweeners and adolescents, the narrowed eyes of mall security. Most of all, I was to ignore the dervish whirling around me.

After several trial runs, I knew the route and my moves were falling into place. I was adding less and augmenting what we'd agreed upon. Zepilov's coaching became less adamant. Yet something was off. We both felt it.

"We need something," Zepilov muttered.

As we walked back to the starting point for our final trial run, we passed a men's clothing store. The windows were filled with mannequins wearing dress coats and shiny leather shoes. Zepilov stopped to comment. It seemed he was always commenting.

"There's something exquisite about that pose," he said, pointing to one of the mannequins. "Something crisp and indifferent. That is the pose of a hero."

He was beginning to annoy me. "I don't know. A little too plastic."

"All heroes are plastic."

We walked into the store, wandering the aisles, ignoring the clerk's offer of assistance. And then I found it: the attaché. A slim, brown leather case, unadorned. Shiny and new. It felt great in my hands. The perfect weight. Its color played off my burgundy sweater with just the right counterpoint.

"Yes, the missing object," Zepilov muttered. "It completes the narrative. You have an excellent eye!"

He purchased the attaché, then we walked quickly back to the starting point for my hero's journey. I was to carry the bag with me on my route, he instructed, shifting it from one hand to the other. I must never set it down. It was a part of me, an extension of my mind and thinking.

"It is your very essence," he explained, "like Arthur's Excalibur. It is the thing that defines you."

I thought about that. "You know, things don't work out too great for Arthur."

"Yet Britons await his return. The greatest form of nostalgia!"

We walked back to the starting point. It was time for the final run-through, the one that counted. Zepilov asked me to remove my mask.

I should have seen this coming. Neither of us had stated up front our intention, but after several rounds of rehearsal I'd hoped the precedent was set. And by the way my mask perfectly matched my sweater.

"Can't we keep it?" I protested. "Sort of a pandemic period piece?"

"Absolutely not. The hero's face is half the story."

"Maybe I consider this one of my contributions."

"Remove it!" he snapped.

I hated him then. Yet, given how far we'd come, and how deep into this I was, I could hardly refuse. I pulled the loops from behind my ear and stuffed my mask into my pocket.

"If I get Covid…"

"Action!" Zepilov barked.

Some of my frustration and hostility must have shown through. As I made my way through the mall, Zepilov was no longer spitting out orders, only exclamations. "Yes! Excellent! Just like that!" I moved from storefront to storefront, through the now-familiar plazas and hallways. I stood in line yet again for pizza, turning away at the last moment. The clerk waved a hand and groaned, "Ah, buzz off."

As scripted, I ended up at an exit, between two sets of glass doors, where I was to stand as if trapped. I didn't like that ending; it seemed wrong for the story as I understood it. This hero didn't want to be stuck in limbo; this hero wanted a vindication, a vanquishing. If there were unsettled questions, he'd demand answers. He didn't ask permission; he took what he wanted. As this feeling welled inside me, I felt less like an actor and more like whomever I was playing, this peripatetic post-capitalist pilgrim. One of us, I'm not sure who, wasn't finished.

"Follow me," I ordered Zepilov. "One more shot."

Unscripted, I marched off before he could mutter a protest. I strode into the palm-lined central courtyard, full of a cross-section of everyone at the mall: teens; parents and small children; grandparents and retirees; workers on their lunch break. I barged through them like an explorer claiming a new territory. In the center of the space, as if on cue, the sun intensified, and a brilliant column of light shone down on me.

"Yes!" Zepilov shouted as he spun around me. "Lift your chin!"

The camera clicked and clicked.

"Turn left! Move the attaché to the other hand!"

Zepilov dropped to his knees. I threw my shoulders back, lifting my chin like one of the mannequins he so admired. After a furious final flourish of lens snaps, the camera fell silent. Zepilov stood and, with surprising theatricality, bowed deeply.

"Thank you, that was tremendous."

Spontaneously, the circle of mall attendees broke into applause.

The other man turned to them, a plastic smile fixed upon his face, waving and nodding in acknowledgement. They confirmed something he'd never doubted, some entitled sense that he belonged exactly where he was. He was, in that moment, irrefutably the shaper of this tale.

I DIDN'T HEAR FROM ZEPILOV for several weeks. Temperatures fell as we sank deeper into autumn. Sweaters and fleeces came out of the closet. Through it all, I streamed television and made calculations.

I thought often of that day at the mall, puzzling over what Zepilov would make of it. The uncertainty nagged at me, as did a couple of other things.

There was the question of the attaché. After the photo shoot I'd taken it home. We'd both been so caught up in the day's success that neither of us addressed the issue. I thought I might drop it by the gallery for Elise to deliver. Yet I hesitated. Zepilov might have paid for it, but I'd picked it out. It was, he'd declared, an essential part of my character. Some part of me, perhaps that man I'd so briefly become, wanted to keep it. But that seemed so bold.

Then there was the question of the charges. The fact that I hadn't come to a clear agreement with Zepilov troubled me. He had two years to follow up. He could act at any time. I needed a clear and definitive answer.

I emailed Zepilov, nominally checking in about the photo shoot. Two weeks later he replied, inviting me to visit the campus gallery the next afternoon. They were installing his new show, and he had some images to show me.

When I arrived Elise was there, her hair pinned up and an electric blue scarf arranged elegantly around her neck.

"Oh, it's you!" The warmth in her voice was new, and I liked it greatly.

Zepilov stood in the middle of the gallery, in his baggy pantsuit, ordering someone on a ladder to adjust a track light. It shone on an image of a man in dirty jeans standing before a worn-looking tent under a highway overpass, one of the sprawling homeless encampments in Oakland. Other images showed the man walking around Jack London Square, reaching into trash cans, or standing on a street corner with a hand-lettered sign.

I wondered about the ethics of using a person's suffering as a vehicle for art. But maybe it wasn't genuine suffering. Maybe that man was just another actor, the hero of another story.

In another sequence, a single mom stands wearily in the middle of a cluttered living room wearing a nurse's outfit. A toddler sits at her feet, mesmerized by a smart phone. In another, she's at work, fully masked up, leaning over a hospital patient hooked up to a ventilator. The worry and empathy in this nurse's eyes, it can't be feigned. In the next photo, she's in the queue at a local food bank, her son in a beat-up stroller, again transfixed by a smartphone.

Other series focused on fast-food and warehouse workers. Others still, wealthy golfers, or bankers sipping cocktails in the View Lounge of the Marriott Marquis in San Francisco.

I felt confused. How did the story in my photos relate to these others? Country club matriarchs and unkempt homeless guys; portly bankers and single, working moms. They were all so different, yet equally true. There was something unsettling about it. Maybe that was Zepilov's point.

I looked around the gallery. A woman stood on a ladder, stenciling the show title in bold, black letters.

DIMITRI ZEPILOV
CONFERENCE OF VICTIMS
ABUSE AND CONQUEST IN LATE CAPITALISM

Zepilov approached, beckoning with a hand. "Come. I will show you."

On the back wall were mounted a series of large color prints, all of me at the mall. Me in line for pizza, or standing before the large, color-coded map. In another I walk briskly past a shop window filled with mannequins. Then I'm encased behind a wall of glass doors. And so on.

In the center of all these prints stood the image of me in the palm-lined courtyard, washed in sunlight. One foot is slightly before the other, a hero mid-journey. The attaché is in his right hand, partially hidden behind a leg. The line from shoulder to hip is powerful; this man moves with great purpose and confidence—chin slightly lifted, gaze off in the distance. Behind him stands a distant ring of fellow shoppers, their eyes fixed on him. A small child in a jumper has her mouth agape in wonder.

"That picture makes the series," he said. "Maybe this whole show. The shot you called for!"

I smiled sheepishly. I didn't know where that impulse had come from, but I knew we were both glad it happened.

Elise approached. "That one is really special. I think we're looking at a lead image." She turned to me. "What do you think about that? Are you ready for your fifteen minutes?"

"I'm not sure what we're talking about."

Lead images go out on flyers and e-blasts, she explained. They go on the cover of the catalog. They're sent out with the press release, that sort of thing.

"Your face is going to be everywhere!" she said, patting my shoulder.

I'd never been on the cover of anything. The thought of it terrified me. I looked again at the picture. It was me, yet it was not me. I was playing a role, only in that moment I distinctly recall not thinking of it as a role. I had become, however briefly, another person—an unexpected transformation. Gazing at the image, I felt again that power, that self-assurance. I knew I wasn't that man, not literally. It was me playing that man. There was something intoxicating about it, like a daydream gone rogue, a private fantasy that you granted yourself but shared with others. You might escape, just for a moment, the wailing and the worries of your world.

Of course, those worries would be waiting for you the moment you returned.

I turned to Zepilov. "Before this goes any further, I need to ask you two things."

He lifted a bushy eyebrow. "Yes?"

"Your court case. The charges against me. What do you plan to do?"

He gave me a quizzical look. "Forgotten, of course."

Before that could even truly register, he asked me what the second thing was. I'd planned to ask what he wanted me to do with the attaché, ready to defer to his wishes. But, caught up in the moment, I simply declared that I was keeping it.

There was an awkward, silent moment as my face flushed bright red.

Zepilov burst out laughing. "Has that been bothering you?"

"A little."

He put his hand on my shoulder. "It could only belong to you."

Relief washed over me. There'd been that bit of awkward, unfinished business, but I'd followed through and gotten my answer. More importantly, I'd surprised myself by making a declaration. Sometimes you just have to tell the universe what you want, and make it happen.

ZEPILOV COMPLETED THE INSTALLATION of his show and attended the opening, where he delivered a lengthy précis on late-stage capitalism and nostalgia. This project was decidedly political. He hoped the images would spur reflection, discussion, and ultimately action. Questions were asked. A graduate student noted the juxtaposition of gross income disparity, with some images so gritty and realistic, and others so arch and ironic. Was the work a critique of capitalism, or merely complicit in its ulterior motives? A lengthy, serpentine answer followed. Finally we broke for wine and cheese out in the courtyard, where we could gather without masks. I saw Zepilov in animated conversation with a ring of students.

A reporter from the student newspaper interviewed me. How had I become involved in Zepilov's project? What did I think of my depiction? Had I been aware of the famous '89 opening at Gallery X in West Berlin, featuring a performance by Einstürzende Neubauten?

I blurted out some nonsense about the poetry of the bureaucracy, trying to parrot Zepilov, then stopped mid-sentence. I was out of my league. About identity, social roles, and art, I only have questions.

Elise stepped in, her answers nimble and brisk. Zepilov had elevated street photography to another level, something on par with sculpture or painting. Think Jeff Wall.

Satisfied, the reporter lunged after another target.

"Thanks." I sipped my wine. "This Sauvignon Blanc is good."

She stabbed a cube of cheese with a toothpick. "It's a Pinot Grigio, and I buy it at Costco."

We both laughed. I asked how she felt about the show.

"Now that things have opened back up, foot traffic is going to skyrocket. There's a buzz about this. He's already lined up galleries in San Francisco, L.A., and New York. Every one of them is going to mention where the show premiered."

That kind of proximal data could be useful in establishing distal goals, but even I knew better than to say as much to a pretty curator at a party.

"Sounds like news you can use."

"Precisely." She planned to lobby her dean for a larger, better located space, one that could attract bigger audiences. She would need to hire an assistant.

"Necessitating a budget increase," I suggested.

"You *are* a bright boy."

I felt that tingle in my fingers, the anticipatory sense of where a data set was pointing. During the pandemic, it was a rare sensation.

"I could help," I offered. "Review your data. Ensure accurate projections. Plus, I know every budget person on this campus. I can get a draft on the right desk for a preview."

Elise raised a finger to her chin. "Yes, you can help. I'm pushing the cross-disciplinary angle. Admin in the arts, that sort of thing."

I looked down at my half-empty glass. "I'm no artist."

"Zepilov told me about the shoot, how you selected the attaché. How you took control of that final scene. He's impressed." A moment later she added, "That's rare, by the way."

"I don't know how to explain it," I muttered. "It was like someone else was in control."

She folded a paper napkin in half. "It's called acting, and apparently you're a natural." She was involved in community theater, she told me, an avant-garde troupe that did some edgy stuff. They were always on the lookout for new talent.

That didn't exactly sound like my thing, but then neither had Zepilov's project. I'd agreed to participate for a wholly unrelated reason, yet something magical had happened. There was a lesson in that.

"Let's go out for a coffee," I proposed. "We can discuss your gallery plans and you can tell me about your theater group."

Elise smiled. "What's your Tuesday look like?"

I NEVER SAW ZEPILOV AGAIN. He wandered out of my life just as he'd wandered in, an imp in a baggy pantsuit. A few weeks later a package arrived at my office. It was a framed print of the photograph. Zepilov had signed and dated it on the back.

Elise tells me it will be worth something before long, and I should take good care of it. Of course I will. But what it means to me can't be measured in dollars. For once, the numbers are meaningless. Zepilov drew out of me an unexpected energy. I won't try to name it.

I suppose I wanted to thank him for that. Perhaps one day I shall.

AS A DATA ANALYST, I PREFER STASIS over volatility. I like predictability and routine. I favor a closed system with known parameters. Only then can projections be made with a reasonable degree of accuracy. Only then do the numbers behave themselves in predictable patterns. Only then can I sit before my laptop with a hot steaming double soy latte and tell you what you'll be doing, statistically, a year from now.

There is an art to making predictions. Opening yourself up to the process is the first step. It's like when you're looking at a Jackson Pollock painting. At first it seems like a big, random mess. But the longer you study it, the more you get pulled in, entranced by the movement, color, and energy. (Elise has helped me with this.)

I feel that way when I receive a good data set. Study the numbers carefully enough, and there are little leads, call them hooks, that pull you in a certain direction. But the numbers alone can't do anything. They need me to arrange them into a proposition, a prediction. It is a process almost sacred, and I am here to tell the tale.

Elise makes fun of me. She says I'm a palm reader with a calculator. She's not far off.

We've been dating for three months. I have a role in an upcoming production with the Rogue Theater, an outdoor staging of a Brecht play. Elise's gallery proposal is under review. These are difficult times; every budget on campus is tightly scrutinized. But word on the street is she stands a good chance.

Amidst all the sickness and the suffering, the distress and the doubt, I remain hopeful. For what? I'm not exactly sure yet. A better world, wiser friends and family. Less bluster and bullying. An end to this pandemic. My world is already better with Elise in it. Will it go any further? For once I can't render a prediction, but it feels good. Stay tuned.

Buxiban Blues

Teachers come and go like hands in a card game. Ordinarily, when one quit Will shuffled the deck and drew a new card. Since Covid, nothing was normal. The hiring pool of English-speaking expats had stagnated. For a while, no new foreigners were allowed into Taiwan. Once the numbers stabilized, some foreigners were let back into the country, but only with the right paperwork, and only after completing a strict quarantine period. Every cram school on the island competed for the teachers who remained.

The demand hadn't gone down. Will still had full classes and often a waiting list. Parents insisted that their kids learn English and were willing to pay a handsome tuition; Will wanted to provide them with that service.

And so, when one of his star teachers abruptly quit, lured by a headhunter from Taipei, Will was stuck. He had a full class ready to start in a week and he was short a teacher. He combed through the recent interview files, but there was nothing worth pursuing. The good ones had already found something. Will had long ago learned not to lower his hiring standards. Forget the schmoozers and the boozers and the starry-eyed backpackers; he needed someone who wanted to work.

On the TeaLit website he found some fresh prospects. He put an ad up. The most promising applicant was Margaret

Zhang, with a Master's in International Languages and a TESOL certificate, both from Cal State. On paper, she looked great. But with a name like Zhang, he knew. He just knew. But he called her in. He didn't have a lot of options.

She aced the interview, easily handling his questions. She knew the Cambridge PET. She understood his syllabus. Start Monday? You bet. They took care of the paperwork. She lingered in the front entryway of the school, chatting with her new boss.

Margaret was short and petite, with an easy smile. Her parents had grown up in Taichung, Shalu District. Born and raised in Stockton, she was as ABC as it gets. She hadn't been to Taiwan since she was a kid, visiting grandparents.

"Planning to stay a while?" Will asked.

"At least a year," she said. Living in Taiwan was a dream long deferred. Then she asked how long Will had been there.

Ten years in Taiwan, he said. Taichung for the last five, where he started Sunflower Academy.

"I have to admit, I didn't expect a white owner, let alone an American."

Will smiled. "I'll be there Monday to introduce you, sort of smooth the way. It'll help, trust me."

Margaret raised her eyebrows. "Are the kids that rough?"

"It's not the kids," he said. "It's the parents."

She laughed at that, a good sign. She was a newbie, unprepared in certain ways. Once she was in the classroom, he had a hunch she'd make it work.

She showed up on Monday afternoon wearing a simple dress and flats. No nonsense. Twenty young students sat attentively in their blue plastic seats, eyes up front. The mothers sat along the back wall, arms crossed. Will introduced himself in Mandarin, explaining the schedule and the curriculum. He presented Margaret as an American and a native speaker of English, reciting her credentials and education, which he stressed were top shelf. The kids in her class were very fortunate. The parents should be pleased.

Then Margaret stepped forward, said "Hello" in English, and began her first lesson.

In the front office, Will checked in with Shu-lin.

"Two families have already asked about switching to another section," she informed him.

"Tell them the other sections are full."

"But they're not. And the parents will talk."

"We have to give her a chance."

"They want a laowai," Shu-lin said. A white foreigner. "She needs to impress them quickly."

Will nodded. "I'm guessing she's a hard worker."

"She'll have to work twice as hard to impress those moms."

Will sat in on a couple of lessons that first week. Margaret knew her stuff, and her rapport with the kids was genuine. They liked her. The parents would come around, he felt sure of it. She might just make it.

SUNFLOWER ACADEMY. LU MEI-HUA HAD picked the name. She said it suggested new growth, warmth, and openness. She also designed the graphic, a bright yellow flower, its face turned innocently up to a radiant sun, arms thrown back. Will thought it looked childish, but Mei-hua insisted. Of course, she was correct. People regularly commented on the image, so much so that he eventually printed a line of T-shirts that sold well.

He'd also worried about the political allusion, but Mei-hua assured him it wouldn't hurt. The 2014 Sunflower Student Movement had been popular, culminating with students occupying the Legislative Yuan in Taipei. The nation rallied behind the students, who successfully delayed review of the Chinese trade pact in question. Their buxiban, opening a year after that event, looked hip and progressive. He had Mei-hua to thank for that.

IN TAIWAN IT'S UNDERSTOOD that you must sometimes relinquish individual desires for the greater good. Asking a country to mask up, or to wash their hands regularly, or to stay socially distant, or to report with whom they'd come into contact—this is no imposition. "This is your country, and it's up to you to save it" is almost a national motto.

It was hard to say anyone got lucky during Covid, but Will sometimes felt that of all the places he might have been when the global pandemic hit, Taiwan was the best. The nation's lockdown had been among the earliest and the strictest in the world, and it had worked. After an initial spike of infections in March and April, things tapered off to a trickle. As Europe and the States braced for second and third waves, re-imposing lockdowns, Taiwan kept its borders closed and its people free and healthy. Most restaurants and bars were re-opening in May. By mid-summer, life had mostly gotten back to normal.

But life was not back to normal for Will. And on another, more personal level, everything he saw made his stomach twist. Social compliance. Submitting to the will of elders. At once the thing that saved and doomed them all.

MARGARET COMPLETED THE FIRST five-week unit, and only two families pulled out of her class, about average. She was reliable and dependable. With her on the roster, plus his other stalwarts, the school was in good shape. Classes were nearly full. Shu-lin kept the numbers ends of things in order. The buxiban almost ran itself.

Almost. Will hadn't taken a vacation in three years. He ran the school six days a week, year-round. They only closed for national holidays, the longest being the Lunar New Year and the Tomb Sweeping Festival, but Will rarely traveled then. Train tickets sold out quickly and the island's highways were jammed to a standstill.

To celebrate, Will took Margaret out for a drink. They sat on an outdoor patio at a bar in the West District, overlooking the Calligraphy Greenway. It was October, which meant the days were still hot and humid, though it had started to cool a little overnight.

The waitress approached and asked Margaret, in Mandarin, if they needed anything.

Margaret smiled awkwardly. "Xiè xiè."

Will waited a beat, then said that they were fine. He complimented the waitress on her bracelet. A smile washed across her face. She'd just bought it and wasn't sure what to think about it. Now she felt better.

When the waitress had left them, Margaret shook her head and said, "That right there. When they look at me, expecting me to be fluent. And if I open my mouth, they're like, 'Why is your Mandarin so bad?' That's when I feel the most removed."

"You've only been here a few weeks. Give yourself time to adjust. Take a language class."

"Your Mandarin is really good."

"I get by," Will said. "I understand nearly everything I hear, which is huge. But my reading level is fundamental. That's an issue if you're running a buxiban."

"Do you like running the school?"

"I do," he said, "but it eats up all my time. I love Taiwan, but sometimes I feel like I only get to see a narrow slice of it. There's a part of me that's ready to move on." He swirled the ice in his drink. "I shouldn't tell you that."

She gave him a warm smile, which heartened him.

"What would be next?"

"That's what I'm trying to figure out."

"Well don't figure it out too quickly. I'd like to teach for you for a while."

Will smiled. "That's good news."

Her phone screen flashed with a notification. "Sorry." She picked it up, read the message, then fired off a quick reply. She dropped the phone into her shoulder bag with a mild look of disgust on her face.

"Everything all right?" Will asked.

"Fucking Chinese Tinder."

Will laughed. He knew it well.

"I'm kidding. It's Auntie. She texts constantly. I'm starting to see why my mom never came back to Taiwan after Nai Nai died. Her sister is a nag."

Will turned his gaze toward the park below. "Family can be difficult."

"She says I look Chinese on the outside, but she can tell. America has ruined me."

"Ruined you? How?"

"According to Auntie, the 'Chinese gene' is looser, more adaptable. She says Westerners are rigid, inflexible. We like having things planned out."

Will laughed. "She might be right!"

Margaret flicked a cocktail napkin his way. "Don't agree with her! She's massively KMT, you know. She has a picture of Chiang Kai-shek in the living room."

"Well, she's not alone."

"I had no idea my family were Nationalists. Growing up, all I ever heard was how great the KMT was. I never doubted it, you know? I didn't know shit about what's going on here."

Margaret's phone flashed again. "I'm not even looking at that."

"It might be a hot date."

"Fuck you," she said, laughing.

It was time to leave. Will's flat was in Xitun District, on the way to Shalu, so he joined her on the BRT. The bus was hot and crowded and they had to stand apart from one another. When he stepped off the bus at Donghai Arts

Shopping District, he gave her a wave, but the bus was so crowded, he wasn't sure if she saw him.

LIKE MANY FOREIGNERS, WILL HAD started out ten years ago on Nanyang Street in Taipei, the "Buxiban Boulevard" offering the nation's largest concentration of cram schools. Back then, new on the island, his Mandarin still rough, it was comforting to be around so many foreigners. A quick trip to the 7-11 or Family Mart for a coffee before class, or lingering outside of the convenience stores after a night of teaching, sipping a 500 ml Taiwan beer, became a ritual. It became a group of friends, a support network, and, yes, a dating pool for some. There was a lot of turnover. Wave after wave of newbies. That meant a lot of opportunity. Will made a name for himself by simply showing up on time, working hard, and always saying yes. Picking up the extra Saturday class that had just been dropped by some kid who'd flown off to Chiang Mai. Covering for the dude who couldn't pry himself from his stool at the Brass Monkey, where the most boring expats hung out to watch NBA games, eat American-style burgers, and drink shots of Jack Daniel's. (Really? That's why you came to Asia?)

At one point, Will was working at three buxibans, filling every available hour with teaching, plus some solo tutoring on the side. It was not a sustainable lifestyle. The money was good, the contacts were invaluable, but he had no life. All he did was race from one lesson to the next.

Then one of his bosses, Yen Hong-wei, took him out for dim sum, followed by rounds of Kaoliang liquor and Taiwan beer. Hong-wei wanted to hire Will to revamp his school's curriculum. The position would be long-term, with predictable shifts, steady hours, and a taste of admin. Will reminded Hong-wei that he had no training in education theory, curriculum design, or teaching. Whatever he'd learned, he learned it the hard way.

Hong-wei waved him off. "What I want is a hard worker, someone who is dedicated and cares about the students. I've hired and fired a lot of teachers. You're one of the best."

The years Will spent working for Hong-wei were his true introduction to Taiwan. He got better at teaching. He learned a thing or two about the curriculum, but mostly he learned the business end of it. Watching Hong-wei navigate the demands of parents, the temperamental whims of instructors, hiring and firing staff, and how to spot and retain the good ones—it was a crash course in management. By the end of his second year, he thoroughly understood the machine. Hong-wei knew this, and that's why he left Will in charge of his school for three months while he took his aging father across the strait to Jiangxi Province. Will kept everything afloat and running smoothly—with the assistance of the newly-hired front office secretary, one of the school's former students, Lu Mei-hua.

Will and Mei-hua spent long hours keeping the buxiban running. Not just running, thriving. Mei-hua was sharp and efficient, and an excellent liaison with the parents. She was also beautiful, with a bob haircut and a wry smile. Dating a co-worker came with certain risks, but the tension between them was inescapable. One night, after having bid goodnight to the last parent and locking the doors, she let him kiss her.

"You've been dreaming of this moment, haven't you?" she asked him.

His face flushed. "Haven't you?"

"I knew all of it long before you did."

He smiled when he thought of that moment now. A fond memory, yes, but also predictive. Mei-hua, always a step ahead.

Upon his return, Hong-wei paid them each a generous bonus. He took them out for a grand dinner and told them, "You two could run your own school now!"

Will had thought of it. Taipei was the biggest and most lucrative market, but it was intensely competitive. Margins were thin and rents were high.

Mei-hua suggested they consider Taichung, her hometown. The third-largest city in the nation was growing faster than a Goat Horn pepper, attracting more foreigners every day, drawn by the expanding business market. She had family there, a network to build on. Her uncle was in real estate and could help them scout out locations.

"You'd partner with me?" he asked.

"A laowai is good for business," she said. "You run the classroom, I run the office."

He understood what Mei-hua meant. To be a white foreigner in Taiwan was to carry a form of privilege. He'd gotten his first teaching jobs without any real training or expertise, simply because he was a white native speaker and therefore pleasing to the parents. Once he was hired full-time by Hong-wei, National Health coverage was offered, as well as help securing his Alien Resident Card. When he studied Mandarin at a local university, he was given a stipend by the Taiwan government—money unavailable to "overseas Chinese" students, a Taiwanese-American friend pointed out. He'd argued his way out of traffic tickets, and even once onto an overbooked airplane, displacing a seated passenger. He didn't like to abuse it, but he couldn't deny it had helped him. He certainly wasn't above using it from time to time.

Will and Mei-hua started making regular trips on the HSR to Taichung. It was densely packed, with glittering glass towers and bustling shopping districts. In an effort to spread the cultural assets around the nation and to encourage tourism, the government had built the National Theatre, the National Museum of Natural Science, and the National Museum of Fine Arts in Taichung. The city's infrastructure was a little behind, but they had big plans. Rents were cheaper than Taipei, and the cram school market was less competitive. There was ample room for newcomers.

Mei-hua's uncle Wei-ting helped them locate a building in central Taichung. The owner was a good friend and, as a personal favor, locked the rent for an extended period—an incredible deal that Will could never have negotiated on his own. As Mei-hua frequently reminded him, family meant everything in Taiwan.

He and Mei-hua grew closer, agreeing to move in together. They rented a flat in the Xitun District, a short BRT ride from the school. Will felt grounded in Taiwan in new ways. He doubled down on his language studies, enrolling at the Tunghai University Chinese Language Center.

He thought he could stay in Taiwan forever. He had a Taiwanese girlfriend he was crazy about, a growing, stable business, and a support network. As he approached thirty, the only thing he wanted that he didn't have was a family. Focused intensely on growing their business, and content for the time being with the status of their relationship, he and Mei-hua avoided the topic. The buxiban was their priority for now.

But the question gnawed at him. His parents had divorced when he was in his teens, his dad and older brother moving to Colorado and Will staying with his mother in Florida. No one seemed happy about it. Yet Will had known happy families and wanted to be part of one. He had a hunch it might be some sort of cosmic rewrite of his crappy childhood. He could be the dad he never had.

Five years younger, Mei-hua wasn't as keen on the topic. Young people in Taiwan delayed marriage, she told him. Birth rates were at an all-time low, a national topic of conversation. (And, for some, a worry.) She probably did want to get married and be a mother, she admitted, but not yet. Not now. This wasn't the time. She loved Will dearly, but he must be patient and wait.

MARGARET ALWAYS DISMISSED HER students promptly at eight o'clock, teaching to the bell—always a good sign, and the surest way to keep parents happy. Will usually hung around after the last class to chat with families and to help Shu-lin close up.

That evening, Shu-lin needed to leave early to check on a sick child at home. Margaret offered to help clean up. When they'd finished, she threw herself into one of the sofas in the lobby.

"I'm exhausted! Those kids! Today they had me working."

"You're doing great," Will said. "Shu-lin talks to the parents. They don't lie to her. They're saying good things."

Margaret smiled. "So you're not worried?"

"You're one of the most qualified teachers I've ever hired. You never miss a shift. Your classes are full." He leaned a shoulder against the wall. "My only worry is whether you're going to jump ship."

"I've looked around," she said. "You pay what the other guys pay, plus I like working for you. And I've heard that some schools underpay Asian Americans, offering the white teachers more money."

"That's true, but not at Sunflower." He picked up a stray pencil from the office desk and placed it in a cup. "In fact, if you stick around for six months, I'll give you a raise."

"Why do you have to make things so hard?" She picked up her phone. "I mean, Pizza Rock is looking for delivery drivers."

"How are you on a scooter?"

"I don't have a driver's license."

"Better stick with teaching."

Will locked up and together they walked down the concrete steps to the busy street, below. Will said he was in the mood for grilled squid and fish balls.

"Where do you go for that?" Margaret asked.

"Only one respectable place to get it on a Friday night. Fengjia Night Market."

"I've heard that's a good one."

Will stopped, feigning shock. "Auntie hasn't taken you? It's only the best night market in Taichung."

Margaret frowned. "Auntie doesn't go anywhere."

"I knew it was bad," he said, "but not this bad. Let's go, you're coming with me."

THEY MADE THEIR WAY SLOWLY down the crowded streets of the night market, drifting with the crowd, stopping whenever either of them saw something interesting. Will got his squid, the meat marinated in soy and garlic, then grilled on a skewer and sprinkled with chili powder. Margaret had never tried an oyster omelet. She liked fried taro balls and the red bean cakes, dorayaki. They stopped at a street bar to purchase cocktails in a bag: a gin and tonic for Margaret, and a whisky and soda for Will. They browsed a few shops offering clothing, sunglasses, and bags, though neither bought anything.

At the far end of the night market there was a vendor selling Tainan-style eel noodles, one of the island's more famous dishes, and the classic eel soup: an entire eel coiled up in a bowl, head to tail, in a savory broth. Margaret wouldn't touch the soup, but agreed to split a bowl of noodles. They watched the chef prepare them, starting with a handful of raw onions and garlic, sprinkled with chili pepper, and then the eels, fried in a wok with sauces. Served over a bed of noodles, piping hot, the eel meat was mild and flavorful, a little salty.

"This is delicious!"

"No offense, but Auntie isn't doing right by you," Will said. "Taiwan is all about the night markets."

"Leave it to the white guy to introduce the Asian American to Taiwan food culture."

"That I can do."

"Tonight one of the mothers told me she didn't believe I was American. I told her I was born and raised in California. I'm as American as they come. She told me that my nose isn't high enough, and my eyes are too black."

"Taiwanese can be blunt."

"The funny part is, most of the time, what I'm experiencing here—it's really powerful. I feel more Taiwanese. The 'weird' parts of me are normal. In the States, I've always stood out. You're always the Asian kid."

"It must feel comforting."

"People don't stare at me on the street, or ask me where I'm from, at least until I open my mouth. But in other ways, I'm more mixed up than ever."

"How so?"

"In the States, my mother never says she's Chinese. She always identifies as Taiwanese, and so do I. But then I get here and I realize it's complicated. What does it mean to say you're Taiwanese here? Or Chinese? Auntie insists we're Waishengren, but she's never been to the mainland. I asked my mom about it and she said, no, we're a mix of Han and Hoklo blood. No one ever told me that. Auntie won't even discuss it."

"An ancestry test will sort that out," Will said. "But if your aunt is a hardcore Nationalist, she might have her reasons for claiming Waishengren."

Walking back to where he'd parked his scooter, Will noted that it was a clear night. The usual haze had lifted, and the night sky shone. That was rare enough. He began to drive west into Xitun District, on the way to dropping Margaret home. Their banter that night had been so easy, most of it light and fun. They were becoming friends. That felt good. It allowed him to push aside some of the shadows, those miserable months alone in his tiny flat. His social circle in Taichung had revolved around Mei-hua, and when she'd left, everyone dropped him.

Ghosted him, it's called now. Yes, he felt like a ghost.

"Do you want to take a little detour?" he asked. "I want to show you something."

"Can we get another drink? I'm having a good time and I don't want it to end."

After stopping at a convenience store to buy a couple of tall beers and a small bottle of Kaoliang liquor, he drove south on Youyuan Road, out onto the Dado plateau, to the Wanggaoliao Night View Park. There, they joined a scattering of people perched on the steps, or sitting on blankets on the green, grassy hillside. Below them the city sparkled, the tightly clustered towers of downtown a glittery swirl in the endless river of light stretching all the way north to Taipei.

They sat quietly for a few minutes, sipping beer.

"There's so much Auntie hasn't shown me," Margaret said. "I feel lucky I've met you, Will."

She leaned forward to toast, clinking the lid of her beer to his.

"Probably shouldn't do that," Will said. "Covid and all."

"Whatever. We teach in a cram school with sixty kids every day. Where's that sorghum?"

Will passed her the liquor bottle. Margaret poured a generous splash of the Kaoliang into a paper teacup.

"I know you're, like, my boss and everything, which kind of sucks right now because I'm having the most fun I've had since I arrived on this island, but speaking off the record, Saturday classes suck! These people are crazy! School all day. Four hours of cram school every night, and then Saturday classes! Those kids don't have a life! What is the motherfucking deal?"

She tossed back the Kaoliang, then chased it with a swig of beer.

"It keeps my fridge full," he said.

"Yeah, of Taiwan beer!" She took another sip of the sorghum, then puckered. "Oh god! It tastes like an old sock."

Will took the bottle and stashed it away. He had to drive, and the Taiwanese DUI laws were no joke. Plus, Margaret was beginning to sound a little sloppy. Fun, if they didn't have to drive in the city or teach in the morning.

"The dating scene sucks," Margaret announced. "Are all Taiwanese super shy? Or is it just me?"

"Once you learn Mandarin things will improve."

"Shu-lin says you're not dating right now."

"True."

"She says you like Asian women."

Will frowned. "Most guys in Asia like Asian women."

"She says she knows why you're not dating but won't tell me. She says to ask you myself."

He took a long pull off his beer. The city lights below looked now like a net, sparkling blue and white, everything caught, everything tangled into one twinkling mess.

"This is me asking," Margaret said.

"I was in a long-term relationship with someone I wanted to marry. Then it fell apart."

"Oh shit, I'm sorry," said Margaret. "A local girl?"

He pulled at the collar of his sweatshirt. "A Taiwanese woman, yes. We started the school together. She came up with the name, Sunflower Academy."

"That's why Shu-lin has only worked there for ten months."

"Ten months," he said, staring at the foam on his beer can. For ten months he'd felt locked in place, frozen in his pain and loneliness. Easily the most miserable ten months of his time in Taiwan. Way harder than those early, lonely months after his initial arrival. At least then he believed things would get better.

"Damn, that's hard."

"It rocked me," he said, "more than I care to admit. Talking to you helps."

Margaret smiled and bounced her shoulders, playfully.

"Did you have anybody in the States?" he asked.

"I dated a woman in Sacramento for a little bit. But that dried up like an old prune. She was the prune, by the way."

Will laughed. "Okay."

"I'm bi, not that you were asking."

"Thanks for sharing," he said. "Wait, that didn't come out right."

But she laughed. He liked how often, and how easily Margaret laughed. She wore her cares lightly, a bright lesson.

"You're a big nerd, do you know that?"

Will shrugged his shoulders. "I've been called worse."

"Where's that sorghum."

"I thought you didn't like it."

"It's a means to an end."

He pulled it out of the bag. "I can't drink any more. I have to drive you home."

"You're a party pooper, too. Aren't you having fun?"

"I am having fun. But I have a school to open at eight a.m."

She poured herself another generous splash of liquor. "Here's to dirty socks and queer pride!"

"I don't often think of those two things at the same time."

"Ha! Stick with me and I'll blow your motherfucking mind!"

They talked for another half hour, then Will drove Margaret home on the scooter, dropping her off at the top of the block so Auntie wouldn't see her niece getting a ride from a man. That would only start another round of interrogation. On the ride home, climbing up the big hill from Shalu to Xitun District, Will thought about Margaret. He liked her. He liked spending time with her. He wanted to keep her around.

He wasn't attracted to her, not in a romantic way. He'd already done the work/love thing and it hadn't exactly ended well for him or the school. Anyway, he wasn't ready to date. He needed more time. That, and something else. Something new in his life. A game changer.

As he crested the hill the city spread out before him, a glittering jade ocean of lights nestled in its round valley below. A city alive with promise, there at his fingertips, yet somehow just out of reach.

WILL LEARNED QUICKLY HOW IMPORTANT family was to Mei-hua. Her uncle, Wei-ting, was a jovial, airy man prone to great laughter and lightness. Will liked him immediately. His help was invaluable, securing not only the lease on the school, but also navigating endless rounds of paperwork with first one government ministry and then another. Then the utilities: phone, internet, and power. He had contacts to help procure office and school room furniture. And he knew the best beef noodle shop in all of Taichung. The cooks sang out his name as he walked in the door.

Seeing Mei-hua with her uncle, laughing and joking, heartened Will. There was a side to her he hadn't yet seen, a warmth and vitality, maybe a touch of youth. (She wasn't old at twenty-three, but an old soul.) Simply put, without the help of Wei-ting, there was no way Will McCarthy could have moved to Taichung and started a new business. No way.

"That's the value of family in Taiwan," Mei-hua said. "They're there for you. They will do everything for you."

"I've always understood that in principle," Will said. "But to see it in practice."

She smiled. "It's more profound than you can know."

Mei-hua's father was a smart man, very successful in shipping. But he struck Will as a little dour, a little distant. When the family hosted a big party at the Howard Prince Hotel in Taichung, celebrating Wei-ting's birthday, Mei-hua made a point of seating Will next to her father. Will tried to make conversation, but Chih-wei only returned clipped answers. After the food had been served, he left their table to drink rice wine with his brother. Will couldn't help feeling he'd been snubbed. Thankfully Mei-hua's cousins, also at the table, politely steered the discussion to brighter topics.

Will asked Mei-hua about it. She acknowledged that her parents were wary about their relationship. "Give them time," she counseled. "They'll come around."

Then she kissed him, washing away his worries.

Mei-hua stayed close to her parents. She saw them frequently, making the long bus ride across the city to Beitun District most Sundays. Will often joined her. The family usually went out to lunch at a local place run by a friend. The food was delicious but they always ordered too many plates. If the ladies wanted to go shopping afterwards, Will followed along, trying to be of good cheer. The mother and sister made an effort to include him. Chih-wei rarely accompanied them.

By the end of that first year, Will begged off most Sundays. It was his one day off from work, and he didn't always want to spend it with his girlfriend's family. He stayed home at the flat in Xitun District, doing his thing.

One evening Mei-hua was late returning from a visit to her parents. Her sister made the long drive across the city to drop her off, very rare. It was clear that Mei-hua had been crying. Will held her for a long time, soothing her. He invited her to share what had upset her, but she just shook her head.

"Please don't ask," she moaned.

"I love you," Will said. "Something happened tonight. What was it? Why won't you share it with me?"

It took a bit of pleading, but finally Mei-hua shared it. She spoke in a low, quiet voice, almost a monotone. There'd been a long conversation with her parents about the school, about her role in it, and about her future.

"What did you tell them?"

"I told them that what they see me doing now is what I hope to continue doing. To work hard for the school, to make it successful, to keep it thriving."

Will brushed a crumb from the tabletop. "Weren't they really asking about us?"

"They have questions, yes."

Will sat forward. "What kinds of questions?"

Mei-hua stared off into a corner of the kitchen.

"Why do they only want to talk to you? Why don't they want to talk to me?"

Mei-hua broke down then, weeping into her palms. He knew enough to give her time. Though it seemed that's all he did: give things time. Wait and wait, playing some long game with the parents, letting Mei-hua do all the messy middle work. He felt like a pawn, thwarted by unseen forces.

He had to remind himself of the basic situation: he loved Mei-hua, and she loved him. They simply had to show that to her parents, to convince them of its power and durability. When it came to business, the school was doing well and Will would be happy to show the Lu family the books, or whatever they needed to see to be assured that Will was a hard worker, successful, and not about to quit.

A year later little had changed. Will understood that the parents had reservations, but how long do you have to pander to that? At some point you just press forward and tell them what's going to happen. Maybe it should be up to them to rise to the occasion, not the burden of Will and Mei-hua to cater to the parents. He yearned to give old Chih-wei a piece of his mind.

Mei-hua gave him an icy look. "Don't you dare. That would be a betrayal. Not just of them, but of me." She lectured him, again, on filial piety and a daughter's obligations to her parents. He must let her take the lead on this issue. Case closed.

Will relented. What choice did he have? He understood filial piety intellectually; the concept was clear. But how it worked, how it felt, what it might lead one to do… there was something there, even after those years in Taiwan, he failed to fully understand. But he knew Mei-hua understood, and he had to trust she'd find a way through it all to get them where they wanted to be. He had to trust her.

SATURDAY, MID-DAY, AFTER THE KIDS had left and Shu-lin had clocked out, Will found Margaret sitting in the waiting area.

"What's up?" he asked.

"I can't go home to Auntie. We had a huge fight this week and she's really mad. She'll hardly talk to me. I have to move out of there."

"Probably a good idea. You should look around."

Margaret stared at the floor, slowly shaking her head. With her budget she could only afford something low-end, she said, well outside of the city center. Will suggested she ask around with the other teachers. Somebody always needed a roommate. He went about his business, closing things down. Ten minutes later, when he returned to the lobby, Margaret was still there.

"It's time to lock up," he said.

Staring at her phone, she said, "Trump just tested positive."

Will shook his head. "He refuses to wear a mask. He thinks injecting bleach will kill the virus. Why am I not surprised?"

"Do you think he'll be re-elected?"

"Why not? America is just stupid enough."

"It's worse than 'stupid.' Hate crimes against Asian Americans skyrocketed after he was elected." She threw her phone into her backpack. "Last month some rando walked up to my sister on K Street in Sacramento and yelled at her to go home. Go home? She was born in Stockton!"

"A vote for Trump is a vote for white supremacy."

"The U.S. is rotting," she muttered. "I'm glad I'm in Taiwan."

"I don't know if you read the papers," Will said, slinging his backpack over a shoulder, "but Trump is more popular than Biden here."

Margaret screwed up her face. "Why?"

"They like him because he stands up to China."

Will turned the lights out and locked the doors. Together they walked down the stairwell and out into the bright afternoon sunlight. Will asked if she had any plans for the weekend.

"I know exactly no one on this island except the people I work with and my aunt. I'm going to treat myself to a bubble tea and then go barricade myself in my bedroom and cry while watching Taiwan Netflix. How about you?"

"I was supposed to meet a friend out at Wuqi Fishing Port," Will said, "but he bailed. Join me for a plate of oysters?"

On Will's scooter, they rode out to Qingshui District. They browsed the huge indoor market, with fresh cuts of fish laid out on ice, along with crab legs and squid and eel. They strolled the wharf, looking at the colorful fishing boats. They ended up at an outdoor café, where they celebrated the weekend with a plate of raw oysters and two large Taiwan beers. The oysters were colossal. Will drizzled a little vinegar and fresh-squeezed lemon over them, then a ribbon of pepper sauce. The oysters were mild and smooth, and they took their time eating them.

A few tables over, a group of local fishermen were loudly laughing and joking, their table littered with empty beer bottles and stacks of spent shells. Every time the waitress tried to clear them away, the men waved her off. They wanted a record of all they'd consumed.

One of the fishermen caught Will's eye. He smiled and raised a glass of beer in salute, and Will raised his. With a smile, they both drank.

"Another first for me," Margaret said. "The Taiwan coast. Which is odd, because I live less than a mile from the water. But I never see it in Shalu."

"You need to go a little further north. The Gaomei Wetlands are worth a visit."

"As usual, the white guy has the 4-1-1." Margaret sipped her beer. "You should be a guide."

Will laughed. "If I thought I could make a living at it, maybe."

"How long did it take you to feel at home here?"

"A few years," he said. "But it's different for me. People don't look at me the way they look at you. I've always been the outsider."

She looked over her beer at him. "You like that."

"I accept it. I know where I fit in, and where I don't. I have a certain level of privilege, which can be useful. But I also know that the language, the history, the culture—none of it will ever be mine. I don't have to wrestle with some of the things you do."

"But you had a Taiwanese girlfriend. You got pretty deep into it."

"Deep into something, all right." He took a long sip off his beer.

She sat forward. "I'm dying to hear more about it."

He had to ask himself if he was ready to talk about it. Well, after ten months, why wasn't he? Apart from a few of his oldest friends in Taiwan, all up in Taipei, he had almost no one to share it with. Or maybe he'd simply spent too many months hiding in plain sight, using work as a crutch to pretend he was too busy to deal with it. Telling himself to be tough, to push through the heartache, the humiliation, and the loneliness. As if simple endurance were all it required. Typical stoic male bullshit.

Opening up a little, sharing the story—it was a way of letting go. Or least a step in that direction.

"I'm ready," Will said, dressing another oyster. "I just don't know where to start."

"Where is she now?" Margaret asked.

"She's out in Beitun District with her parents. She's got a new job, working for her dad." For several months Mei-hua was still a business partner at Sunflower, he explained, paying her share of rent and utilities but also grabbing her share of the profits. Will had been slow to fix that, mostly because he knew he not only needed to buy her out; he needed a local business partner to take her place.

"It's nearly impossible to run a business in Taiwan without a local partner, someone who can navigate the policy and paperwork. Legalese in Mandarin is way outside my scope."

"What did you do?"

"I convinced my former boss in Taipei, Yen Hong-wei, to partner with me."

"How did Mei-hua handle all of this?"

Will ate his oyster, then stacked the empty shell on a discard plate. "I haven't seen her since she left."

"Ouch."

"I understand. We've both been hurt. She's trying to move on."

"And you?"

He topped off their glasses of beer. "It's over, I get that. I just don't know what comes next. I wake up, I go to work. I come home. I'm stuck in a loop."

"It's called depression. I know something about that."

Will traced a bead of moisture along the base of his beer glass. "What do you do about it?"

"Spend a thousand hours in therapy. Get new habits and hobbies. Move to Taiwan."

"I don't think I'm ready to leave this island."

"You know you're not stuck here."

Will lifted his beer and smiled. "I've never felt so elegantly stranded."

The fishermen at the next table over were getting up to leave, smiling and laughing in solidarity. One man called to Will in Taiwanese, a phrase he didn't quite catch. Something about "brother" and "good to see you." Another came to their table and placed a tiny orange flower before Margaret. He spoke very rapidly, bowed deeply, then left to join his friends.

"What was that?" she asked.

Will smiled. "He compared your beauty to that flower."

She picked up the flower and gave it a sniff. "Great, the first guy to hit on me in weeks and I can't understand a word."

The waitress came and asked if everything was all right. Will thanked her and said they were ready for the check. The waitress smiled and said that the fishermen who'd just left had already covered it.

"They paid for our lunch?" Margaret asked. "Who were they?"

"Admirers," the waitress said, in English.

WILL DECLARED THAT IT WAS TIME to speak to Mei-hua's parents. She warned him it would be a bad idea, but he insisted. They'd been a couple for five years. They were business partners and lovers. They lived together and worked together and had a right to plan a life together. And hadn't she just confirmed it for him? Mei-hua wanted to marry, she wanted kids. They wanted these things together. Why couldn't they work together to make it happen?

They both knew the answer.

Will suggested they run off to Hong Kong and elope. Her family would come around, sooner or later.

"That would be worse than a slap in the face," Mei-hua said, somberly. "My parents might never speak to me again."

"What if you accidentally got pregnant?"

She cocked her head. "I'm not playing games with my father. We need his blessing."

"Then we need to speak to him. Together."

She covered her face with her hands. "I can't, Will. I'm not ready."

She would never be ready, he understood this now. "Then I need to speak to him. I have it all laid out in my mind. I'll bring the school ledgers. I'll bring our savings account statement. Doesn't he want to be a grandfather?"

Mei-hua resisted for weeks. Will was patient but persistent. He was ready to settle down. He felt it in his bones. If there was some sort of sticking point with her parents, he wanted to address it, not hide from it. He had a hunch, call it a certain confidence, that Chih-wei could be persuaded. He was a businessman, after all. They would reach some sort of agreement.

Mei-hua, openly frustrated at being pressured on two sides, finally relented. On a Sunday afternoon she took Will to Beitun to discuss the marriage. Will wore his best trousers and shirt, and even a tie. It felt a little like a job interview.

Mei-hua led him up to a family altar on the second floor of the house, a room Will had never seen. She kissed him, wished him good luck, then quietly walked downstairs to await the verdict. He'd wanted to address the parents jointly, but Mei-hua assured him this would be a conversation between men only.

Mei-hua's mother knelt before the altar, chanting softly, bowing and offering prayers. The Buddha, made of burnished bronze, sat in the lotus position, eyes lowered, hands folded in the cosmic mudra. A silky thin taper of smoke rose from one of the incense burners. Will knew the family was Buddhist, though Mei-hua was not an active practitioner. Will was not a person of faith; he'd never thought to ask about any of it.

Chih-wei sat stiffly upright in a chair. Will sat opposite him. Chih-wei asked questions in Mandarin. What were his intentions? How did he intend to make Mei-hua happy?

Will spoke of their commitment and affection, the rare quality of true love, but the father cut him off. He began a long, circuitous discussion on security, stability, and permanence. Will was patient; talking around a thing was often a feature of Chinese conversation. Finally, Chih-wei concluded his oration with one simple question.

"How will you support her?"

Money. He wanted to talk about money. Will was prepared for this. He began to recite the annual profits at Sunflower, slender but consistent. From his bag he extracted printouts of his business ledgers and copies of his bank statements, all available for review.

Being successful at business was good, Chih-wei said, but that wasn't what he wanted to know. "A man cannot support a family without property. What do you own? You rent your school building. Are you going to buy a house? An apartment in Taichung? You don't even own a car."

Will felt a spike of panic. He might be able to afford a car, but he couldn't afford to buy an apartment or a house, let alone buy commercial property. Chih-wei knew that and was making it hard.

Chih-wei lectured Will on the need for stability, for permanence. Where was his family?

"My mom lives in Tampa, Florida," Will said. "My dad passed away eight years ago. I have a brother in Fort Collins, Colorado."

"Do you speak with him?"

"Once a year," Will said, looking away. "We're not close."

"Why is that?"

Will resented the question. He felt it was none of Chih-wei's business, though clearly Chih-wei felt differently. Refusing to answer wouldn't help.

Will recited the sad story of the family breaking apart, the parents each taking a son. "I rarely saw my brother after that. Instead of growing closer, we grew apart. I guess we never fixed it, not entirely. But it wasn't exactly our fault, at least initially. Our parents made that decision."

Chi-wei seemed to consider this point. "Does your mother work?"

"She runs a print shop with her second husband."

"Do they own it?"

"They own their shop, but a franchise owns the parent company."

"Does your mother ever visit you in Taiwan?"

"She's never been here."

"Do you visit her in Florida?"

"I've been back twice."

"Twice in ten years." Chih-wei folded his arms across his chest. "You're alone here. You reject your family. You have little wealth. And you want to marry my daughter."

"I don't reject—"

Will paused, taking a deep breath. He felt things sliding out from under him. He must not lose this moment. He sat forward in his chair.

"Lu Chih-wei, with respect, I love your daughter and she loves me. Isn't that enough? Our business is doing very well. I have a robust savings account. In time, we'll accomplish all the things you desire of us. But let us marry now. Let us give you a grandchild. Let us celebrate. Our love is pure."

"You think pure love is enough."

"Yes."

Chih-wei gave him a long, hard look. "Marriage is about security."

Then he stood and walked out of the room.

FOR THE REST OF THAT WEEK Will and Mei-hua hardly spoke. A gloomy silence hung over them, dark and foreboding. The next weekend she rode the bus out to Beitun alone. She did not return for three days, missing work.

When she did return, he fixed her supper and they spoke over the table. In a dry, almost business-like tone, Mei-hua confirmed what Will suspected. Her parents did not approve of her marrying a white foreigner, at least one without property or money. Chih-wei considered Will a vagabond, a waif, not to be trusted. He forbade her from marrying him. They could continue to date, but at this point Mei-hua felt that even that was disrespecting her father's wishes.

"Don't say that," Will replied. "He doesn't want us to marry. I get it." They'd back off the issue. Will could afford to buy a car. Wei-ting could help them find an apartment to purchase. In another two or maybe three years, things might look different. They could try again.

"The main thing is we're together, you and me." He reached his hand across the table and she placed hers in his. He gave it a squeeze, but she did not reciprocate.

"Hey, talk to me."

Her eyes cast down to the table, Mei-hua shook her head slowly.

Will's throat tightened. "Don't do this."

She brought the back of a hand to her mouth. "I wish you hadn't spoken to him. Now things have been said, a line has been drawn. My father is firm."

She sat back in her chair, withdrawing her hand.

A few days later she packed up her things and left the apartment, moving back into her parents' home. She stayed at Sunflower Academy for another three weeks. It was horribly awkward and strange. She avoided talking to Will, avoided eye contact and chat. She wanted to pretend that their relationship had never happened. He told her it didn't have to be like that; they could still be friends.

But they couldn't be lovers, they couldn't be friends, and, in the end, they couldn't even work quietly side-by-side.

And then she was gone. Absent. Vanished. He knew he'd never see her again, never hear from her. Privately, he cursed her father and his old-fashioned ideas. But mostly he cursed himself for not listening to Mei-hua in the first place. She'd counseled him to lay low, to be quiet and patient. Right from day one, she knew how to play it. He'd pressured her, forced the question, and gotten the answer he deserved.

His Taiwanese friends listened to the story in a respectful silence. Nothing about it shocked them. Lu Chih-wei might be old school and conservative, but he was hardly alone.

His expat friends told him to shake it off. There were any number of Asian women in Taiwan keen to date a white guy, plenty of other fish in the sea. He'd find another woman and Mei-hua would fade from memory.

But it wasn't like that. Will was heartbroken, yes, but also stunned and humiliated. The whole experience made him question to what degree he'd come to rely, consciously or unconsciously, on his white privilege. Did he really think he could move to Asia and everyone would bow to his demands? Who was he? Why was he so shocked? He lived in a culture he only partially understood at best, speaking a language he struggled to master, ignorant of a deeper set of values, beliefs, and customs. Should it really come as a surprise to learn that, lo and behold, he was not welcomed by every Taiwanese family he met? There were some who viewed him with doubt and suspicion, who regarded him as an outsider, an unwelcome guest.

And there was one man in Beitun District who, when asked, said no. No to this white man. No to his daughter seeking his approval to marry a laowai. No, no, no.

IN DECEMBER, STRICT NEW MASKING policies went into effect as new cases of the coronavirus spiked across the island. Luckily, cram schools remained exempt, one of the few exceptions. By the end of the month, as case counts continued to rise, new entry restrictions for foreign nationals were announced. Will knew what that meant: another tightening of the labor pool for the cram schools. He needed to hang onto Margaret at all costs.

In the States, Trump lost but was stirring up his followers with the tale of a rigged election. Audits and recounts turned up nothing, yet the conspiracy theories ballooned.

A few weeks later, a violent mob stormed the U.S. capitol. Will watched the footage in a state of outrage. Grown men dressed in antlers and buffalo hides; racists carrying Confederate flags into the Senate; and militia members chanting "Hang Mike Pence!" All of them bent by a lie, a conspiracy theory launched by a man who could not admit that he lost, that he was a loser, that he'd been rejected. Why couldn't he admit it and move on? Quit clinging to the wretched past. Quit trying to convince yourself it might come back to you. Move on.

ON A FRIDAY EVENING, AS HE and Margaret closed up the classroom, Will made a simple offer.

"I have an extra room. The flat is quite small, but I can cut you a deal for a few months, until you sort things out."

"I can't do that," Margaret said. "It'd be too weird."

"Suit yourself. I wouldn't offer if I didn't think it would work." A moment later he added, "I don't mind telling you, it's been a little too quiet lately."

"Let me think about it."

By Monday she'd made up her mind. Her only question was how soon she could move in. She didn't have a lot of stuff. Shu-lin got her brother to lend them a car for the afternoon and, one artful packing job later, she'd moved up the hill from Shalu to Will's flat in the Donghai Arts District. There was a terribly stiff, awkward good-bye with Auntie. Margaret swore she'd never visit the woman ever again.

He set Margaret up in the small back bedroom, a room he'd used for storage. She brought with her a ukulele. He enjoyed hearing her soft strumming in the bedroom, her slow, plaintive melodies. He invited her to bring it out into the living room. The music enlivened the apartment, as did her presence.

After a week of living together, he made a dinner for the two of them: braised pork and vegetables over rice, with a nice bottle of wine he'd picked up at Taisuco. They ate and talked of that week's lessons, some boisterous students, and a funny joke Shu-lin had shared about tea leaves.

"I have to tell you," Margaret said, staring down at her glass of wine. "This week has felt restorative. I can't believe how toxic things had gotten with Auntie."

"It's been pretty easy having you here."

"I don't drive you nuts?"

"Far from it." He drizzled soy sauce over the last bites of his meal.

She looked up from her wine. "Thank you."

Will nodded and smiled. They were two loners and outcasts, each lonesome and sad, each struggling to find new footing in the world. It was enough to celebrate that, to find someone who could accept that in you and, perhaps, because of that, in themself. They could be lonely together, or lonely in the presence of one another. They could be friends, helping each other, lifting each other's spirits. It didn't need to be anything more than that; that was enough for now.

Packing Out

1

On the third morning, Jon stayed inside the tent, spiraled deep within his sleeping bag. He would linger as long as possible, avoiding the cold and drizzle. Outside, he heard his father working around the fire pit, boots scuffling across soggy ground, the busy clatter of pots and pans. Campfire smoke drifted through the tent, light and musky.

"You alive in there?"

Jon groaned.

"Get your ass up. I'm making breakfast."

Rain splattered the tent shell in bursts, like buckshot. Ten minutes later, his father barked again. The eggs would be ready and he damn sure better be out there to eat them.

"Can I eat in the tent?"

"No food in the tent! You know that."

Jon was slow to pull himself out of the sleeping bag, slow to look for his duck boots, slow to don his rain pants and jacket. Maybe he could just skip breakfast, though when Dad cooked you had to eat or he took it personally. Not like Mom. She hated cooking now, no longer nagging if he left a meal half-finished.

By the time he managed to pull himself out of the tent, food was on the table. Reconstituted scrambled eggs, two sausage links, and half of an English muffin. A dollop of margarine sat off-center, melting into the warm bread.

His father waved a spatula at him. "Sit down and eat."

"I have to pee."

"You haven't peed? Christ, hurry it up! I'm soaked to the bone out here cooking, and you haven't even taken a whiz!"

Jon scampered a few yards down the path leading out of the campsite, towards the pit latrine. He lowered the waistband of his rain pants with a thumb. Urine foamed on the spongy earth, steaming in the damp air. How quiet this little dell in the woods was, covered in fern and moss. A sanctuary of sorts, a world of blankets, covering the ugliness.

He returned to the campsite and slid into place at the table. Across from him, his father's plate was already empty. Jon nibbled at his food. The sausages were cold. The eggs were tasteless and rubbery. His father pointed to a small bottle of Tabasco on the table. Jon soaked his eggs in the fiery red sauce and did what he could to choke it down without meeting his father's gaze.

After eating Jon made his way down the hill to the lake-shore to collect a pot of water for washing. The lake was flat as glass, covered in a silvery mist. He crouched on a stone spit, studying it. He envied such stillness; he ached to feel such peace. But it was impossible. All the shadowy stuff churned inside him, a desperate, roiling mess. He felt one way about it in the morning, and another in the afternoon. Nothing could be settled, it seemed.

He closed his eyes. *No dark things.*

HIS FATHER HAD HIS TACKLE BOX open on the picnic table. He held up a bright yellow bucktail jig. "Wash those dishes, then grab your rod."

"Fishing in the rain?"

"You want to waste another day sitting in that tent?"

At least it had been dry. He'd read about Huck and Jim on the river, two friends on the run, fleeing a desperate, stultifying world. Best part of the book so far. He wished for it never to end, but he knew it would. Things always fall apart.

His father produced his fishing hat, with its enormous visor like a duck's bill. He cracked a goofy grin. "Those fish are hungry. The rain actually helps!" Jon nodded as his father recited the familiar facts—cold fronts and barometric pressure, insect behavior and organic runoff. Yes, the fish would bite. Yes, you know more than I do. Yes, I'll do what you say. It was their oldest ritual, the one thing that hadn't changed after the divorce. It was certainly the reason Jon was there with him now. Fishing and blood. What else did they have?

HE'D STALLED AND RESISTED, procrastinating his packing until his mother finally shouted that unless he had his pack filled by bedtime, she was going to take every damn piece of electronics in the house and bury it in a box in the back yard for a year: iPod, iPad, iPhone, 3DS, and X-box.

"I don't have an iPad."

Her finger jabbed in the air like a lance. "Go to your room!"

She sat in the chair opposite his bed as he packed, texting on her iPhone. Blue light flickered across her face.

"I don't see why I have to go," he growled.

"This is him reaching out."

"It's crap."

"Only if you treat it like crap. It could be great."

"Five days in the woods? Tell me how that's great."

Busy with a text, she was slow to reply. "Male bonding."

"What a joke."

She lowered her phone, holding his gaze for a moment. Then the blue light returned.

Jon folded his arms. "You don't care."

"I do care. But I don't have a say."

"Which is totally effed." He studied the jumbled mess of clothing on his bed. None of it made sense. "I'm just this thing you pass back and forth, one more thing to fight over."

She sat silently, thumbs thrumming across the iPhone screen. Sometimes he wanted to smash it right out of her hands, screaming at her to look at him, to touch him.

"He says you turned on him. He says you kicked him out."

The phone finally fell to her lap. "Did he tell you that?"

"Is it true?"

"No." She ran a finger along the edge of her smart phone, as if caressing it. "I can't believe he said that."

"I overheard him telling someone." Jon searched his laundry for a sock, the missing partner to the one in his hand. "Will you and Dad ever get back together?" The eagerness of his question embarrassed him.

She looked at him with wet, red-rimmed eyes. "Baby, I've told you."

"But I still don't understand."

"I can't," she whispered, slowly shaking her head. "Maybe someday you'll understand."

He threw the single sock into a corner of his closet, forever an orphan. He might understand if his parents would talk to him. They exploded in each other's faces, screaming out how they felt about one another, but all they ever did with him was circle around a thing.

His mother was wounded and scared, he knew that. Still, he'd hoped for reconciliation, that she could at least imagine the possibility. Now, perhaps for the first time, he understood that it was beyond her imagination. She had no imagination. Like a forest after a ravaging fire, it would be months, years before she returned to life.

Wadding up the remaining clothes on his bed, he began jamming it all into his pack, everything helter-skelter.

"It won't fit like that," his mother observed.

"I'll make it fit."

"You won't find anything."

"There's not as much to sort out as you think."

THEY FISHED IN A COVE CARPETED in lily pads and banked in slender green reeds. They sat in opposite ends of the canoe. Jon cast into deeper water, while his father worked the shore. Wary of startling the fish, they remained silent.

In late morning the rain weakened to a drizzle, and by noon it had stopped. The clouds lightened. Soon there were patches of blue sky poking through. Jon felt the warmth of the sun on his neck. They removed their rain jackets. His father rolled up his flannel shirt sleeves, exposing his muscular forearms, covered in a skein of black arm hair. Within the past year, the silky tendrils on Jon's own arms had thickened and grown longer.

His father turned. "What're you looking at?"

"Your hairy arms."

He laughed. "Yeah, just you wait. Your grandpa was a hairy son of a bitch. Runs in the family."

"Tell me about him."

His father made a short cast and reeled it in. "Hard guy to get to know. He worked the ore boats. Wasn't around a lot."

"I know that," Jon said. "Did he take you fishing?"

His father smiled. "He did." He spoke of his favorite memories: long, lazy afternoons trolling for walleye, shore casting for trout, or netting smelt. "That's why I do this with you. Sort of a tradition, you know?"

Jon nodded, then reeled in his line. His plug was fouled with stringy weeds. He cleaned it, then began carefully sorting through the tackle box, searching for the right lure. It was time for a change.

BACK AT CAMP, THEY STRUNG lines between trees and hung their wet clothing to dry. Jon's father lay down in the tent for a nap. Jon returned to his book. He read the scene where

Huck, confronted by slave catchers, lies to protect Jim. Later he feels guilty for not having done the right thing, yet he knows that handing Jim over would've been just as bad. There is no correct answer, it seems. Right or wrong, both carry a cost. So how do you choose? *I was stuck*, Huck concludes. *I couldn't answer that.*

Jon sat up in his camp chair. He read the scene a second time. Amazing, he thought. There it was, right there. His mind felt electric; he couldn't sit still. He walked down to the lake and gazed across the water, rippling with waves, the sunlight sparkling, almost holy, beacon from an undiscovered country. One day he would go there.

IN THE LATE AFTERNOON, they again set out to fish, this time on foot. Jon worked a tiny cove far from their campsite. He found a clearing between two ancient fir trees and stepped to the shore. He knew the smaller pike would be in shallower water. The larger pike would be out in the middle and along the points of the cove. He used a red-and-white Dardevle spoon, casting up high. Just before the lure hit the water, he jerked back on the rod, snapping the line so the lure slapped the surface, a trick his dad had taught him. It attracted bigger pike, triggering their feeding response.

He was at it for forty minutes with nothing to show. Mid-autumn was a funny time to be fishing for pike. It depended on what the muskies were doing in the lake. Muskies swam in the deeper, colder water and when they moved out the bigger pike would, at this time of year, move into that deeper water. He might need to be out in the canoe. He might need to be fishing for something other than pike. He might need to be on a different lake. Or on a wholly different adventure. Maybe floating down the river on a raft with a friend.

He checked his watch: four o'clock on a Saturday afternoon. He was tired and hungry, hadn't bathed in three days, and the mosquitoes and black flies were eating the living shit out of him. But hey, this was his dad's idea of "guy time," getting away from it all, the big step back. They were supposed to be getting to know each other again, re-bonding.

Whatever. A bunch of bullshit. Wow, his dad felt guilty for walking away from the family. He took a week off work to bring his son up to the Boundary Waters… in fucking October! They had the place to themselves, however many millions of acres of lake and forest, but that just meant the mosquitos had nobody else to pick on and you could pretty much count on rain.

His thoughts were arrested by the sound of a loon calling from across the lake, its wail piercing and plaintive. The sound lingered in the trees, at once the most beautiful and the most mournful thing he'd heard in these woods. He longed to hear it again, and a few minutes later he did. Now farther away, the song was quieter, softer. A haunting echo, the memory of a song.

ACTUALLY, WHEN HIS FATHER had made that comment—that Jon's mother had turned on him—it had been to one of his girlfriends, Vicky or was it Gwen. (None of them stayed around for long.) The two of them sat out in the kitchen one Saturday night, drinking and talking, their voices loud. Jon lay in his bed in the narrow utility room, hastily converted to a boy's bedroom, the back half haphazardly piled with boxes. When his father said it, Jon knew it was a lie. He also knew his father believed it. There was no version of the story where he was plainly at fault, where he accepted blame.

The next morning Jon rose early. The house was quiet. He walked down the hall and peeked into his father's bedroom. Janice—that was her name—lay stretched out naked beside his father. Jon stared at her back and bare ass, dimpled with fat. Her skin looked flabby and pasty white, nothing like the glossy skin he'd seen in the pictures on his father's computer.

Jon stepped back. A board creaked. His father's eyes flew open.

"Close the fucking door!"

Jon slammed it shut and threw his old man the finger.

SEVERAL TIMES JON SWORE it would be his final cast, but he cast again—eternal hope of the fisherman. When the pike hit, he knew it was big. The fish took line and Jon heard the drag on his reel and tried to slow it down as the fish swam toward a log. Jon worked the fish in, thrashing, to the shore. The Dardevle was pinned tightly into the lower jaw, bristling with heavy teeth. Jon removed the lure with a pair of longnose pliers, a gift from his father on his eighth birthday. He strung the fish through the gills and immediately set out for camp.

His father was down along the shore, cleaning a smallmouth bass. Blue-gray innards sat in a small, wet pile. He sawed off the fish head with two vigorous strokes of the knife. He smiled when he saw Jon's catch.

"Atta boy! Now we have a meal. You clean that up and I'll pan fry these suckers."

Jon scaled the pike, then gutted it. He tossed the offal along the shore for the gulls or raccoons. He rinsed his hands in the cold, clean water. He brought his wet, glistening fingers to his nose, savoring the smell of the lake: earthy and damp, fresh but also a little musty from the reeds and lily pads and leaves. The odors of camping—lake water, wood smoke, fish frying up in the pan—these might be his favorite things about it, what he would remember best.

He stood before the lake, studying its coves and outcrops. Trees crowded the shoreline, ablaze in autumn oranges, yellows, and reds. So many hidden areas, secluded spots. It was oddly comforting, when you thought about it: you can't see the entire lake all at once, a case of limited perspective. He liked knowing there were hidden pockets, safe spots where you might hide from others.

Last year, during the divorce, his parents were constantly shouting and throwing things and slamming doors. Mom lay in bed half the day, sobbing. Dad was gone a lot. When he was home he sat alone at the kitchen table under the fluorescent light, drinking Jim Beam out of a jelly jar, lame '80s rock music playing on the radio, staring sullenly at the dark brown oven door like it might open up and tell him something, answer some question about why, about who was to blame, about what to do next. But the oven never had anything to say, never opened its mouth, cold because no one had bothered to cook a meal in weeks. All they ate was crappy take out. For once Jon could eat whatever he wanted: KFC, Taco Bell, Pizza Hut. His mother let him eat in the living room with the television blaring. Just clean up your mess. She couldn't be bothered.

A horrible year, one long opera of tears and shouting, but mostly silence. Three people in their tiny, one-floor house each pressed into a different corner, alone. A terrible stillness, heavy as a stone, pressing down on each of them. Until one of them left.

And then, gradually, things changed. His mother started to clean the house again. She read Jon's report cards. His third quarter grades were poor. In the thick of the fighting, with neither parent paying attention, he'd quit doing homework. He skipped days, feigning illness at home or playing hooky, wandering in the trees along Congdon Creek or walking out to Como Park, napping on a picnic bench. What difference did it make?

His mother was shocked. She knew she'd dropped the ball, but what the hell was this? Jon made some remark about no one else caring, so why should he.

"You want to repeat sixth grade? Because if you get another quarter of this, that's what'll happen."

"Who fucking cares." A stupid thing to say, but he was trying to hurt her.

She narrowed her eyes. "It better be you, baby."

HE WALKED UP THE NARROW, winding path between the ferns, climbing the short hill to their campsite, perched on a bluff overlooking Arrowhead Lake. His father had a fire going, a thin blue spiral of smoke rising into the birch and maple canopy. The clouds had cleared off, leaving a brilliant teal afternoon sky. On the table stood an aluminum flask. Dad was in a jolly mood, whistling as he tended the fire. The bass lay on a plate, split into two clean filets. In a bowl beside it, corn meal with a pinch of red pepper.

"Nice catch," he said, looking at Jon's fish. "I dated a Chippewa girl once. She sucked the heads and ate the eyeballs."

"When was that?"

"Years ago."

"You still dating Tanya?"

"No," he said, sharply. "Too much work." He poked at the fire with his stick. "Your mother seeing anyone?"

"She says she's through with men."

He laughed. "Yeah, we put her through the ringer. Me first, and now you." He picked up the flask and drank, lips narrowing as he swallowed. "How 'bout it, huh? That storm blows in, three straight days of rain, but then we get this one nice day. Not even one. Half a day." He slid the flask into a pocket of his vest. "Are we fucking camping, or what?"

"We are fucking camping, Dad."

Already his speech was changing: a little louder, a little slurred. Jon had only been down at the shore, cleaning fish for twenty minutes. But then his father probably had the flask with him all afternoon. It was their last night in the woods. Why not tie one on? The rain might have sucked, but at least his dad had been sober.

Jon deboned the pike, then cut it into small filets, which they covered in corn meal and dropped into a hot pan. The meat cooked quickly, turning white. They ate it with a dash of Tabasco. The fish tasted of the lake, a little earthy. Baked beans were next, syrupy and sweet, the perfect follow-up.

After that they felt full and content. They sat around the fire as the afternoon light faded, dusk slowly rising out of the shadows. His father sat in his camp chair licking his fingers and sipping from his flask. Jon kept mixing lemonade, going heavy on the sugary powder, leaving a sediment in his cup. Camping was the one time he drank the stuff.

"How's your mother doing?"

The question surprised him. "I don't know. Better, I guess."

"Glad to hear it."

They listened to the gentle crackling of the fire, which needed tending.

"You think about her?" Jon asked.

"All the time. We talk, probably more than you know."

Jon dug a fingernail into the nylon fabric of his camp chair. "About what?"

"You, mostly." His father sat quietly for a long moment before turning to him. "We lost something, each one of us. But it won't do any good to wish for it back."

"But if you're talking, maybe—"

"Jon," his father cut in, sharply. "It ain't coming back."

Jon swirled the last sip of lemonade, then poured it into the fire. It sizzled on a log. "You're mad at her. You think she turned on you."

"Why would you say that?"

"I heard you talking to that woman, Janice, in the kitchen."

His father screwed up his face, thinking. "The fuck you listening in on me for?"

"I wasn't. You were talking loud, you and that drunk bitch." He sat back in his chair, huffing.

"The walls in that place are pretty thin." His father looked down into the fire. "It was a mistake having her over. You're not ready for that. That was stupid of me. I'm sorry."

Jon studied the endless dance of orange flames flickering up and down, swaying side to side.

"I've made a lot of mistakes, Jon. Your father isn't a perfect man. You know that now."

"But Mom never turned on you."

His father sat back, exhaling loudly through his nose. "No, not exactly."

Jon wanted to ask, *Not exactly as in, she did or she didn't? Speak clearly to me for once in your life.* But he said nothing, aware that his father had said more in the last five minutes than he'd said in the last five years, and equally aware that he was now finished speaking.

A minute later, his father stood from his chair, cleared his throat and spat into the fire. "You go down to the lake, get us some water for washing. I'll burn these scraps in the fire."

Jon grabbed the pot. For once he was glad to have a chore, a reason to walk away. At the shore he stood still, studying the ochre clouds streaking the evening sky. The trees were aglow with a special light, beautiful but fleeting, fated to disappear. He thought he might cry. Something was broken inside him. The sadness and fear were there, had always been there, probably always would be. He'd seen it paralyze his mother. But it didn't have to. It could become something else. The question was where to place your hand on it, how to control it, how to make it into something other than a wild horse trampling you.

Jon breathed deeply of the cool breeze blowing south, across the water. His eyes traced the contours of the lake, soft now, half-covered in shadow. His thoughts, like his heart, were a jumbled mess. He longed for the solace of reading, to disappear again into his book. Not only to escape; there were answers there. When Huck discovers that Jim has been recaptured and sold back into slavery, he weeps for his lost friend. He's devastated. But eventually he acts. Out of sadness comes a stronger resolve, a will to change, to help others, to focus on someone other than himself. It seemed as good a place as any to start.

A large black bear emerged out of the woods along the inland shore, perhaps a quarter mile across the lake. Even at that distance it appeared huge, plump and round, with its distinctive tan snout. Jon was electrified at the bear's appearance. He watched it rout along the shoreline near a campsite they'd considered before settling on the island site, which would be more private. The bear sat back on its haunches and lifted its nose into the air, holding it aloft. Then it walked forward, into the lake, and began swimming for the island.

2

They sat in the clearing, waiting. The packs had been hastily strung in the trees, a dozen feet overhead. His father sat at the end of the picnic table. It probably smelled our campfire, he said, and was coming to have a look. These bears were pretty tame, used to dealing with campers. Easy to scare off. Just let him handle it.

Jon was nervous. A bear was nothing to mess with. They were on its turf, not the other way around.

And then it was there, entering the campsite from the trail that led up from the shore, its black hair glistening and wet. They hadn't heard a thing, not one sound.

Jon's father stood and picked up the soup pot and metal spoon. "Stand up straight," he said. "Stay behind me and a little off to the side. Don't turn your back on him." He started banging the spoon on the pot and shouting at the bear to scram, buzz off, get the hell out of there.

The bear stood still on the edge of the campsite, regarding them, then moved forward, slowly, head low, sniffing. Jon and his father backed off, giving it space. It moved to the table, nosing around the fire pit, where it found something on the ground.

"Damn, those fish scraps."

"Didn't you burn them?"

"I dropped the plates. I thought I picked it all up. Now he thinks we have something."

He stepped forward, banging loudly on the pot and shouting.

"Dad! Be careful."

"I've done this before."

The bear sniffed around the perimeter of the fire pit, moving slowly, indifferent to the camper's clamor. Jon felt tight and nervous, his body stiffening with fear. Yet his father appeared loose, almost like he was having fun. He pounded and hollered, whooped and shouted. The bear continued its methodical search, sniffing along the tent, back around the picnic table, and then across the clearing before pausing at the foot of the tree bearing their packs. It sat back on its haunches, sniffing up in the air, then raised itself up on its hind legs, placing one paw on the pine tree. Erect, it stood six feet tall, its movements oddly human.

"Oh, no you don't!" his father barked. "You don't want to do that!"

"Is it going to climb the tree?"

"He's thinking about it."

His father stepped forward. The bear lowered itself to the ground. It rolled its head, turning towards them, making a strange kind of huffing sound. His father stomped a foot and roared.

"Dad!"

His father was screaming now, banging ever more quickly. He stepped forward again.

The bear rose like a black wave, knocking his father flat to the ground and tousling him, teeth bared, before charging into the blackness of the forest, through the brush. Gone, vanished. The forest was eerily silent.

His father lay on his back, flat on the ground. He groaned. Jon darted forward, dropping to his knees. Blood dampened his father's shoulder. "I can't feel anything," his father said. "Is it bad?"

Jon breathed quickly, in sharp, shallow huffs. He couldn't speak, frozen in disbelief and fear. This terrible, unimaginable thing had just happened.

"Jon, look at me. Tell me how bad it is."

Jon blinked, staring down at his father. "I can't touch it."

"You have to. You have to bind it up, clean it."

Jon picked at his father's torn shirt, saw the blood already soaking the shoulder. He moved the fabric and saw the open wound—two or three gashes, like he'd been slashed with a knife. There were more along his right rib cage and forearm. In the minutes that followed, Jon did his best to clean and bind the wounds, following his father's instructions. His dad seemed remarkably calm and clear, though he said it was beginning to hurt. He wasn't sure he could sit up yet. Jon dabbed at the wounds, cleaning them, then applied a crude compress, wrapping it all with a couple of shirts.

"We have to break camp," his father said.

"Is it coming back?"

"No. I challenged it, which was stupid. He spooked and ran. He'll wait a good while before coming back. We need to leave at first light. I gotta see a doctor."

His father lay in the tent, head propped up on some bags, his arm in a sling and his side and shoulder wrapped in the make-shift bandages. He directed Jon's actions, telling him what to pack and where to put it. The entire break-down of the camp was now on Jon's shoulders. His father couldn't help. The initial numbness and shock of the encounter gave way to a rising sensation of sharp, burning pain. Even rolling over made him cry out.

Jon checked repeatedly for cell phone reception, but they were out of range, just as they had been since leaving the out-fitter four days ago. The stark fact of their isolation terrified him; his back and shoulders were tight and stiff. Adrenaline coursed through his body in rude surges. It helped having chores to do, the packing and stuffing and cleaning up. Just keep moving. Push aside the fear, which could swallow him. He mustn't let it.

It was agreed they would break camp at dawn. Crossing the lake in the dark was too dangerous, and anyway they had two portages on their way out that could only be managed in daylight. They would spend the night in the tent, set an alarm, and be off first thing.

Jon couldn't sleep. He listened to his father's labored breathing, the wet, close snorts and snores. He worried his father might die. That possibility hovered before him like an inscrutable, black shadow. He would not, could not look upon it. He must turn his mind from it. But to what?

He worried the bear might return. It would be angry. It had tasted blood.

The wind increased. The tent's rain cover and sides flapped noisily—so thin, just two layers of nylon. No protection at all if a bear attacked. Suddenly, every aspect of their situation seemed stacked against them. The darkness, the wind and rain, the bear. What stood between them and disaster? Nylon. Nothing.

The temperature started falling. The rain began softly at first, then steadily increased, drumming on the tent. His father slept fitfully. The unzipped sleeping bag Jon had draped over him kept sliding off. His breathing was labored and heavy. Jon wanted to wake him, to ask if he was all right, to ask if they were going to make it out of there. It seemed impossible, a long day of canoeing and portaging. How was he going to do it alone? Would his father be able to walk? Their situation struck him as increasingly desperate. Doomed. The fear rose again, racing through his mind in mad circles. He wept, he couldn't help it, but then he felt better. He closed his eyes and concentrated on his breathing, something his mother had taught him after his first panic attacks, right after Dad moved out. In, out. Just breathe.

WHEN THE ALARM SOUNDED it was still dark. Jon didn't think he'd slept at all, not for a single minute. And now it was time to do this, to step out into the wind and rain and move everything down to the water. Rousing his father proved difficult. He appeared groggy. Jon wrestled rain pants onto his legs, then ordered him to sit up. His father moved slowly. Overnight the pain and stiffness had increased. Just sitting up made him cry out, a sharp, piercing, primitive wail, almost child-like. Such naked vulnerability terrified Jon. His father was more seriously wounded than he'd thought. Panic washed over his body, stinging like acid. He felt powerless, incompetent. There was nothing he could do, yet he understood there was really only one thing to do, and it started now.

He got his father out of the tent and sat him at the picnic table, a raincoat draped over his shoulders and head, then proceeded to break camp. He didn't wait for instructions. His father was no longer capable of giving instructions. He sat, head drooping, listing to one side, half-asleep.

The canoe loaded, Jon cautiously led his father down the path to the shore. He arranged the packs so that his father could sit in the bottom of the canoe, leaning back. Jon pushed off from shore, climbed into the stern, and began paddling. He needed something to aim for, like a big pine tree or a rock outcrop on the far side of the lake. You aim for your mark and you just keep paddling, telling yourself you're going to get there, one stroke after another. The scuffed wooden blade of the paddle slices into the lake, wind and water offers resistance, yet the boat moves forward. It's almost an act of faith.

Out in the middle of the lake the chop got so heavy it splashed over the bow, spraying them. The canoe rocked violently and Jon feared capsizing. His father's rain jacket blew off, but there was no way to help him. Jon paddled toward shore, where the water was calmer, but this would make their trip longer. His upper arms, neck and back burned with the effort, yet he must continue.

They reached the first portage and Jon unloaded the canoe. He got his father situated on the shore, resting under a large maple, its crown a fiery auburn. Item by item, he conveyed the load from the shore of Arrowhead up and over a steep hill, walking along a narrow forest path to the shore of Hunger Lake, a quarter of a mile away. The packs were heavy and after four trips there and back, his back ached. He felt exhausted, yet still there was the canoe and also his father.

He lifted one end of the canoe and rolled it over, upside-down, then backed himself towards the middle, lifting it along the gunwales until the center span's shoulder pads were in position, and then, crouching, he lifted the rear end off the ground and stood, the canoe now balanced on his shoulders. Walking up the steep trail with the enormous canoe proved taxing. He was red-faced, his head and torso covered in sweat by the time he crested the hill. Mosquitoes buzzed mercilessly around his neck, face, and ears. At the shore of Hunger Lake he had to rest for ten minutes and catch his breath. He tried his father's cell again. Still no reception.

He walked back to get his father. He was half-asleep, dozing under the tree. Jon roused him. His father was shivering. He had trouble standing. He felt dizzy, nauseated. Jon guided him slowly along the path. His father started panting in short, rapid breaths. His feet slipped on the soft, spongy loam of the pine-shaded forest. They paused several times, but it seemed he could never catch his breath. He just wanted to sit down and rest. But after five minutes his breathing had not slowed and he felt no stronger. Jon pleaded with his father to stand. They had to keep moving.

"I don't think I can," his father said.

"You have to," Jon said, his voice hardening with an impatience that surprised him. "I can't leave you out here."

"No, you can't." His father sat broken on a rock, head drooping. "I'm sorry, Jon. God damn it, I'm no good."

The sound of his father's weeping arrested Jon. He closed his eyes, felt his own tears brimming. There was something surreal about all of this, but there was no time to puzzle over it. They still had two lakes and a second portage to cross. He had to get his father back to the outfitter on Eagle Lake today, by sundown. It was already noon. Jon thought his way through the next stages of their journey, estimating how long it would take. God damn it, they could do it! He could make it happen. He was already making it happen. The truth of it washed over him like a cool wave.

"Come on, old man. When we get to the lodge I'll buy you a big beer."

His father chuckled. "They won't serve you!"

"They will after they hear about this."

He got his father up on his feet and they shuffled along the path and down the hill to the lake shore. Jon made himself a quick PB & J. His father wasn't hungry, but Jon made him sip water. He loaded the canoe and got his father positioned, tucking in the edges of the rain coat he draped over him. He hoped his father would stay dry, but in this weather it was a vain wish.

"That's the best I can do," he said.

"You're doing it," his father mumbled. "You're a good son."

A COLD, DRIVING RAIN PELTED them all along the length of Hunger Lake. Jon's hands were red and raw, his cheeks burning. His father's jacket blew off again, but Jon couldn't stop paddling to fix it. The floor of the canoe was awash in rainwater. He knew his father was soaked, miserably wet and cold.

When they reached the shore of the second portage, his father was half-unconscious. Stepping out of the canoe he lost his balance and toppled over into the muck. Cursing, Jon dragged him onto the dry shore. He unloaded the canoe in the rain, arranging the packs in a line in the order that he would carry them. He beached the canoe and rolled it over, upside down. Dirty water funneled out, soaking into the rocky ground.

Jon knew the portage from Hunger to Eagle Lake was shorter and flatter, just ten minutes one way. The trail was wider and better maintained. But he looked at his father, who sat curled up against a tree, muttering, confused, asking where they were, and he knew there was no time to waste. The packs would have to stay. Someone would come back for them. Jon carried the canoe to the shore of Eagle Lake, then double-timed it back for his father, who inexplicably had removed his rain jacket and fleece sweater. The garments sat in a puddle at his feet, covered in mud.

"What are you doing!" Jon hurriedly redressed his father as best he could. "Dad, wake up! You have to wake up now." But his father was not waking up. He was still breathing, however. Thank god.

Kneeling, Jon slowly pulled his father onto his back. His dad was out cold, pure dead weight, no help at all. Jon staggered to his feet, nearly toppling over, but held his footing. Somehow, he made the portage, shuffling, staggering down the trail, grunting and huffing and cursing the Boundary Waters, all species of bear, and every damn mosquito in the state of Minnesota. At the trailhead, Jon lowered his father into the canoe. He fell forward, unconscious, like a bag of meat.

For one raw second the terror of what they faced shot through him, but it was easier now to push it down. There was a single immediate thing that must be done. He must cross Eagle Lake as quickly as possible. Once he got his father back to the outfitter's lodge everything was going to be all right, and this nightmare would cease. He pushed the canoe forward into the water and began paddling. He would not slacken his pace or pause. He told himself he was a machine. Never in his life had he felt so singularly focused on one thing, one goal, one destination.

3

Jon sat in a kitchenette outside the lodge's tiny triage room, a blanket draped over his shoulder. His hand cradled a half-warm cup of cocoa. In the next room, medics counted out a cadence as they performed CPR on his father. They'd had difficulty finding a pulse after the canoe touched shore. His father wasn't breathing.

Jon checked the cell. Still no coverage, even at the lodge. Someone had called his mother on the land line, but she hadn't picked up. They left a message. He didn't know what else to do but wait. A few minutes later a helicopter arrived with a great, thunderous chopping of the air. A doctor, flown in from Ely, rushed into the triage room. The door was shut after him.

Someone handed Jon another cup of cocoa, though he hadn't finished his first. Down the hallway, two staff members spoke in hushed tones.

"The bear attacked last night, around sundown."

"Between storms."

"They set out at dawn from Arrowhead Lake."

"Arrowhead to Hunger, that portage is no joke. How'd he get his dad over that ridge?"

"I think he carried him."

"And a canoe?"

"He paddled solo across three lakes. I know."

Jon wished someone would talk to him, ask him more questions. He didn't like sitting alone at the table, waiting. He felt a curious mix of exhaustion and anxiety, simultaneously ready to collapse and bracing for whatever came next. He needed to keep it together, like he'd been doing. That was the main thing now. Focus on that.

Several minutes later the door opened and the doctor emerged. He drew a chair up beside Jon. The doctor was young, with a lean, angular face and a short, closely trimmed beard.

"Your father slipped into cardiac arrest out on the lake," he said, "long before you touched shore." CPR had been administered for over thirty minutes, but it was simply too late. The doctor put a hand on Jon's shoulder. "There's nothing more we can do. I'm sorry."

In the terrible silence that followed, Jon focused his gaze on the cup of cocoa cradled in his hand, staring at the chalky sludge, little powdery balls lining the rim, undissolved.

"He's dead." The words felt hard on his tongue.

"You did everything you could."

A phone rang down the hall, an urgent clanging. Someone answered it. "Yes, yes, he's right here." A young woman appeared in the hallway holding a green receiver attached to a long, curly cord, hopelessly tangled.

"It's your mom."

Jon stared at the phone as if it were some strange, foreign object. He felt a stirring deep inside, something bubbling and boiling. Not fear, exactly. He knew fear. That's what he'd felt out on the lake. This was something new, something harder. He wasn't sure what it was, not yet. He only knew it was just beginning, its urgency measured by the pounding of his heart and the racing of his blood.

The woman gestured with the phone. "Jon, can you answer it?"

He must be the one to tell her. Exactly what he'd say, or how he'd say it, he didn't know. He simply saw that this was the next step, and he must take it now. He cleared his throat, pushed back his chair, and rose to accept it.

Searching for Florence

Mais qu'y a-t-il derrière la porte
Et qui m'attend déjà?
Ange ou démon qu'importe
Au devant de la porte il y a toi

But what is behind the door
And who is already waiting for me?
Angel or demon whatever
In front of the door there is you

—Jacques Brel, "La Mort"

The train wound its way into the steep, rugged hills of the Basque Mountains. The sinuous, snake-like movement of the journey, following a sparkling stream, intrigued Van Wheeler. With each blind curve, with each precipitous gorge traversed, he felt pulled deeper into something.

His month in Madrid had been fruitful. He'd delivered a keynote at a small film festival and had recorded audio commentary for an exclusive European Blu-Ray box set. A North American edition would be timed for the release of the third Peter Friar film.

Back in L.A. his producer, Sal Casa, awaited a script. A few months ago, Wheeler had been halfway into it when his laptop was stolen. Stupidly, he had no backup.

He told himself not to panic. He had his scene cards. He had a treatment. He could remember whole passages of dialogue. He sat down at his desk and started typing from page one, confident it would all come back, but it didn't. The dialogue felt wooden. The narrative arc looked more like wet tissue paper. An agonizing period followed, one failed start after another.

Wheeler's mood darkened. The trip to Spain was supposed to clear his head, loosen things up.

Wheeler felt stiff and his lower back ached. He walked to the rear of the train, where he stood on the platform between two cars. A man in a business suit was there, smoking. Wheeler felt the man's stare and knew what was coming.

In perfect English, the man said, "I have to ask. Are you Peter Friar?"

"I play Peter Friar," Wheeler replied in Spanish. "My name is Van Wheeler."

"I thought I recognized you!" The men shook hands. "The chase scene with the Tesla, when it flies off the pier into San Francisco Bay. Brilliant!"

A scene from his first film, *Cold Snap*. Critics likened it to a Bond picture, a comparison Wheeler appreciated but wanted to transcend. He'd consciously avoided those tropes in the second film. No more car chases or whiz-bang gadgets.

They struck up a conversation. The businessman was from Bilbao and made several recommendations for dining in the city, chief among them a certain café in the Casco Viejo. The calamari was legendary. And it attracted the most interesting people. Come to think of it, the last time he'd been there Michael Florence was sitting at the next table. They began talking, and before long Florence invited him to join his table. Dinner with Michael Florence!

Wheeler's first instinct was to call bullshit. Did this man know what he was claiming? No one had seen Michael Florence in over a year. Not that people weren't trying. No doubt the paparazzi were combing the back streets of Bilbao at this very moment.

"You know Florence?" Wheeler asked.

"When he needed a maid I recommended my niece, who cleaned his flat for a time. She fell in love with him, naturally. Michael had no choice but to fire her. I understood."

"He's still in Bilbao?"

"Oh, yes. He's working on a film."

That was news. That was something that, if Wheeler were to break it, would draw attention, and attention is always capital in L.A. But he had to be tactful. He needed more information. He'd find a way to contact Florence quietly.

Wheeler asked about a phone number.

"The number I had is disconnected. He's very strict about privacy. You know him?"

"We have some mutual friends." That much was true.

The man handed Wheeler a business card. "If you find him, tell him Lon Bidarte says hello." Then he requested a selfie, to which Wheeler agreed, though he'd long ago quit smiling for them.

IN THE OPENING SCENE OF *Cold Snap*, Peter Friar bursts into the El Dorado County D.A.'s office, dragging a half-frozen corpse. The D.A., an old pal of Friar's, is shocked to receive the body of Henry Dunstable, wanted for a string of murders.

"How'd you nab him?" the D.A. asks.

"He went for a swim," is Friar's oft-quoted line, delivered with a smirk.

From there, the film jumps back to the start of the search, with Friar in his San Francisco office, frustrated by a string of cold leads. From a near miss at the Ferry Building, Friar tails Dunstable across the Bay Bridge, into Sacramento and then high into the Sierra Nevada. The final scene, a confrontation on the shore of Lake Tahoe, shot in low light and deep shadows, ends in a fistfight. Friar holds Dunstable's head under the icy water as he sings Jacques Brel's "La Mort."

The scene hit a nerve with critics and fans. Is Friar any better than the man he apprehends? He's on the right side of the law, but just barely. Obsessed with stopping Dunstable, Friar ignores all limits. His rage is both an asset and a weakness.

Wheeler's conception of Peter Friar was palimpsestic, each new layer deepening and complicating the portrait. That meant not just producing another successful movie; it meant re-inventing a man of his own creation, making him somehow at once immediately recognizable and thrillingly new.

Sal Casa begged Wheeler to lower his standards, to repeat the formula. That's how a franchise grows, Casa pleaded. A carbon copy of the first two films could double, triple their audience. Once he'd made them all millionaires, he could go off and make his art film.

Wheeler waved him off; he had final say on all artistic aspects of the project. He'd keep chiseling at the marble until the shape he wanted emerged. Every morning he sat down at his desk and reviewed his scene cards. The beats were all there. The scenes were like empty rooms waiting to be appointed. All he had to do was write them. But each time he did the draft felt wooden, forced. There was nothing bold or original there, no innovation. The Friar on the page hewed too closely to the Friar he already knew.

IT WAS A WARM SUMMER EVENING in the Casco Viejo, its cafés filled with laughter and discussion. Wheeler visited the one recommended by Bidarte, just around the corner from the Teatro Arriaga. He ordered the calamari, served with lemon and a glass of vino tinto.

Eventually Wheeler asked if Michael Florence often visited. His waiter, a young man with a sheepish smile, stiffened. "Just a moment, sir."

Minutes later, an older man approached the table, tailed closely by the young waiter. The elder introduced himself as the manager. Was everything to his satisfaction?

"Absolutely," replied Wheeler. "I just happened to meet a customer of yours, Lon Bidarte. He told me Michael Florence is a regular here."

The manager smiled. "Yes, Mr. Bidarte is a good friend. Mr. Florence came often, for a time. He really likes his pintxos!"

"You know him."

"As I say, he was a regular guest. But he's such a big star. He attracts attention. Things became unmanageable. In his opinion." The manager brushed at his sleeve.

"Do you know where I might find him?"

"Oh, I'm afraid I can't—"

The waiter stepped forward and whispered into the manager's ear.

"Of course!" the manager exclaimed, stepping forward. "How stupid of me! I recognized you immediately but couldn't place the name." He praised a scene in an abattoir, where Peter Friar chases his prey amidst the saws and straps. The criminal ends up on a meat hook, but Friar isn't done with him.

"How do you make that blood spray everywhere?"

"Corn syrup and non-dairy creamer," Wheeler answered, "with a little food coloring. Throw a cup of that into a fan."

"What a scene! You're an artist, sir."

Hardly, thought Wheeler. The scene pandered to the blood and gore crew, a cheap move he knew would draw a certain kind of attention. It embarrassed him now.

He brought the conversation back to Florence. "I'm trying to reach him. As a fellow filmmaker."

The manager smiled. "You may be interested to know that I named a dish in honor of our friend, item C3, Anguilas de M. Florence. Would you like to try it?"

Wheeler folded his napkin. "Please."

The manager snapped his fingers, and the waiter darted off to the kitchen. The manager proceeded to share fond memories of long nights at the café with Florence and his entourage, never fewer than a dozen men and women. They ate, they drank, they laughed. For a time, it was a weekly affair. Then word spread and the gawkers started showing up. Florence became uncomfortable.

"I offered to close the café just for him and his friends, but he wouldn't have it. He came just once more and then…" He flicked the fingers of one hand.

The waiter reappeared with Wheeler's elvers, served in an earthenware bowl with a fat wooden fork. Sauteed in olive oil and garlic, with dried Guindilla peppers, the dish was spicy and delicious. Wheeler didn't have to feign enthusiasm.

The manager explained the difficult process of procuring elvers, which were seined out of the estuary. If the dish were served traditionally, it would cost many hundreds of euros.

"What you are eating, my friend, is Japanese surimi fish and squid ink. Few can tell the difference."

"I salute your ingenuity," Wheeler said. He admired a well-executed illusion. He trusted Florence would appreciate the irony.

Wheeler asked one final time regarding the star's whereabouts. The manager took a pad of paper from his pocket and scribbled across it. He tore the sheet and handed it to Wheeler. The Basque poet Arnas Exteberri ran a bookshop just a few streets over. If anyone might know Florence's location, it would be him.

The manager summoned the young waiter, who presented Wheeler with a small glass of Patxaran, compliments of the house. After an obligatory photo, which the manager assured him would be on the wall the next time he visited, Wheeler was allowed to take his leave.

WHEELER SPENT THE NEXT MORNING in his hotel room, drinking espresso and milk as he drafted new pages for his film. Scene cards lay across the bed like puzzle pieces. He picked one, read it quickly, then started writing dialogue rapidly, line after line, filling a page. He stopped to re-read, then crumpled it up. He had a nice little pile of paper in the corner of the room. He'd leave the maid a good tip.

Visualize. He had to visualize the scene in his head. Damn! He'd never had this problem in the past. The first two films had been written quickly, almost recklessly in their initial stages. Of course he'd had less pressure on him then. He didn't expect the films to be a hit. He had no one expecting magic. Just an avalanche of ideas that he worked furiously to arrange.

Wheeler stared at the empty page. In his head, in his heart, he felt a great, yawning emptiness. Within it swirled an energy, just out of reach, a ribbon of sinuous black ink—a force, an energy he yearned to catch, to control, to command. His fortune, his future, his fate, written in his own hand.

Michael Florence knew a thing or two about commanding fate. He'd made a name for himself in a string of witty, feel-good comedies. He became known for a certain kind of performance. He attracted a certain kind of script. When he announced that he'd write and direct his next film—a religious drama—eyebrows were raised. No one expected him to deliver in a "serious" role, but deliver he did, winning best actor for his depiction of Martin Iverson in *The Gift*.

In a famous scene, Iverson logs timber in the Catskills. He and his followers have purchased an old Arts and Crafts colony which they plan to restore as a religious commune. It rains endlessly. Mosquitoes plague them. Rats infest the buildings. People are weary and dispirited. A group of dis-satisfied parishioners approach Iverson, announcing that they're leaving the commune. Iverson lays down his axe, wipes his brow, and delivers the speech that earned Florence an Oscar. Standing on a hillside, rain streaking his face, he redefines the group's mission, proclaiming the commune a chosen project, and he its divinely appointed leader. Before that speech, Iverson was a mediocre preacher with a half-formed mission. By its end, he's a prophet.

Wheeler had watched the scene a dozen times. It was well-filmed, yes. The dialogue was stirring, to be sure. But none of that accounted for the scene's haunting, elegiac power. What flummoxed Wheeler was that he couldn't detect any of Florence's familiar tics or mannerisms. He'd completely reinvented himself for the role, as if learning to act anew.

Whatever that quality was, Michael Florence had it, and Van Wheeler was going to find this man and draw it out of him, like some medieval physician with his leech.

Is that what he'd become? A parasite?

So be it.

AS AFTERNOON SLID INTO EVENING, Wheeler sat at a quiet pintxos bar, enjoying a few small plates as he read Arnas Exteberri's *Ruptura: poemas de la separacíon*. The language was muscular and frank. Yet the poems were of an era, a snapshot of a Spain deep in the past, or so it seemed to a twenty-first century Californian. Wheeler wondered how Spaniards regarded the work; he trusted Basques revered it. In 1970, in defiance of the Nationalists, Exteberri started a bookstore and a press for publishing Basque literature. He was jailed three times. No wonder Florence sought him out.

The next morning, Wheeler made his way to Exteberri's store. The aisles were narrow. Its shelves reached to the ceiling, teetering with books. Behind the counter stood a tall, slender man with a voluminous white beard, an open ledger in his hands.

"Mr. Exteberri?"

The silver head rose, his eyes a dazzling, mystic blue.

Wheeler introduced himself, then asked if the poet could sign his copy of *Ruptura*.

"Gladly." He scribbled a quick inscription. "You like Basque poetry?"

"It's new for me. But I loved your work—in translation, of course. I regret that I don't have the Basque."

"Your Spanish is good," Exteberri said.

"Thank you." Wheeler dropped the book into his shoulder bag. "I'm told you know Michael Florence."

"Who told you that?"

After Wheeler named the café manager, Exteberri admitted it was true. "Florence is a friend and, I might add, a great customer of this shop."

"He visits frequently?"

"Not since he moved to Getxo. He has a salon there. He's invited me, but I don't travel much these days."

"I'd love to visit. Could you put us in touch?"

Exteberri frowned. "He avoids the press. He's sick of the paparazzi. You're all a bunch of nosy salamanders."

"Oh god no," Wheeler said, introducing himself as a fellow filmmaker. Exteberri had never heard of him. Wheeler emphasized this would be a meeting of peers, not press.

"I'm afraid I can't help you." Exteberri turned, moving towards the back of the shop.

Wheeler recited from memory:

> *See how strange*
> *how sad*
> *familiar things may be*
>
> *Look where Christ is still*
> *suffering*
> *who would help you*
> *if you asked him:*
>
> *you cannot ask him.*

Exteberri turned, trembling. "That poem was once printed on the front page of a Basque newspaper. The next day, Franco sent its editor to prison. I was already there."

Wheeler paused, unsure what nerve he'd touched.

The bell on the front door tinkled as it opened. A young couple entered. Immediately they stopped, puzzled looks on their faces. The boy was tall and lean, with an angular nose and dark eyes. The girl had a soft, round face and an energetic smile.

"Van Wheeler?" the boy said, in accented English.

"Yes." He felt pleased to be recognized by his true name.

The couple stepped forward. They were big fans.

"The scene in the ice bar, with the women drinking martinis in parkas," the boy said. "The tables, the glasses, the bar—truly, it was all ice?"

"All ice. Shot in Alaska in July," Wheeler answered. "Chena Hot Springs, just outside of Fairbanks."

"And then the swordsman popping up," the boy continued, "slicing them to shreds!"

Wheeler frowned. It was a key plot twist in the second Peter Friar film, *Thin White Rope*, but he winced at it now. The spectacle and oddity of the moment drove the scene, not its characters. People always liked the wrong bits.

Exteberri lingered behind the counter, smiling. The old poet was eavesdropping.

"I like Audrey Lodge," the girl said. Lodge had appeared in the second film. "I hope you bring her back."

"Friar is through with sidekicks," Wheeler quipped.

"You should make a movie about her."

The statement arrested Wheeler, unsure if it was a subtle criticism or a plea. He offered the couple a quick selfie before sending them on their way.

"They know your work," Exteberri said. "It's gratifying, isn't it?"

Wheeler smiled. "Sometimes."

Exteberri slid a paperback across the counter. "Read this next, compliments of this shop."

The cover showed a dark, mountainous forest. *Espíritus de Bizkaia: ficciones de Ler Biskarret.*

"Look up Biskarret in Getxo. He's close to Florence." The poet scribbled a quick handwritten note. "Tell him Exteberri sent you. And good luck with your work."

IN *THIN WHITE ROPE* PETER FRIAR is under review. Audrey Lodge is assigned to tail him. Friar resists Lodge, but her persistence proves to be formidable. She's not out to stop Friar, only to hold him accountable. She keeps close tabs, following up on every scrap of paperwork.

Friar resents this. He tells her to back off. He has his own way of doing things.

"There aren't two standards of justice," Lodge fires back. "We all play by the same rules."

"You think the creeps I chase play by the rules? Wake up. If you want to nab them, you have to get a little dirty."

Friar finally evades her and dons a disguise. For the next thirty minutes, the old Friar is back, breaking rules and busting skulls as he closes in on his suspect in Las Vegas. In a strip bar, Friar, disguised as a bouncer, watches his mark toss singles onto the stage for a masked dancer wearing lingerie and silk scarves. As articles of clothing come off, the shower of singles increases. At the end of her bit, the dancer slides into the man's lap and, without much apparent effort, leads him to the private booths where the lap dances occur.

Friar bluffs his way into the back of the club. Timing his entry for maximum effect, he bursts in only to find the dancer has the suspect face down on the ground, cuffed, and is reading him his rights.

"Call a squad car," Audrey Lodge orders Friar, "and hand me my bra."

The scene thrust a previously unheard-of Beryl Monroe onto many people's radar. At the moment, she was shooting a rom-com with Clifton Glover, best known for playing Clifton Glover in every damn movie he made. Talk about predictable. The film would surely be a hit, elevating Beryl's profile.

Sitting at his hotel bar that evening, nursing a Scotch on the rocks, Wheeler thanked himself for including an option in Beryl's contract for a second film. This comforted him greatly, because something about that girl's comment in the bookstore had stuck with him.

You should make a movie about her.

He took out his notebook and started jotting down ideas. Friar and Lodge could be full-fledged partners, the odd couple bit. It wouldn't be about sexual tension; Friar was twenty years older and each had a romantic companion. It would be about old school versus new, the changing of the guards. He sketched out new scene ideas for a few minutes, excited by the possibilities.

But taking the spotlight off Friar, or just sharing it… that was a risk. Friar was incontestably the center of the first two films. You needed a big ego and a stubborn streak to succeed in Hollywood; Wheeler had both. Perhaps with the help of his expensive L.A. therapist he might persuade himself to step back.

Or perhaps he could simply admit that he had nothing to show for a new script. Sal Casa needed to see something when he touched down at LAX, or there'd be hell to pay.

Wheeler didn't put much stock in fate, but he was a deep believer in the power of intuition, a gut sense of what's best in a given moment. Intuition doesn't present long, serpentine arguments. Intuition prompts action and rewards spontaneity, relying on courage and wit. It's a mix of things—the conscious and the unconscious, the ego and the id. All his success to date had come from trusting that inner feeling, an urging beyond language or reason, what could only be described as a yearning.

It was time to try something new. Something like what Florence had pulled off. A hunger, a curiosity, a ferocity of ambition. Something no one saw coming. How in hell had Florence done it? What were the obstacles? What would Wheeler need to look out for? What sage words of advice could Florence offer? There was only one way to find out.

WHEELER RODE THE METRO NORTH to Getxo, proceeding directly to the address Exteberri had given him, a tavern. The Raven proved to be an exquisite find, a place of dark wood and dim lights. Wheeler needed a moment for his eyes to adjust. Something moody and menacing played on the sound system—Nick Cave's cover of "Wanted Man." A young man with a head of voluminous black hair, wearing a turtleneck of all things, sat alone at the bar, working on a laptop. Wheeler considered taking his phone out to snap the image, it was almost too perfect.

Wheeler approached. "Ler Biskarret?"

The young man didn't take his eyes from the screen. "We don't open for another hour."

Wheeler placed his copy of *Espíritus de Bizkaia* on the bar. He praised the final story, set in the late nineteenth century, of a haunted baserri and its brooding ghost, a Basque Nationalist murdered by Spanish soldier. A naked political allegory, but charming nonetheless.

Biskarret closed the laptop. "The Spanish translation is crap."

"It won the Belido Prize."

"Which means it sold a thousand copies in Madrid." He laughed. "Why do you think I run a tavern?"

"Never scoff at success," Wheeler said.

Biskarret studied Wheeler for a long moment, then smiled. "Peter Friar drinks vodka and tonic, yes?"

"He does, but Van Wheeler prefers Scotch on the rocks."

Biskarret walked behind the bar, grabbed a bottle off the shelf, and poured them each a drink.

"I'll be honest with you," he said. "I detest plot of all sorts. I only watched *Thin White Rope* in order to sleep with a woman."

Wheeler laughed. "I could make a joke about a double climax."

"Beryl Monroe is exquisite. I dream of her sometimes."

"Yes," Wheeler said, laughing. "I've been thinking about her lately."

"Where is she now?"

For once, Wheeler was glad to have a bit of Hollywood gossip to share. It pleased Biskarret, and soon they were into another round of drinks. Then he asked why in the world Van Wheeler had sought him out.

"Exteberri sent me." Wheeler placed the poet's note on the bar.

Biskarret didn't even glance at it. "And?"

Wheeler returned the note to his pocket. "I'm told you're an acquaintance of Michael Florence."

"What if I am?"

"I very much want to meet him."

Biskarret shrugged his shoulders. "He can be hard to find."

"But you know where to find him."

"More like he knows where to find me," Biskarret said. "He pays a handsome price for me to host his private parties. But I haven't heard from Michael in weeks. He's late paying his tab, now that I think about it. Too busy reading Basque history."

"Books from Exteberri. Research for his new film."

"Yes. Some sort of historical epic—all plot," he said, frowning.

"Tell me about it."

It starts in Euskadi, Biskarret explained, just after the first Carlist War, the end of Basque home rule. Seeking a new beginning, a family emigrates to California just as the Gold Rush begins. They lose everything.

Wheeler sipped his drink. "Sounds cheerful."

"That's part one. Michael has hinted at a second part, more contemporary. The Basque diaspora today, sheepherders in Reno, that sort of thing. But no one has seen any of that."

"Almost sounds like two films."

Biskarret slapped at the bar top. "You should tell him that!"

"I'd love to. Can you arrange a meeting?"

"That's not how Michael works. He calls when he needs you."

"But you're in touch. You've read his script."

"Part of his script. He sends it via courier." Florence is a recluse, Biskarret said, obsessed with his project. In the age of email and Google Docs, he works on a vintage typewriter, banging out pages for a small circle of readers. When he wants feedback, he sends a draft around. Then he throws a big dinner party at The Raven and all the readers offer feedback. Each script must be returned in full, every page accounted for.

"He's a bit paranoid. I mean, it's 2019. He's never heard of a camera scanner?"

"Oh my god," Wheeler said. "You have a draft on your phone?"

"Just one scene."

"Show me."

Biskarret waved him off. "I'm not nearly drunk enough."

"Then let me buy you a round."

"Forget it. I have to open this bar and earn a living. God knows short stories don't pay."

"Write a novel," Wheeler said.

"I told you I hate plot." He walked around the room, opening blinds and arranging chairs.

Wheeler, a little drunk now, felt desperate. He was closer than ever. He couldn't let this lead go cold.

"Listen, I really need to get in touch with Florence."

"I might hear from him any day now, but who knows? Give me your number. Maybe I'll sneak you into his next salon."

"I fly to L.A. in a week."

"That's too bad."

"Can't you call him?"

He shook his head. "You don't call him. He calls you. That's how it works."

"Well then I'm fucked."

Wheeler walked to the men's room to relieve himself. Over the urinal was a photograph of a tall, narrow, red-brick house on a street corner, its door a stark white and its shuttered windows a Hunter green. "Poe House, Baltimore" read the caption.

A place easily found, Wheeler mused, marked for all to see. How fortunate.

When he returned, Wheeler handed Biskarret a card with his international phone number, just in case. Biskarret told him to drop by some evening for dinner. They made the best American burgers in all of Spain.

"I'm only eating Basque food while I'm here."

Biskarret's eyes widened. "Of course! I should have thought of that."

Confused, Wheeler wondered if he'd misspoken.

Biskarret took a step forward. "Do you like marmitako?"

"I don't think I've had it."

"Stewed tuna, a Basque summer staple. You must try it, trust me. The best place to get it is at a certain café in Portugalete, across the estuary."

"Okay. I like adventures."

Biskarret described a narrow, cobblestone street in the old quarter. There Wheeler would find a tiny yellow café with a few tables out front, on the ground floor of a rather old apartment building. He worked his phone as he spoke, thumbs flying.

"I just texted you a pindrop on Google Maps. These are horribly small apartments, you understand. Not modernized. No elevator. Most people wouldn't want to live in such a place. They would only appeal to very particular kind of person."

Wheeler smiled. "I understand."

He opened his phone and pressed on the maps link. The location was six kilometers from his present spot. The café was closed that evening but would be open the next.

"I think I know what I'm doing for dinner tomorrow."

"Enjoy the marmitako," Biskarret said, "but don't tell them who sent you."

THE NEXT MORNING, WHEELER SAT at a café in the Algorta neighborhood, at the foot of a long flight of stone stairs, overlooking Puerto Viejo, the Old Harbor. He had a table in the sun, sipping a café con leche. He enjoyed watching people walk along the waterfront, parading before the string of colorful dinghies anchored there.

He re-read his new script pages. Audrey Lodge, now Friar's work partner, finds a key piece of evidence in a case. Lodge decides not to share it, but to act on it herself. This leads to a meeting at a Napa Valley winery between Lodge and a major player in the scheme under investigation. The dialogue in that scene, even in its rough state, had energy. Lodge is willing to play a deep game, gaining the vintner's trust. Already Wheeler envisioned the next scene and its key plot point on the waterfront in Sausalito.

He ordered another café con leche and quickly wrote a draft.

When he finished, he re-read everything. Nearly thirty pages, all very rough, but it was a start. And not half-bad. At least he didn't immediately want to destroy it. Audrey on the page made him curious; he felt a keening urgency to know more about her: what she would do, what she was capable of, how far she'd take things, where her limits were.

The more he thought about it, the more he liked it. A film with a strong, independent female lead, rare enough in the crime genre. He had a chance to reboot the entire game.

The only problem was that it had nothing to do with Peter Friar.

Was that a problem? Why was that a problem?

You should make a movie about her.

What Wheeler wanted was the thing Michael Florence had shown him: the confidence to break the mold completely, to re-invent himself from the ground-up. You don't make a film like *The Gift* by falling back on the patterns you know; you make it by establishing a new pattern. Wheeler didn't know just yet what he was after, but he had a hunch that finding Florence would give him the puzzle piece he'd been missing. He just had to reach out and take it.

WHEELER HAD THE TAXI DROP him in Las Arenas, at the foot of the Vizcaya Bridge. He felt edgy with anticipation. The bridge spanned the Ibaizabal estuary, hovering over the water like an enormous iron arachnid, its gondola dangling from so many silken threads, gliding silently over the water. He lingered at the foot of the bridge, reading plaques about its designer, Basque architect Alberto de Palacio, and his innovative use of lightweight, twisted steel cables.

Yes, thought Wheeler, there's an artistic sensibility for you: soundly built, trim and functional, yet remarkably elegant. His next film would embody all these qualities. He was more excited than ever about its possibilities, though also sobered because he knew how much work it would entail.

He would have to convince Sal Casa that a film focusing on Audrey Lodge was worth bankrolling. Beryl Monroe he trusted would be eager to sign on, especially if the Clifton

Glover film made a splash. Thank god for Clifton Glover! He was training Beryl as a lead actress, making Wheeler's job easier. He knew she could carry a scene; now she would have to carry an entire film.

Wheeler decided to walk across the bridge. He paid the toll and stepped into the iron cage of an elevator that lifted him to the top of the eastern tower. He walked out onto the long, narrow span, a stiff onshore breeze blowing through his hair. He studied the spectacular view: a bustling industrial shoreline giving way to the rugged cliffs of Aixerrota, then widening into the bay.

A distant, watery horizon cannot fail to stir dreams. Wheeler felt confident he was moving in the right direction. Peter Friar, he now realized, was a solved puzzle. What Wheeler had done with Friar was invent a character he could embody, essentially a moral philosophy he could present with some authenticity. Friar was a righter of wrongs, but was himself deeply flawed, driven by anger and restlessness. There were depths there, but he'd sounded them. Now they felt more like limits, like the walls of a mine into which he could only sink to deeper, darker depths. But it was still the same mine.

With Audrey Lodge everything felt new. Focusing on her would expand the possibilities of the franchise. Or take him beyond it. Perhaps he was starting a new franchise. The thought at once terrified and excited him.

Surely Michael Florence felt similar worries prior to making *The Gift*. Surely there'd been that moment of doubt. What held him back? Nothing! Here he was, hidden away in Spain, reinventing himself yet again. A Basque historical drama! To find him meant to confirm undeniably that Wheeler was making the correct choice. Florence could not fail to see the wisdom in this move.

He walked off the Vizcaya Bridge, entering Portugalete full of determination, wholly awake and aware. Blood coursed through his veins with new intensity, thrumming in his ears. He walked briskly through the busy streets, turning one corner and then another, until finally he stood at the foot of Victor Chávarri Kalea, a narrow lane closed to motorized traffic. There he slowed his pace, strolling the ancient walkway, half in shadow, half in sun. Shop clerks leaned in doorways. Old men shuffled along, hands clasped behind their backs. Shoppers lingered at windows, admiring displays. Baskets of vibrant purple flowers hung around the windows of a café, where patrons sat in the sun, enjoying coffee. The steep walls of the buildings stood close on either side, a canyon of yellow and blue and crème. Above the shops, the apartments' balcony doors stood open to the early evening air. Yes, things were slower here, just a step removed from the bustling inner city, from the noise of traffic. A bit of the old ways lingered, hovering in the air like cigar smoke.

Wheeler advanced slowly, looking for the yellow café. What he found was a tall wooden construction fence protruding out into the street, covered in bills and ads. Scaffolding clung to the building's walls like vines, wrapped in sheets of opaque plastic. Deep inside the structure he heard rotary saws and sledgehammers, things cracking and being torn down. Men shouting. Scrap was tossed out empty window frames, landing in dumpsters with a terrific clatter.

He checked the map on his phone. This was the precise spot.

No yellow café.

A shopkeeper in an apron stood across the street, smoking a cigarette. Wheeler asked if this was the site of the Café Amarillo, the one famous for its marmitako.

"Gone," the man said, "in a big fire."

"When?"

"Two weeks ago." The man described a sudden and terrific conflagration, incinerating everything. No one died, praise God, but those who escaped had no time to save anything.

Only what they could grab in mere moments. And that beautiful building, one of the oldest in this historic neighborhood, gutted.

"Did you know any of the tenants?"

"I've run this carnicería for twenty-two years. I grew up here. I know everyone."

"Did you know Michael Florence, an American leasing a flat there? He may have gone by another name."

The man shook his head. "Too many rentals, worse now with Airbnb. I suppose you can't stop it, but it disrupts our neighborhood. All the coming and going. It was better ten years ago." He flicked his cigarette out into the street, then turned and walked inside his shop.

Wheeler stood alone in the street, listening to the hammers pounding, watching scrap drop into the giant, yawning dumpsters. Florence had vanished, fleeing a disaster. Did he have time to grab his precious pages? Or were they lost in the fire? Was he, too, starting over with nothing? Nothing but ideas and intuition.

Yes, thought Wheeler, how utterly perfect. The absence of everything: the café, the flat, the man. Yes, of course, just exactly as it should be. And this sweet old building, stripped down to its core. Only the essential structure would survive. A process of rebuilding would follow, using all new materials, following new plans. It was time to move on, time to build new rooms in new styles, modern and efficient. There was no point looking back. What was lost was lost, never to be recovered.

IT WAS LATE AFTERNOON AND THE BAR near Bilbao-Abando station was crowded. A pair of women stood near the back, casting glances Wheeler's way. It didn't feel awkward or intrusive. It helped that they were both attractive, dressed up a little, and around his age. He smiled and gave them an encouraging wave.

The women moved his way. "We've figured out who you are," one of them said. "Peter Friar."

"He's expired," Wheeler said. "I once played him in the movies, yes."

His statement didn't phase them, an encouraging sign. He let the women shower him in compliments, naming their favorite scenes. For once, he didn't second guess them or feel uncomfortable. He laughed when he should laugh, and spoke with gravity and a sense of artistic determination when it seemed appropriate, basking in their appreciation.

He asked them if they remembered Audrey Lodge.

"She's brilliant," one said. "So sexy and strong. Is she coming back?"

"Very much so."

The women nodded. "And when is your next film?"

Wheeler stared down at his Scotch, studying its coppery color. "I've just started the new script. I'm flying back to L.A. to finish it."

"How exciting!"

They chatted for a few more minutes, until Wheeler's phone pinged, alerting him that his train was ready to board. He paid for his drink, consented to a selfie with the admiring women—he even smiled for it—then strode off, moving closer to home and all that awaited him.

Parallel Lines

1

G rant hated the desert for its monotonous brown emptiness; for the ugly, squat prickly pear cactus, like some old man's ear, sprouting stiff hairs; for the withering, snake-like pica with its dangerous thorns; and for the dust. When the winds blew, great clouds of it rose up like some wicked story out of the Bible. The windows had to be shut and you couldn't go outside. Afterwards everything would be covered in a fine, granular film. Disgusting.

Everything around him looked exactly like he felt: lost, empty, forlorn, and utterly miserable. In contrast to what his mother had said, finding new friends in El Paso proved difficult. Joining a new school late in the year meant everybody already had friends. They didn't need him. And he wasn't good at reaching out, hobbled by a shyness that felt as foreign to him as these brown hills.

Shortly after their arrival, a neighbor knocked on the door. She introduced herself as Mrs. Sergeant John Dupree. Beside her stood her son, Wade, a tall, lean boy wearing cowboy boots and a western shirt. They went to the same middle school, and Wade would be pleased to show Grant the shortest walking route. Before Grant knew it, his mother had thanked Mrs. Dupree for the offer and the boys had agreed to meet at the corner the next morning.

Wade was a talker. He spoke in a loose, rolling drawl, a voice paired to the emptiness surrounding them, filling it with a seemingly endless stream of information. His family had been in west Texas for over a hundred years. His grandfather had a cattle ranch near Midland-Odessa. His father, a retired marine decorated in the last war, now managed rental properties for off-base army housing near Fort Bliss.

Wade was fond of jokes, mostly about faggots and retards. He also hated Mexicans. Half of Morehead Middle School was filled with wetbacks, he said. "They ought to fill one of them school buses and drive 'em the hell back to old See-you-dad Juarez. Give a white man a little room to breathe. Some clean air, at least. They must wash in that cologne they wear. And how's about the motor oil those dudes pour on their head? I'm like to think they's a nation of faggots."

Shocked, Grant didn't know what to say. His mother had taught him that when you don't have anything nice to say, you say nothing at all. It was true that the Chicano boys wore a lot of cologne and pomade, but it never bothered Grant. Actually, he was fascinated by the boys in the bathroom. They stood before the mirror, endlessly stroking their hair though it already looked perfect, speaking Spanish to each other as if no one else existed.

"You wear hair oil?" Wade barked.

"Hell no."

"You a faggot?"

"Shut the fuck up."

Wade laughed. "You're all right for a Yankee."

The boys walked through a residential neighborhood, cutting from one street to another in a confusing zigzag. They arrived at the school and went their separate ways. Grant walked to class feeling odd. Something about Wade irritated him, yet he didn't know what to do. Do you just come out and tell him to shut up? Do you call him a racist? Or do you ignore it? Grant figured the best thing, for now, was to ignore it. At any rate, he didn't think he could figure out the route home on his own. He needed Wade, at least for a while.

AT RECESS, THE CHICANO KIDS hung out in one corner of the yard, playing soccer. The boys wore tight white T-shirts, blue jeans, and steel-toed work boots. The white kids played basketball in their Pumas and Izod shirts, white athletic socks pulled up to their knees. In the lunchroom, the Chicanos sat in one corner, laughing and speaking in Spanish. The whites sat on the other side of the room. And in the classroom, the Chicanos sat in the back, clustered together in a few rows, rarely speaking. The white teachers never called on them. There were, it seemed to Grant, two playgrounds, two lunchrooms, two classrooms. Two schools.

Except in Spanish. When Grant had entered the school and signed up for classes, the guidance counselor had enrolled him. "You'll need it, trust me."

Grant joined the class cold, no preparation. The kids were six months ahead of him. Some had been studying it for years. And then there were the native speakers. In this class, they sat in front and the white kids sat in the back, quiet, as the Chicanos did all the talking. The teacher, a Chicana herself, laughed with her muchachos, cracking jokes in Spanish and touching them on the shoulders.

Grant felt lost, helpless. There was no way he could catch up. The teacher handed him a book and some worksheets and told him to start by playing some cassette tapes at a table in the back corner of the room. He listened to the introductory lessons, wearing boxy black headphones with thick rubber pads that pressed against the side of his head.

Hola. ¿Cómo estás? Yo me llamo Grant.

He scribbled best guesses on the worksheets and dropped them in the teacher's basket. He never saw them again. He came to hate the class. La maestra ignored him. He cursed her, just as he cursed that moron of a counselor who'd enrolled him, what an asshole. But mostly he cursed his father for taking a job in this dusty hellhole of a town.

Grant quit trying. He didn't turn in the worksheets, didn't log any minutes on the cassettes. One day the teacher approached him with her grade book. They sat at a table in the back and reviewed his scores. He was failing the class. "You've quit trying, muchacho. Why aren't you turning in the work?"

Grant hesitated before telling her he never wanted to take Spanish in the first place. The counselor had forced him. "No offense," he quickly added.

She smiled, thank goodness. "Listen, tengo una oferta." If he agreed to try his best, turn in all the worksheets, and log his listening minutes, he would pass the class. And she would assign him a tutor, one of her best students. "She'll help you get the work done and, who knows, maybe you'll learn un poco de español."

Grant agreed. His only alternative was to fail the class, for which his father would slaughter him.

Melinda Díaz had a broad smile and warm brown eyes that seemed to pull Grant closer. He had no trouble listening to her, no trouble at all. When she asked him to complete a worksheet, he did it. She corrected his answers, asked him to try again, and he did.

She sat next to him, reading over his latest effort, her head bowed, pencil in hand. Grant gazed at her smooth brown neck, the wispy tendrils of black hair, the delicate lace pattern of her shirt collar.

Melinda handed his work back. "I don't know why you're failing this class. You're doing pretty well."

"I'm doing better now," Grant replied.

"Where are you from?"

"Marquette, Michigan. How about you?"

"I was born in El Paso."

"But you're originally from Mexico?"

Frowning, she cocked her head to one side. "I just said I was born here."

He looked down, blindly, at his worksheet. He felt like crawling off in a corner and curling up like a pill bug.

"Lo siento," he said, quietly. It was one of the few phrases he'd learned.

A moment later, she said, "I bet it's different for you here."

"You wouldn't believe."

"Do you like studying Spanish?"

He lifted his chin. The girl he'd just insulted was staring at him, but not with anger. She was curious about him. He was definitely curious about her.

"I do, if you're teaching me."

She smiled. "Mi familia es de Chihuahua."

"Mi familia," he repeated. "My family…"

"…es de…"

He sat up in his chair. "Your family is from Chihuahua."

She told him that her parents were both from a small village there, many miles south of Juarez. Her grandparents lived on a horse ranch. Had he been to Mexico?

"Not yet."

"You should go. It's very beautiful."

"Maybe you can take me."

She narrowed her eyes. "Eres demasiado atrevido."

Grant laughed. "What's that mean?"

"It means you'd better study Spanish!" She tapped the next worksheet with her pencil. And so he did.

IT WAS THE YEAR OF *Parallel Lines.* The record by Blondie was everywhere, and "Heart of Glass" was constantly on the radio, holding at number one for weeks. Grant loved the pulsating, disco beat. His older brother Robbie had the album and Grant often sat in Robbie's room with him as the record played. On the cover, a blonde diva stared down the viewer, stunning in a white silk dress, hands on hips, eyes locked as if demanding an explanation, a mysterious white ribbon wound around one arm.

"Sexy as hell," Robbie informed him.

Behind her, the five male members of the band stood in black-and-white suits and bushy hair, looking like a Beatles cover band on a coffee break. One wore mismatched Chuck Taylors, one black and one red. Grant figured that would be him, if he were in the band.

Robbie was a fan. He had all of Blondie's albums and laughed at Grant for adoring "Heart of Glass." Robbie said that was their sell-out song. Every band did it sooner or later, sucking up to the puds who liked disco. Grant didn't care. That one song deep in the middle of side two leapt up at him. He could listen to it over and over, and often did.

One afternoon as Grant wandered around the playground during lunch recess he came upon a group of kids sitting around a picnic table. Melinda was there, leaning over a yellow plastic transistor radio. "Heart of Glass" was playing. Grant paused by the table to listen. One of the kids said something sharp in Spanish. Melinda said, "No la cambie! I like it." The song played on. It was the radio edit, with the "pain in the ass" line omitted, which Grant belted out anyway. The table exploded in laughter and he walked off, feeling something close to good, maybe better.

That night he borrowed Robbie's album and begged a blank cassette off him. He recorded the LP on his father's hi-fi, listening to the entire thing on headphones. The next day in Spanish class he inserted the tape into the cassette player, queued to the hit single. Feigning difficulty understanding a lesson, he asked Melinda to help him. She put the big, boxy headphones on and pressed play. Immediately her eyes lit up and a broad, white smile flashed across her face. She listened for a bit, then took off the headphones.

"What are you doing?"

He pressed eject, slid the tape into its case, and handed it to her. "Para tu."

"Para ti," she corrected. She took the tape and read the label. "The whole album? Thank you."

Grant leaned closer. "You mean gracias."

She swatted his shoulder. "Fresco! Now you better sit down and do some real work or la jefa is going to be on your case again."

It'd be worth it, Grant thought, walking to his seat.

WADE AND GRANT WALKED HOME together that afternoon. It was much warmer now, the afternoons in April ten degrees hotter than when he'd arrived in March. Grant was sweating in the mid-afternoon sun.

"Why you hanging around that greaser cunt?" Wade asked.

"What?"

"That girl in your Spanish class. I hear you sit with her in the back all the time, just the two of you."

"She helps me with class work."

"She wants you to knock her up so she can have a half-white baby and stay in the States. Probably wants you to fuck her mom, too." It sounded so stupid and outrageous, Grant burst out laughing. As they approached the street corner where they usually parted ways, Wade invited him to come over for a few minutes. "Got something to show you."

Grant began to stammer an excuse, but Wade tugged at his arm. "Real quick."

He followed Wade down the street and toward a sand-colored ranch, plugged into a suburban cul-de-sac just like Grant's, where the houses all looked identical, and the cars in the driveway were all newish and mostly domestic, and the trees were all juvenile. A mind-numbing vision of sameness, with one glaring exception: out front of Wade's house stood a white flag pole. The stars and stripes flew atop it, then the flag of Texas, and finally that of the marine corps.

"Nice flag pole," Grant quipped.

Wade's "thank you" betrayed no awareness of sarcasm. Every morning at six it was his job to raise the flags, he said, and he had to have them down and folded correctly by sunset. As a kid he'd had to stand and watch his father do this; once he turned twelve, it became his responsibility. And when he had kids, it would be theirs, too.

"You sure you'll have kids?" Grant asked.

"It's a white man's duty," Wade said. "That and serving our country. The day after I graduate high school, I'll be on Parris Island, I can guaran-damn-tee you that. That's if I choose the marines. I might go navy. Daddy says the navy is all right. Anything but army."

He took Grant inside. Mrs. Dupree was there, watching soap operas and ironing shirts. Grant said hello and made a little chit-chat, like his mother had taught him, before Wade led him down the hall to his father's study. It was a dark room with the heavy curtains shut. A little halo of afternoon sunlight limned the two windows, bathing the room in a soft, golden glow. Wade showed him a large case containing a collection of rifles, twelve of the finest vintage Winchesters, Remingtons, and god knows what else. This was his "legacy." He'd shot every gun in that cabinet; he'd also disassembled, cleaned, and oiled them. But don't even think about asking to handle one. They were off-limits. Hell, he wasn't even supposed to let Grant look at them without Daddy's approval.

Wade took a step forward and whispered, "This is a very special favor." His ash blonde, crew-cut hair and eyebrows appeared almost colorless in the ambient, golden light.

Grant saw that Wade expected an acknowledgement of this great kindness. "Uh, thanks."

Wade put his hands on his hips and nodded, a big, reedy smile on his lips.

The next day after school, Wade told him that he and his father were going shooting on Saturday. "Daddy says I can invite you."

"You already asked him?"

"I told him you saw the guns," he said. "He was pleased to hear you respected them and the flags. I've told him all about you."

"You have?" Grant didn't know what to think about that.

"Daddy says we should be polite and welcome you to this great state. We can show you how to value it, show you what's important. Be at my house tomorrow at ten, all right?"

Grant walked home in silence, unsure about how to get out of this, or even if he wanted to get out of it. The only gun he'd ever handled was at summer camp, shooting targets with a .22 caliber rifle. Shooting those big guns—it might be kind of fun. But Wade made him uneasy. And he'd never met the father. He didn't know what to do. He walked home and told his mom, who was surprised.

"I had no idea you wanted to shoot guns."

"I don't know if I do. But Wade is so into it. His dad is too, apparently."

His mother uttered a groan. "Let me call over there and talk to Mrs. Sergeant John Dupree." She went into the master bedroom and closed the door. A few minutes later she emerged, announcing that it was all perfectly legit. They were visiting a gun club. They'd wear safety gear. Sergeant Dupree was a certified instructor and taught gun safety to kids. A local officer in the NRA. "This is Wade reaching out to you."

If only she knew. But he couldn't tell her some of the things Wade had said. Parents—they never know anything that matters.

WADE'S FATHER LOOKED LIKE AN OLDER, wizened version of the son: tall, lean, with deep-cut lines surrounding his mouth. He had the ash blonde hair, cut in the boyish flat-top. He also had tattoos on his forearms from his days in the marines.

They stood in a stall at an outdoor shooting gallery, shaded from the mid-day sun. Across a sandy field stood a row of targets, and behind it a large earthen berm. Grant watched as Sergeant Dupree stood, solid as a statue, legs spread, holding the rifle steady, firing off several rounds in quick succession. Each shot erupted in an ear-piercing explosion. Even with protective headgear, it was deafening. As the sergeant worked the lever, spent cartridges leapt from the receiver, careering over his shoulder. He paid it no mind, no mind at all.

And then Wade, who shot at a slower pace, his shoulder jerking back with each discharge, but he kept the rifle level, taking aim and firing off a half dozen rounds in quick succession. The sergeant had landed six bullets in a tight cluster near the center of the bullseye. Wade's shots were more widely scattered, but all within the black compass scope of the target. Now it was Grant's turn.

The wood of the rifle stock was glossy and smooth, polished to the proverbial shine. The barrel and trigger mechanism were equally fine, rubbed in a light coat of gun oil. This was a Winchester Model 1894, the sergeant explained, an icon. He reviewed how the gun operated. Grant noted a solemn reverence as the sergeant spoke. Wade stood a few feet behind them, arms folded across his chest, nodding in agreement.

Grant stepped up to the white line. The target seemed a mile away, a tiny white piece of paper with a black dot on it, impossibly small. He raised the rifle, following the sergeant's instructions. It was so heavy! He tried to line up the sight, taking aim on the target, but he was having trouble just holding the gun still. Not that he'd know if he were on target or not. He brought the bead as close to the bullseye as he could, and then he pulled the trigger.

The thunderous explosion punished his ears. He staggered backwards, as if hit by a bus. Suddenly Sergeant Dupree had one steely arm wrapped around Grant's chest and his right hand gripping the rifle stock, steadying it. Wade was face-down on the ground, hands over his head. Grant felt dizzy and disoriented.

Other shooters stood out in the alley, watching with big grins on their faces, nodding and chuckling at the show in stall sixteen.

"Sorry," Grant mumbled.

"I told you she'd kick," the sergeant said. "Now you know what I mean. You'll be ready next time." He reviewed how to stand, how to absorb the percussive force of the weapon in the upper shoulder. He held the rifle forward. "Try it again, son."

Grant stared at the weapon, more terrible now in every way. He thought of refusing, but the hard look on the sergeant's face dissuaded him. And the smirk on Wade's face made him reach for the gun and step to the line.

Later, they sat at a table out front of a Dairy Queen, eating soft serve. Grant lapped at his vanilla-chocolate swirl, his ears still ringing from the gunfire. He felt as if by simply surviving that afternoon he'd accomplished something significant, something he would never have to face again.

"You got one on the paper," the sergeant said.

"But not in the flippin' target!" Wade yelped.

The sergeant shot him a hard look. "Grant's not shot before, Wade. And what have I said to you about civility in discourse among your equals?"

Wade's smile evaporated. "Sorry, sir."

The father turned to Grant. "I'm pleased to give you this opportunity. Every American boy should know how to use a firearm. It's his constitutional right." The sergeant carefully licked around the base of his vanilla cone. "I'm glad that you and Wade are friends. It's getting harder to find people who share our views."

Grant wasn't sure what the sergeant was talking about. He kept his attention on his cone.

"Has your family found a church yet?" the sergeant asked.

"We don't go to church."

The sergeant gave him a long, penetrating look. "Not at all?"

"We go to the Texas True Bible Church," Wade announced.

"Every Sunday at ten o'clock," the sergeant continued. "We'd be happy to introduce you to the congregation, Grant. The teaching is true." He gave his cone a big lick, then added, "You'll find a lot of good, clean, like-minded folk."

"How about tomorrow?" Wade asked.

Grant paused for a moment, frozen not with indecision—there was no way he was attending their church—but with uncertainty how to respond. Finally, he said he'd have to check with his mother.

The sergeant nodded. "That's right. Your parents are more than welcome to join us. Do they share your views?"

"What views?"

The sergeant crunched into his sugar cone. "On the race."

Grant looked to Wade, who smiled and nodded.

"I must admit I was surprised," the sergeant said, "you being a Northerner and all."

The full weight of his previous silence settled on him, heavy and foreboding. He felt paralyzed, then stupid. He stared, helpless, as a line of ice cream ran down his finger.

Later, at home, he was taciturn, unsure what he could or should say to his parents. The phone rang and Grant answered. It was Mrs. Sergeant John Dupree, inviting the family to join them for worship. Grant handed the phone to his mother, then held up his arms in a big X, shaking his head. His mother nodded, then chatted with Mrs. Dupree for a minute before politely declining the invitation. "Perhaps another time!" So easy.

His mother sat next to him on the sofa. "What's your friend like, exactly?"

"I don't know."

"What do you mean you don't know? You just spent an entire day with him."

"I don't know if he's my friend."

"Oh, I see." She explained how, sometimes, after you got to know someone a little better, you discovered that they weren't your cup of tea.

"And then what do you do?"

"You move on. Find different friends."

"I don't have any other friends. And neither does he, apparently."

"You just worry about yourself. You're new here, finding your way. It's okay to shop around."

The problem was what to say to Wade. A simple no thank you will do, his mother suggested. But somehow it didn't seem that easy. How do you tell that to a kid that you see every day, who lives one block from you, who walks the exact same route to school with you? The solution came easily enough when Grant told Wade he was going to start riding his bike to school. This allowed him to leave a little later, missing Wade, and to take a different route, following the streets. It was cool in the morning and the ride was actually pleasant. The ride home in the afternoon sun was punishing, but a price worth paying if it meant he could avoid Wade.

2

On cool spring weekend mornings, before the sun scorched the land in its fiery kiln, Grant hopped the low stone wall encircling the back yard and walked into the desert. He crossed ridges and climbed into and out of arroyos, winding between cacti and creosote. There were paths cutting this way and that across the open desert floor, littered with coyote scat. There was a dry riverbed, lined with scrub brush and stunted trees, their trunks littered with trash from the flash floods that rose up after big storms.

The landscape fascinated him. What he'd once written off as a wasteland was, in fact, possessed of a subtle beauty. In his biology class, he learned that much of the life in the desert took place inches from the ground, in the short cacti and under rocks, or even below ground. Wherever a little shade and moisture could be found, away from the punishing sun. Grant decided to look a little closer at things, to explore more carefully, to see what he could find. The desert did not disappoint. He found papery, translucent snake skins; watched a striped bark scorpion scamper between rocks, carrying its giant, lobster-like pincers and that fearsome, coiled tail; and once discovered a walking stick bug, almost undetectable as it clung to a tree branch, perfectly still and unmoving.

One morning, on the floor of an arroyo, Grant watched a tarantula fight a giant blue wasp. The wasp circled the spider, moving in quick bursts. The spider lifted two legs, as if ready to strike. The wasp, as big as Grant's thumb, waited, its shiny, iridescent wings poised and alert, glistening in the sun like stained glass windows. It sprang forward, its abdomen curving down, extending its stinger towards the spider in sharp jabs. The spider spun and skittered out of the way. The wasp, moving in brilliant bursts, orbited around it, striking and jabbing again and again. The intensity, the ferocity of this exchange, thrilled Grant.

After several rounds, the spider slowed, only turning partially as the wasp continued to dart nimbly. The spider gingerly lifted one leg just barely off the ground, like a feeble auctioneer. The wasp leapt atop the spider, sinking its stinger deep inside. After that, the tarantula did not move, apparently killed. Minutes later, the wasp, not even half the size of its prey, began dragging the spider across the sandy desert floor. Grant watched in rapt attention, in thrall of the victor.

Later, in the family's *Encyclopædia Britannica*, he read that the spider was not dead, but merely paralyzed. Its assailant, a tarantula hawk wasp, deposited its eggs directly into the spider's living body. The wasp larvae slowly ate their way out, eventually killing the host as they grew. Brutal, but in the curious way nature sometimes worked, necessary.

Everything about that incident fascinated Grant. Never again would he take the desert for granted, or misjudge it as barren and empty. He just had to learn how to look at it.

IN '79 SASSON JEANS WERE ALL THE RAGE, and no one wore them better than Melinda Díaz. Every time Grant saw her in the hall they smiled at each other. She was all he could think about in math, in English, in science. He looked forward to Spanish and the minutes they'd spend together in the back of the classroom.

He thought he might be going nuts. He'd never felt like this about a girl. He literally could not get her out of his head. At lunch recess that day he sought her out on the playing field. He found her at the soccer bleachers, where the Chicanas sat and watched the boys play a lunchtime round of shirts versus skins. The white kids generally hung out by the basketball courts, which had more shade. White kids rarely walked onto this part of the field, unless they were in a large group. But Grant was feeling bold. He stood at the foot of the bleachers, waving and smiling. Finally she came down and said hello.

"What are you doing here?"

"I wanted to say hello."

She tilted her head at him. "Hola," she said, flatly.

Someone shouted out something in Spanish. Laughter rippled across the bleachers. Melinda waved her hand dismissively without looking back.

"Walk with me?" he asked.

"I need to get back to my friends."

He nodded, masking his disappointment. She turned and began to walk back to the bleachers. Then she stopped and said, "You can walk me home today, if you want."

He smiled. "All right."

After school Grant lingered by the bike rack, standing in the shade. Melinda had told him she'd meet him there, but the bell had rung minutes ago. He hoped she hadn't forgotten. And suddenly there was Wade Dupree. He wore silver aviator sunglasses that gave him a look at once comical and menacing, like a hayseed sheriff out to prove something. Grant gave a little groan as Wade approached.

"Hey there," Wade said. "What you up to?"

Grant shrugged his shoulders. "Nothing much." Wade was the one person Grant didn't want there when Melinda appeared.

Just then a door flew open and Melinda emerged with a group of girls. "¡Mira, ahí está él!" They burst out laughing. The group stood near the door in a tight circle, Melinda hidden somewhere in the middle. Grant was confused. This was where they'd agreed to meet, but he knew better than to approach the group; she must come to him. When the group began to move across the basketball court, shuffling away in one big herd, Grant understood. He was not alone. He was with Wade.

"I have to go," Grant said.

"Who's that, your wetback girlfriend?"

"Shut up, Wade."

Grant rolled his bike away, following the group as it moved across the basketball court, hoping Melinda would peel away. Maybe at the gate, but then he realized he was screwed. He couldn't get his bike through the gate's rotating arms. He would have to ride back across the court, to the bike entrance.

"Go back to Mexico!" Wade shouted across the court.

One the girls shouted something sharp back in Spanish. Then she turned to Grant and hissed, "Why do you hang around with him?"

Grant stopped, squeezing his handlebars furiously, watching the girls slip, one after another, through the gate, away from him.

THE NEXT DAY, IN SPANISH CLASS, Grant sat at the back table, feigning work on an assignment, waiting for Melinda. She avoided him. Only when the bell rang, amidst the bustle of students gathering their things and leaving, was he able to approach her. He spat out a quick, awkward apology for yesterday, nothing like the more graceful script he'd planned. She cut him off. "Meet me today in the parking lot of El Martillo Hardware. You know the place?"

He did. It was several blocks from school.

"Don't forget," she said, smiling. He knew then he hadn't lost her. Not yet.

Walking together along Shadow Mountain Drive later that afternoon, they made awkward small talk. They walked slowly, traffic rushing past them in hot droves. Grant asked if she'd listened to the Blondie tape.

"Es muy extraño."

"You don't like it."

"It's just weird," she said, laughing.

"It's eclectic," he replied, parroting his brother. "New wave, ballads, pop, and disco. Everything that's any good is happening in New York. That's where I want to go to college." He mentioned other New York bands that his brother liked—Ramones, Talking Heads, Television—but none of them seemed to impress Melinda.

"What about you?" he asked. "Where do you want to go to college?"

Melinda shrugged her shoulders. "Probably UTEP."

"You don't want to leave? You would just… stay here?"

"This is where we're from." She smiled, that one-hundred-watt smile that could not fail to warm his heart. "My parents wouldn't want me too far away."

They paused under the shade of a large, leafy mesquite tree, before a sprawling apartment complex with clusters of two-story units. Melinda pointed up to the Franklin Mountains in the east. "Mira. The thunderbird. You can really see it today."

"See what?"

She indicated with a finger, and suddenly Grant saw it, the reddish, V-shaped wings visible against the brown ridges of the mountains, its head cocked to one side, like a figure in a cave painting.

"What is it?" he muttered.

The thunderbird is a mythical creature that fights against the bad spirits of the underworld, Melinda explained, a defender of man—but also his judge. "They say he's resting there, watching. Waiting. One day he will awaken and return, and the wicked shall be punished."

Grant sputtered out a laugh. "You believe that?"

Melinda swatted his arm. "Don't make fun of me!"

"But do you believe it?"

"Papí says we should not forget the old stories. They exist for a reason." Her face looked so sweet just then, her round, brown cheeks so perfectly smooth, and that playful twinkle in her eye, he might just believe anything she told him.

"Melinda, I'm sorry about Wade."

"Everybody knows he's a racist."

"I'm not."

"But when people see you with him, they think you are."

He kicked at the dry patch of lawn, piss yellow and stiff. "Somebody needs to tell him to shut up."

Melinda cocked her head. "Who, like you?"

"Maybe."

"It might be better that way," she said. "The cholos at Coronado High aren't going to let him talk like that, nunca." She thanked him for walking her home. She had to go now, she said. She had chores to do before Mamí got home.

"Can I walk you home again tomorrow?" Grant asked.

"Sí," she said, smiling. That word lingered in his ears, ringing like a chime, as he biked home. Feeling strong, he pumped straight up Indian Bluff Road, climbing the steepest part of it without stopping.

HE COULDN'T TALK TO MELINDA AT RECESS. Except for walking her home from school, he couldn't speak to her or see her. Her friends, her parents, her siblings, her race made her off limits. They saw each other in class, when she sat with him in the back, helping him—less frequent now, as his grade had pulled back into the C-range. In fact, he was flirting with a B. When he complained to la maestra that he still needed Melinda's help despite his climbing grades, she smiled and told him, "Siéntate y haz tu trabajo, muchacho."

Several days a week Melinda let him walk her home. As long as they were out in the open, walking down Shadow Mountain Drive, they were fine. But, always, they parted ways under the shade of the mesquite tree at the edge of her apartment complex. One day Grant asked if he could walk her to her door.

Melinda's eyes widened. "Estás loco! If Mamí sees us, sería el infierno."

"Let me meet them."

"No way. Papí would kill you. He'd kill me. You have no idea."

"Because I'm white," he said.

She gave him a sympathetic look, like he was a poor fool just catching on. "What are you mad about? We're not even dating." Then she turned and darted off.

He waited a half-minute after she'd disappeared around a corner, thinking about what she'd said. The next day at school he asked for her phone number. She gave it to him instantly. He felt powerful, confident he'd made a move in the right direction.

It was a Thursday. His mother had started volunteering at a local charity shop in the afternoons. Robbie worked after school, flipping burgers at the Charcoaler on North Mesa. His father never came home before six. Grant usually had the house to himself for a couple of hours. He was expected to get himself a snack, hit the homework, and then he was free to watch TV, read a book, whatever. Just be home when his mother arrived.

He sat in the kitchen staring at the yellow rotary wall phone. His mother had added an extra-long cord to the receiver so she could walk around the kitchen with it wedged on her shoulder. He waited until he estimated Melinda would be home. Then he waited ten more minutes. And then he called.

He watched the rotary spin out each number, an interminable wait. Then a buzzing, then the throbbing ring, and then her voice, bright and warm in his ear. "You didn't wait long to call me." She didn't sound annoyed.

They talked about all sorts of things. She wanted to know what Marquette, Michigan was like. He told her about playing ice hockey on outdoor rinks in sub-zero temperatures, and shoveling twelve feet of snow each winter. He asked about Chihuahua, Mexico. She described Christmas on her abuelo's rancho, when the family came together—tios y tias from New Mexico, Oklahoma, east Texas, and of course parts of México. The women worked together in the big kitchen, making home-made tamales the old-fashioned way. He'd never tasted anything like it.

They talked for over an hour, until Melinda told him she had to get off before Mamí came home.

"She can't be mad at you for talking to someone on the phone," Grant said.

"If I'm on it for more than a minute she'll want to know who it is. And if I'm speaking English, she can guess. And then I will have a lot of explaining to do. I told you, you have no idea."

"Can I call again later?"

"Tonight? Are you crazy?"

He waited for a moment, wrapping the yellow phone cord around his finger.

"Tomorrow, same time," she said, and then she hung up.

He ran down the hall and threw himself onto his bed. He was over the moon, hung up, hogtied. He didn't know how to explain it. He thought he might be crazy. Almost certainly, he was in love.

He called her the next day, and the day after that. Their conversations were long and intimate. Grant had never talked to a girl in that way, sharing things. She told him he was a good listener. The other boys she knew, especially the Chicanos, were not good listeners. Grant understood this to mean that she was falling for him. He had already fallen for her. He wanted nothing more than for her to be his girl. He realized that it was complicated. But Robbie had told him, yes, there were some mixed-race couples at Coronado High, and, no, it wasn't totally weird. That was all Grant needed to hear.

3

Exploring the desert one morning, Grant discovered a small campsite, with a firepit lined by stones, and a blackened metal grill. It was a nifty little spot, tucked in among some large rocks, just out of sight. The ground right around the fire had been swept clear of large stones, an ideal spot to lay out a sleeping bag. Grant thought about bringing his camping gear there and spending the night, studying the desert in darkness. He wondered who might show up. Hobos? Bank robbers? It became a central spot in his adventures. He might spend an hour sitting in the shade of one of the big rocks, reading. He sometimes packed a lunch.

Because he visited it so often, he noticed changes. Someone had been there recently, had cooked in the firepit and left a tin can in the ashes. He found large plastic water bottles there, sometimes full and sometimes half-empty. Who would leave behind water in a desert? Another time he found a threadbare blanket and a flannel shirt, neatly folded and stacked, as if someone expected to return.

THERE WERE TWO LINES IN THE school cafeteria. One was usually burgers, hot dogs, or pasta. The other was always Mexican food. For a dollar and change, Grant could buy a plate of it, and once he'd tried it he never ate anything else. He loved all of it, the burritos, tacos, and tostadas. Carnitas, pollo asado, y carne asada. It was all insanely good. School lunches were supposed to be horrible! But no one had told the lunch ladies that.

One day they served enchiladas verde, and after one bite Grant thought he'd lost his mind. The sauce was so spicy and fresh, and the chicken and cheese so perfectly done, he rooted around in his jeans pockets to make sure he had enough money to buy a second plate. When he got in line the lunch lady gave him a funny look, like she'd seen him already and why was he back?

"Uno más, por favor," he said. "Muy bueno, muy bueno!"

The lunch lady gave him a big smile and handed him another plate. "Me gusta ver un niño comiendo."

As he sat at the table, eating his second plate, he overheard some Chicano kids. "Look at the güero!" He knew they were speaking in English so he could understand them.

One of them called to him, "You like that, hombre?"

Grant looked up, unapologetically smiling. Their laughter seemed warm and accepting, not condescending.

At lunch, Grant started sitting near the Chicanos. Not with them, but on the fringes of where they sat, a row behind them or a few seats off the side. No one bothered him. Ordinarily, no white kid sat near the Chicanos. Certainly none sat with them. The white kids didn't hang out on the soccer pitch during lunch, didn't walk near the bleachers where the Chicano kids hung out. It just wasn't done. There were, however, Chicano kids who could cross the color line, hanging out with the white kids at lunch, or on the basketball courts. These were the ones who spoke excellent English, who dressed like the white kids, whose parents went to their churches and joined their book clubs and drove the same kinds of cars, lived in the same neighborhoods, listened to the same music and watched the same movies. They'd assimilated, a word Grant had never heard before moving to El Paso. You heard people talk about the Chicanos assimilating into white culture. But never, he noticed, talk of whites assimilating to Mexican culture. Odd, since about eighty per cent of El Paso was Chicano.

When he mentioned this to Robbie, his brother rolled his eyes, like he was surprised his little brother was finally catching on. "That's because white people don't assimilate. They don't learn about other cultures. They are the culture."

That was, Grant supposed, the story of Texas. But Robbie said you could take it even further back: to the original thirteen colonies and the nation's western expansion. It started with the land, which, once taken, was never returned. "If you believe you own something, then anyone else who is there is a threat—even if they were there first," Robbie said.

The stark, stinging resonance of this point floored Grant. He'd seen what Robbie described, and yet it was like he somehow hadn't seen it. He'd been blinded by something, he wasn't sure what.

"You're just white," Robbie sneered.

"You are too!"

"Yeah, but if I've learned one thing since moving to Texas, it's this: don't let it dupe you into believing you're special, or that you deserve anything. It's what separates you from the rednecks."

Grant buried his face in his hands. "I wish we'd never left Michigan."

"You think it's any better up there? Ask the Chippewa."

Damn, Grant thought. God damn.

ONE AFTERNOON WADE DUPREE SLID into the seat across from him in the school cafeteria. "Saw you walking your bike today," he said.

"Flat tire," Grant said, looking down at his lunch plate, not making eye contact.

"You can get your Mexican friends to fix that. They like working shit jobs."

Shaking his head, Grant picked up his tray and moved to another table. Wade followed him.

Grant shoveled another couple of bites into his mouth, and then cleared his spot. He walked out onto the playground and wandered around for a bit, looking for a group of kids to blend in with. But he hardly knew any of them. He'd distanced himself from both the whites and the Chicanos by being seen with Wade Dupree. He'd have to find some way, any way, to break that association. Grant wandered over near the tetherball courts, never used by anybody. A kind of no man's land between the soccer pitch and the basketball courts. In between. It seemed apt.

And then, perhaps inevitably, Wade stood before him.

"What the hell do you want?" Grant spat.

A strange half-smile arose on Wade's lips. "You been avoiding me."

"So what."

"I thought we was friends."

"We're not."

"On account of all them wetback girls wanna get inside your jockey shorts."

"Is that all you think about? Fucking one of them?"

"I wouldn't never fuck them dirty whores!"

"Then why do you talk about it all the time?"

Wade gave him a little shove on the shoulder. "What's got into you?"

"I don't want to hear your racist bullshit."

Wade lifted his chin. "You turned pussy on me."

Grant flipped him the bird and started to walk away. Wade blocked him. Grant grabbed Wade's upper arms and tried to shove him out of the way but couldn't move him. Wade swept his foot out, catching Grant off-balance, and then pushed him down.

Wade loomed over him, legs spread and hands on hips. A group of kids stood at a distance, watching.

Wade spat on the ground. "Get up so I can whip your ass proper."

Grant took his time standing up, trying to figure a strategy. Wade was taller than him and stronger. Grant knew he had only one chance to gain the advantage, and he took it. He kicked Wade in the groin, sending him staggering backwards, hands grabbing at this crotch. Grant sprang forward, delivering a sloppy roundhouse punch. Wade stood dazed for a moment, giving Grant momentary hope that he'd finished, maybe won, but then Wade erupted, knocking Grant flat on his back and pinning him to the ground. Wade rained short, sharp blows on Grant's face in a staccato rhythm, like a machine gun. Grant's arms were pinned at his sides. He thrashed, trying to rock Wade off, but Wade was too wiry and strong.

Then came the whistles and the adults. A yard duty peeled Wade off Grant. Another lifted Grant to his feet. He felt disoriented, weak-kneed. He tasted blood on his lips, metallic and salty. His right eye throbbed. Only then did he realize a sizeable crowd had formed around them, witnessing the fight.

The vice principal wasted no time. Grant was tagged with a week's worth of after-school detention and a referral in his permanent file. Wade, who had a record of fighting, was suspended. In fact, he never returned to Morehead Junior High. Grant didn't see him around the neighborhood. Later he learned that Wade's father had shipped him off to a military school in New Mexico, where his son might learn a measure of discipline and respect.

The next day at school, a group of white kids sat with Grant at lunch, eager to hear a breakdown of the fight. How did it start? How many punches had Grant landed before Wade pinned him? It was universally acknowledged that Wade had kicked Grant's ass, which initially embarrassed him, but as the kids kept talking he realized they were on his side. By just getting into it with Wade, he'd scored major points. There was no ambiguity about whether Grant and Wade were friends.

From that day forward, Grant had a group to eat lunch with. They started hanging out during the recess periods, too, and meeting up on weekends to ride BMX in the desert plains, building elaborate tracks with huge jumps and tight turns. Now Grant couldn't wait to get out in the dust and sand. He often had scrapes and bruises on his elbows and knees from wipe-outs, the stuff of great lunch table yarns.

Unfortunately, Grant's parents didn't share the boys' enthusiasm for the fight. In addition to the round of after-school detention, Grant was grounded for the week and his telephone and TV privileges were taken away. He couldn't walk Melinda home or talk to her on the phone. He couldn't watch *Fantasy Island* or *WKRP in Cincinnati*, his two favorite shows. It was a long, miserable week. He spent it reading Executioner novels in his room, a new passion. *Colorado Kill-Zone. New Orleans Knockout. Texas Storm.* Robbie mocked him for reading trash, but something about Mack Bolan's vendetta against the mafia thrilled Grant. Bolan was unwavering and resourceful, a vigilante who lived by his own rules, eternally the outsider. And he always won his fights.

The next Monday, when Grant was no longer grounded or sitting in detention, he asked Melinda if he could walk her home. She said that he could.

They met at El Martillo Hardware and followed their usual route, talking about the fight with Wade. She herself hadn't seen it, but she'd heard about it from some of the boys who had watched. The Chicanos had no sympathy for Wade and were glad to see him suspended.

"You made a name for yourself, amigo," she said. "El vato blanco."

The fact that she felt that way thrilled him. It had all been worth it, every damn minute of the detentions and grounding.

When they got to the mesquite tree, Grant, out of habit, stopped. "Melinda, I have something I want to say."

She pressed a finger to his lips, a gesture that both startled and delighted him. She gestured with a nod of her chin towards the apartment complex. "Espera un momento. I want to show you something. Vamos."

She led him down a walkway between the large units of the apartment complex. They cut down narrow alleys and crossed dusty courtyards with sun-bleached, dead yellow grass, stiff and brittle. She stopped before a tall wooden fence. She unlatched the door and opened it slowly, the door creaking on its hinges. Inside was a small yard. Along one wall of the fence were wire mesh cages, stacked one atop the other. In each cage was a pair of pigeons, their heads silvery gray with bands of iridescent green and lavender. The males were larger and darker.

"My father breeds them," she explained. Every night when he got home from work, the first thing he did was feed and water his birds. He talked to them. They all had names. On weekends, when he had birds to sell, he drove to east El Paso, to some people he knew there. "You can always tell when he has a good day. He'll take us out to eat and let us order anything on the menu."

They lingered, watching the birds as they strutted around their cages, pecking at the floor. Melinda sprinkled a little food for them, speaking softly. It might sound funny, she told Grant, but this was one of her favorite spots. Being with the birds was so calming, so quiet. Their apartment was loud, with her three sisters and her parents all sharing such a small place. "Do you have a spot like this?"

He told her about the campsite he'd discovered in the desert, about the firepit lined by stones, about the empty tin cans and the water bottles. It would be awesome, he said, to camp out there one night, drinking in the stars and the cool night air.

She laughed. "You might have company."

Grant brightened. "You'd come with me?"

"Not me, tonto. Los mojados."

"Who?"

It was slang for the workers who crossed the border without papers. The Mexican equivalent of wetback, only it wasn't so much of a put-down when fellow Mexicans used it to describe one of their own. "Your campsite is for the ones who are passing through, traveling farther north, up to New Mexico or Colorado."

Of course. He should have guessed as much. He felt stupid and naïve. "How do you know things like that?"

She looked him in the eye. "Because that was my parents twenty years ago."

They had their papers now, she added. They were legal. But like so many before them, they walked across El Rio Bravo, as the Mexicans call it, searching for work and a new life in Los Estados Unidos. For them, it had worked out.

Each of their four children had been born in Texas, U.S. citizens by birth.

"You think that's bad?" she asked.

"No, I don't," he said. "Thank you for telling me."

A bird strutted up to the wire mesh of its cage, its beady eye fixed steadily on him. "I'm not that different," he said. "Almost everybody here is from somewhere else, if you go back far enough."

"But it's not the same," Melinda said. "Your people, they took and took. Now they think they own everything. They look down on us. They hate us."

"I don't hate you."

"You're different," she said. "You're not like them."

"It's going to change," he said. "It's going to get better."

She shook her head, slowly. "Papí says America will never accept people with brown skin."

He frowned, unsure what to say to that. He wanted them to be wrong, but he knew they might be right. More immediately, he understood how little he actually knew about Melinda Díaz. More than ever, he wanted to know everything about her.

"What did you want to say to me before?" she asked.

He had planned to ask her to be his steady girlfriend. He'd prepared a thrilling speech about true love. He'd understand if they needed to keep it hush. They'd be secret lovers, writing long, flowery letters declaring their passions, and—

He couldn't say those words now. He'd sound childish and naïve. Worse, he might insult her, the last thing he wanted.

He reached for her hand, brushing his thumb slowly, gently across her smooth skin. "You're the best thing that's happened to me in this town," he said. "I think you're the reason I moved here."

She smiled at him. "Eres loco," she said, "pero me gustas."

He understood what she said. He pulled her close. She felt warm and soft in his arms. His entire body bristled with energy and excitement. He closed his eyes and breathed in her soft, black hair, savoring every moment of her touch. He knew it was only just beginning.

Welcome Back to the World

Those who awaken
Never rest in one place.
Like swans, they rise
And leave the lake.

—The Dhammapada

The preachings are one thing and the preacher another.

—Montaigne, "Of Books"

1

I walked into my brother's trailer, dropped my bag, and took a look around; I knew that I would not stay long. The walls were covered in beer mirrors and tacky color posters of bikini-clad women advertising tequila. Pizza boxes and empty bottles littered the kitchen counter. A heap of laundry occupied one of two chairs—clean or dirty, I'm not sure it mattered. On the television, a basketball game.

Dennis leaned a hip against the tiny propane range, wearing baggy shorts and a bright red T-shirt advertising Dr.

Kong's Board Wax. Flip-flops, of course. He held up a pint glass filled with tomato juice, a pickle spear jutting from it like a severed digit. "Bloody Mary?"

"It's ten-thirty in the morning," I said.

He looked at his wristwatch. "Is it Tuesday?"

I assured him it was Tuesday, then asked about his plans for the day. He had none.

"Don't you work?" I asked.

"I'm taking the day off. That's the beauty of being your own boss." He took a sip of his Bloody Mary. "It's not every day that your big brother gets kicked out of a Buddhist monastery."

I hadn't been kicked out. I'd explained that to Dennis on the phone when I'd called him the week before. He was razzing me, like always. When we were in high school and I was captain of the wrestling team, traveling the length of California, chasing yet another trophy, my brother used to joke that the reason I didn't have a girlfriend was because wrestlers were always looking to score, but they never made a move unless a referee was in the room. I was also vice president of student government and edited the senior yearbook.

Dennis majored in truancy, mouthing off, and nearly having to repeat his sophomore year. College had never been on his to-do list. It surprised no one when he moved to Santa Cruz to surf. He did surf back then—mostly couches. Dennis drifted from job to job: fry cook, janitor, stock clerk. When he finally settled in at the engine shop, it seemed like a miracle. He repaired lawn mowers, generators, mopeds, you name it. The old guy who owned the place loved Dennis. Actually, most people love Dennis. He's affable and laid-back to a fault, the lowest of low-maintenance people. But the flip side is that you can't convince him to make a plan, let alone stir up any ambition. He's always bounced along, living paycheck to paycheck, happy to be near the beach. Not that he surfs much. It's all about the lifestyle, screw the career.

Dennis sank into his armchair. "So how long you plan to stay?" His calves, like his arms, were covered in an ever-growing mishmash of tattoos. Vargas girls, a Māori tribal pattern, the obligatory yin-yang swirl.

"I don't know," I said. "Long enough to plot my next move."

"Guess those monks don't give you your deposit back when they bump ya."

I sighed. "I left voluntarily, just like I arrived."

"Whatever!" He reached for the remote and began flicking between channels. "Between you and me? Never seemed like a smart career move."

As if he had room to talk! I pointed to a pair of Chinese characters on his leg: 強度

"Is that new?"

He ran a hand over the tattoo, caressing it. "Qiángdù," he said.

"Which means?"

"Intensity." He looked up at me and said, "It's how I live my life."

I barked out a laugh. I couldn't help it.

"Fuck you, Clint."

"Sorry," I said, smothering my grin with a hand. "It's just…"

He turned off the TV and tossed the remote into the laundry pile. "I know it doesn't look like it to you, but there's more than one way to bring it into your life. A good set of waves. A kick-ass sunset while drinking a spicy Bloody Mary at the Crow's Nest. Sex with your lady, if you have a lady, which neither one of us does right now, but we're going to work on that, stat!"

"Slow down," I said. For the last seven years I'd lived with a vow of chastity, not something taken or renounced lightly. I wasn't rushing into anything. Honestly, chastity had not been a major issue for me. It was one of the more comforting aspects of monasticism. People finally stop asking when you're going to get a partner.

"Come on, dude! You're stepping back into the material world—lust, lies, and corruption! Only one way to do it. Jump in with both feet!" He stood from his chair, drained his drink, and set it on the tabletop with a bang. "You know what you need, brother?"

A job, a bank account, an apartment, a car—none of which was close at hand. I shrugged my shoulders.

"Floridalma's shrimp tacos. Best food truck in Watsonville, or Santa Cruz for that matter. Let's go."

I'd also been a vegetarian for the last seven years, though I suspected that would change. I'd always envied the Theravada monks who were allowed to eat meat. Now I had the choice.

We drove in Dennis's Bronco down East Riverside Drive. He pointed to a large building with an arched roof. It looked like a gymnasium. "You know we have a Buddhist temple in Watsonville, right? It's not your order. I stopped and asked them once."

Of course I knew of it, a Jodo Shinshu temple, part of the Pure Land order. I was surprised that Dennis had bothered to ask.

The taco truck was a boxy white food van sitting in the corner of an unused parking lot, the asphalt punctuated with spiky green weeds and trash. The strip mall on the other end was vacant, the shop windows covered with FOR LEASE signs. In front of the truck were a few picnic tables under a vinyl awning, its aluminum legs secured in buckets of sand. The tables were full and the queue was eight people deep.

"This place is always hopping," Dennis said. "It's because it's so damn good! How many you want?"

When I said two, he laughed. "Four. Trust me." Then he told me to find some seats. Lunch was on him. I found seats and held them. Dennis joined me a few minutes later, handing me a tall Mexican beer in a can. I had to smile. It seemed that my brother was intent on overturning every vow I'd lived by as a monastic. But, when you leave that life, you leave behind more than your robes. I popped the top on the beer and took a sip. I don't mind telling you, it tasted pretty good.

"Let me ask you something," Dennis said. "Was it a girl?"

I decided to keep it simple for now. "Nothing like that."

"Cause if it had been me? I'd flunk out in about a day. You won't find me cutting back on the hooch or the ladies."

"Have you dated anyone since Laurel?" Their relationship had lasted three years. I knew she got sick—terminal cancer, discovered at a late stage. Within six months of her diagnosis, she was gone. Her death had rocked Dennis, but just how much, I couldn't say. We hadn't talked about any of it.

Dennis lowered his chin, staring down at the table for a long moment. "A one-night stand with a woman who brought in a blender, which I ended up fixing for free. Nothing serious." A moment later, he added, "I don't usually do kitchen appliances."

"So why do you sound so randy?"

"I talk big," he sighed. "Truth is, I'm off my game. But now that my brother is in town, the two of us—back in the saddle!"

Our order was called. Dennis returned with two plates piled with shrimp tacos. There was no talking, only the bliss of indulging in food that was every bit as good as Dennis had promised. Tender shrimp cooked in garlic and cilantro, with fresh lime squeezed over it and a dollop of peppery red taco sauce. Every bite was a dream.

"Was that good, or was that good?" Dennis asked.

"Better than good," I said, smiling.

"Just keep listening to me," he said, wiping his chin with a napkin. "I won't steer you wrong. And by the way, I come here about twice a week. Get ready to binge!"

I laughed. This was everything opposite to what I'd recently been practicing, but it felt good at that moment.

He raised his beer and we toasted. "Welcome back to the world!"

2

There is a stillness, a quiet, a settled sense of place and purpose inside a monastery. Rising at five o'clock to the chiming of bells, we climb onto our cushions for the day's first sitting. Gongs ring. Incense smoke perfumes the air, musky and close. I settle on the cushion, rocking gently left and right, forward and then back, finding the center. Legs folded, hands in the cosmic mudra, chin and eyes lowered. I follow my breath as it moves through my lungs and into my body, deep into my abdomen. My eyes half-focus on the wall before me, and if I am mindful and diligent, I enter into a radiant stillness, a fertile sense of being and becoming.

Bells ring again and we stand from our cushions. Outside, in the bright morning light, everything seems newly awakened and vitally alive. That is the goal of practice: to take one's clarity and mindfulness off the cushion and into the world, and to sustain it. It's not easy, but I believed I could perfect my practice to the point that this mindset would never fade.

It's a form of faith, a radical trust. I miss it now, more than I would have imagined.

REVEREND MASTER ENO WAS A SHORT MAN, lean and muscular. He must have had an outrageous metabolism because he was not a modest eater. He also drank copious amounts of black tea, morning to night. When studying, we sometimes worked for three hours without a break. His level of attention to any task, large or small, was ferocious. I liken it to drilling down: his gaze was penetrating, insightful, knowing. At times, he unsettled me. Usually he inspired me. In the end, he undid us both.

We met in San Francisco. I was taking a break from social work—the burnout rate is shocking—bouncing between temp jobs, and volunteering at a homeless shelter. I had a room on Polk Street in the Tenderloin. Every morning the sidewalks were littered with heroin needles, smashed bottles, and human excrement, a pleasure for which I paid through the nose.

Eno spoke at a local Zen center, lecturing on the Four Noble Truths, bedrock Buddhism. We're born into a world of suffering, caused by an endless desire for things to be other than they actually are. It seemed he was describing the world to me as I had understood it for most of my life, though I'd never had the language to articulate it. What Eno made so clear and compelling, what sounded liberating on his tongue, what finally woke me the hell up and made me stand in line to shake his hand—ah, he doesn't shake hands, he exchanges bows—was that there was an end to this suffering, and that is by following the teachings of the Buddha.

With a certainty I have felt rarely in my life, I knew I must walk that path. I started visiting Castle Rock monastery on meditation retreats, eventually staying for several months. Before long I had accepted the monastic vows, shaved my head, and been issued a set of robes. I put my things into storage, gave away my car, and moved into the monastery. Rev. Eno gave me my dharma name: Kanshin, or broad heart.

My friends and fellow social workers all thought I'd lost my mind, but I'd never felt so sure of what I was doing in my life.

When it came time for me to request a senior teacher, I asked Eno. This was not customary of a novice. Eno was spiritual advisor to the senior monks, who in turn advised the juniors, and so on. He might have dismissed me, but he surprised me by accepting. He later told me he saw a glimmer of his younger self in me: a yearning, searching soul, restless and already deeply committed—someone who, with right effort, could go far in the practice.

This surprised me greatly. I felt nothing like Eno, who carried a paternalistic air of authority, what the military calls command presence. There was never any doubt who was in charge. I, on the other hand, was a mess of fears and insecurities. Despite this, I managed to squirt out a line about living up to his expectations.

"It's not me you must please," he said. "Be true to your nature. Follow the practitioner's instinct. Look inward. If you are mindful, you cannot defeat yourself."

He was full of sayings like that. I took to recording them in a small notebook, hoping to present them to him one day as a collection of spiritual aphorisms.

I saw in Eno a version of myself as who I aspired to be. He made me believe I could become that person. He made me want to try, perhaps more than I myself wanted to. This was my first mistake.

WHEN I ASKED DENNIS IF I COULD stay for a while, he was quick to agree, though it was clear that he had little more to offer me than a cot in his "second bedroom," in reality a storage room crammed with boxes. The trailer was small, just two bedrooms and a common area, and an unbelievably tight bathroom. "Less to clean!" Dennis boasted, though in practice it proved to be no incentive.

Dennis lived in Watsonville, a farming town known for its strawberries. He owned his trailer, rented the lot, and drove his pock-marked Ford Bronco the eighteen miles to his engine shop in Santa Cruz, which he'd bought from the former owner. It had to be a sweetheart deal. Who can afford to own a shop in Santa Cruz? The place was tiny, tucked in alongside a Mexican bakery on a side street in the Beach Flats neighborhood, one of Santa Cruz's poorest. But locals knew where to take their busted lawn mowers, generators, and chainsaws. His rates were affordable. Dennis was some kind of wizard, capable of fixing anything.

I know nothing about mechanics or engine repair, but even I could appreciate watching Dennis work with his tools.

He moved with a kind of elegance, leaning over the piece, working with his fingers, humming along to classic rock on the portable radio, his jump suit streaked with oil and grease, his long hair tied back in a bandana. The intensity of his focus, combined with his obvious mastery of skills, and the grace and fluidity of his motions—I know it sounds odd, but I was often moved when I watched my brother work. He could tell, and it annoyed him, and so I wasn't allowed to linger at the shop.

Dennis frequently took days off. He surfed a little, when he was in the mood. He watched a lot of TV. He napped. And he read books, good books. He had a library card and he used it frequently. He loved novels. He had good taste, both for the classics and the newer stuff. DeLillo, Morrison, and Whitehead. But also Kafka, Wharton, and Faulkner.

One Sunday afternoon, I sat folding laundry as Dennis watched a football game. I asked him what his favorite book was. He didn't hesitate. *Under the Volcano*, by Malcolm Lowry. "That book will take your head off, dude."

I told him he'd probably given himself the equivalent of a bachelor's degree in literature, just based on the range and quality of what he read.

He laughed. "What a fucking useless idea, a degree in reading books."

"Not reading—analyzing."

"Even worse. If it's good, it's good. If it's not, forget it."

"But there's the why of it. Why is something good? How do we know?"

Fixated by a play on the television, he appeared not to register my question. When the play finished, he took a sip of his Bloody Mary, and he turned to me. "If a thing is good, if it speaks to you, or if it's well-written, or maybe if it's just entertaining enough to hold your interest—isn't that enough? Do we have to scrutinize every little thing in life? Can't you just recognize that something is good and leave it at that?"

"But in order to share it," I suggested, "in order to demonstrate to others what is truly valuable…"

Dennis waved a hand. "Me telling you *Under the Volcano* is the best book of all time isn't going to make you like it. You have to read it and think about it for yourself."

But some people needed help learning what to look for, I continued. Wasn't that the role of a teacher? To be a trusted guide?

He gave me a sharp look. "Do you trust all your teachers?"

He had no idea how deeply that question struck; I hadn't shared with him that part of my story. I quietly folded a pair of boxers.

On the television, a wide receiver leapt into the air, plucking a football out of the sky. The moment his feet touched earth, he was knocked flat by another player. Dennis bolted out of his seat, nearly spilling his drink.

"Holy shit, did you see that? He laid him out! Laid! Him! Out!"

REVEREND ENO ASKED ME TO study the Brahma-viharas, or four perfect virtues: metta, good will or loving kindness; karuna, compassion; mudita, joy for others; and upekkha, equanimity. In our discussion of how best to actualize these virtues, Eno stressed that there were what he called the near enemies and the far enemies. The far enemy is not hard to distinguish. It is the opposite of virtue: ill-will as opposed to good will; cruelty as opposed to compassion, and so on. It's the near enemy that is harder to distinguish. Pandering condescension disguised as joy for others, for example, or indifference masking equanimity.

I knew exactly what he was talking about. As a social worker, I'd served the homeless, the recovering drug addicts, and the teenage single moms. I told myself I was motivated by empathy for these suffering souls, and most of the time I think I was, but there were other times when I sat with one of my clients, hearing their sad story, and I felt something else. Their suffering, their mistakes, their bad luck—I was thankful it was them and not me. I understood, even then, what I was doing: masking self-righteous pity with compassion, a near enemy for sure.

I shared this self-reflection with Rev. Eno, who was pleased to hear that I'd absorbed the teachings so quickly, and that I could point to concrete examples from my lay life. This was the sign of an ardent disciple.

"Thank you, Master." His praise always felt good, like warm sunshine on my shoulders.

At our next meeting, however, Eno seemed stiff and cold. We chatted briefly about an upcoming Buddhist ceremony, Wesak, a celebration of the birth, enlightenment, and teachings of the Buddha. This event always drew a large crowd from the local community as well as dozens more from Sacramento and the Bay Area. Event planning had grown complicated, Eno complained. Frankly, I wasn't sure why he was sharing this with me. I wasn't involved in Guest Services.

I'd been appointed assistant to the bursar, Reverend Keido, one of the Welsh monastics who'd helped found the monastery back in the Sixties. If Eno wanted to talk shop, I had a few things to share—most notably that the monastery was delinquent on several payments for utilities, groceries, and contracting. These folks were getting impatient. I fielded their angry calls, promising them that payment was forthcoming. When I asked Keido about this, he assured me everything was in order; we were just a little backed up. Why were we backed up? Keido couldn't give me a clear answer. At first I worried that he was corrupt, but, when I pressed him, he couldn't recall the names of certain creditors, despite the fact that some had been doing business with the monastery for years. The true answer, I surmised, was simpler: Keido was incompetent. He needed to be removed.

Just when and how to share that with Eno was another question. As a junior monk, I had to tread lightly and respect the chain of command. For all the talk of selflessness and no ego, a monastery is an astonishingly hierarchical institution, and removing a senior monk from a top position could be tricky.

Finally, Eno turned to the topic of my studies. How had I progressed?

I'd been focusing on metta, or loving kindness, I informed him. Selfish affection was one of its near enemies.

"And how did you arrive at that conclusion?" Eno asked.

I smiled. "I practically ate it for lunch every day of my working life."

Nothing about social work is easy. Case workers juggle mountainous client loads over long hours. There are days when it seems like you're dealing with an endless procession of misery. It takes a toll. To get out of the trenches, case workers either transfer to some other state office, or they climb the ladder into middle management, where you're pushing paper and attending meetings as opposed to handling clients.

I chose the latter, and I didn't get there by virtue of hard work. No, I got that promotion the old-fashioned way, by kissing ass. Our district supervisor was a vain, ego-driven peacock who alienated everyone. How this guy made it to management is anyone's guess, but I knew he was my meal ticket, so I buttered him up and then some, playing golf with him, eating barbecue lunches with him, and laughing at his lousy jokes. We even went in together on Kings season tickets. (I couldn't care less about pro sports.)

Sure enough, when an assistant supervisor spot opened up, I leap-frogged over a couple of senior case workers and landed the position. Now I shared an office with this clown, and the long Friday lunches and Sunday morning tee times became a regular ordeal. I'd done it to myself, faking affection for a guy I secretly detested. I solved that dilemma, sort of, by walking away from social work and shaving my head.

"And what did that solve?" Eno asked. "You haven't changed."

The statement surprised me. "Master, please explain."

"You're a sycophant, barging into my chambers to praise me, begging me to be your teacher. Perhaps you have the same aim. You want to become a senior monk, perhaps abbot one day." A smile crept across his face. Was he baiting me? Or was he in earnest? This was a side of Eno I didn't recognize.

"No, Master. My affection for you is sincere."

"Are you sure? How do you know?"

I let his words sink in, felt the sting. Was I being rejected? Berated? This was new and unexpected.

"Have I done something wrong?"

"Yes!"

"What is it? Please tell me so I can correct it."

Eno grew quiet, chin lowered. He looked at the floor as he spoke. "Your fear and disappointment are obstacles to your training. Move past them to what is next."

I felt I should know what was next, but in that moment I did not know. When I admitted as much, Eno's face darkened.

"Do not patronize me! Do not seek my favor! Do you think I'm hard on you? You should be just as hard on me. Don't forget that."

I'd never heard a senior monk talk like that. I didn't know whether to feel shocked, challenged, or honored. Before I could make up my mind, Eno turned away, brusquely waving his hand, dismissing me. I left his chambers, wandering the cloisters in a daze, turning over what Eno had said, puzzling at his deeper meanings. I nearly collided with the vice abbot, Rev. Nanshin.

"Mind your step, friend," she snapped. I recoiled, apologetic, and turned away, crossing into an open yard, where the afternoon sunlight blinded me.

3

I got a job waiting tables at a café just off the Boardwalk in Santa Cruz. I worked a split shift, covering lunch and dinner. Dennis lent me his motorbike, a Honda CB250 he'd restored just for kicks. It was a sweet little machine, perfect for the commute. Parking was never a problem. Usually I spent the hours between my shifts hanging around downtown, but one afternoon I had to make a quick trip back to Watsonville to get something. I ran in, grabbed what I needed, and on my way out met a man wearing a sharp grey suit. A silver Lexus stood at the curb. He asked for my brother. I told him Dennis wasn't in. Could I help in some way?

The man lifted his chin. "Ah, the brother."

I wasn't sure I liked the sound of that. "And who are you?"

"Rafael Jimenez," he said, handing me a business card. "Your brother's lawyer."

We shook hands. I asked if Dennis was in some kind of trouble. My worst fears confirmed, etc.

He looked surprised. "He hasn't told you?"

"Told me what?"

Jimenez had a bright, easy laugh. "I will let Dennis share the news." He turned and began to walk back to his car. "I'll call him, but you know he never answers his phone. That's why I dropped by." He paused, one hand on the door of his Lexus. "Perhaps you can help. Please tell him the farmer has returned."

I didn't know whether to laugh or get scared. "What does that mean?"

Jimenez smiled. "Your brother will explain. He's one of my biggest clients!" And with a wave of the hand, he was gone.

WHEN I GOT HOME FROM THE CAFÉ that night, Dennis was sitting in his chair, reading a library copy of Margaret Atwood's *The Testaments*. A six pack of beer stood on the table before him, three cans already empty.

"How is that?" I asked. "I've heard good things."

"I'm not sure I'm in the right mindset," he said. "Maybe when Trump is gone." He closed the book and set it on the table. "Grab a beer, cop a squat."

He pointed at the chair opposite him, filled with a pile of his laundry that hadn't changed position in a week.

"I met Rafael Jimenez today," I said. "Did he get ahold of you?"

"He left me a phone message. I haven't picked it up."

"Isn't he your lawyer?"

"He brings me down."

"He asked me to tell you something. 'The farmer has returned.'"

Dennis lowered his head and spat out a string of curses.

"What does it mean?" I asked. "I've been wondering about it all day."

He picked up his cell phone from the table. "Give me a minute." While he listened to his voicemail—it was quite lengthy—I went to my room and changed out of my work clothes. When I came out, I found him back in his chair, cradling a can of beer against his stomach. "Let's take a little drive," he said. "I want to show you something."

We drove to La Selva Beach, just north of Watsonville. The tide was out, leaving a broad shoreline strewn with driftwood, flotsam, and twisted, rope-like strands of bull kelp. Gulls hopped and darted about, picking at the piles. We walked barefoot over coarse, cold sand. A strong breeze blew onshore. My bare arms bristled with goose bumps.

Dennis found a dune to his liking and sat down, plunking the remains of his six pack in the sand. He opened a beer and handed it to me, then opened another for himself.

"This was one of our favorite spots," he said. "Me and Laurel."

"I'm sorry I never met her," I said. "What was she like?"

He laughed. "She was the first person in my life who totally got me. She laughed at my stupid jokes. She didn't care if I worked part-time, or not at all. What mattered to her was, when you do a thing, do it completely. No half-assing. That might be fixing some guy's ATV or it might be surfing at sunset. Pay attention to the thing you're doing right now. Bring all your energy and attention to it." He nodded his head, sure of something. "That's what I mean by intensity, bro."

"Buddhists call it mindfulness."

Dennis picked up a stick and jabbed it into the sand. "Whatever you call it, she had it. Big time."

"She sounds pretty special."

"Most definitely. We'd sit out here, smoke a big J, plow through a twelve pack of something—I tell you, the girl could drink—and we'd settle the world's problems."

Dennis explained that Laurel came from a well-off family. Her dad ran a medical supply business—exclusive contracts in Asia, that sort of thing. Her mother was an in-demand architect in San Francisco. They were go-getters, and they expected their kids to follow suit. The older sister dutifully complied, landing a Stanford MBA and was now making a mint selling women's clothing online.

Laurel took a different path. She dropped out of college at Humboldt State to farm weed in the Emerald Triangle for a season, then followed a rock band on tour for a year, before settling into Santa Cruz to pursue her next bliss. Her parents were apoplectic, but—and Dennis assured me this was key—they never cut her off. They badgered her constantly, urging her to finish her degree, but Laurel was nothing if not independent. What looked to her parents like a wasted life was, in fact, the most meaningful of quests. Laurel couldn't settle into a lifestyle before she'd shopped around, trying this and that. Gathering experiences. Life wisdom.

When Dennis met her, she was apprenticing with a ceramicist who lived in the hills just outside of Santa Cruz. He used this ancient Japanese method, some kind of hand-made, super-rare glaze and the very best clay.

"His vases go for five, ten grand," Dennis said, "and he's got a two-year wait list. The dude makes mad money, but you wouldn't know it. His jeans are streaked with dirt. Drives around in a beat-up truck—a '72 Datsun 521, to be exact. Sweet little ride."

The master almost never agreed to train anyone, but he accepted Laurel. She had to go and live on his property. He made her get up at five a.m. to fire his kiln and check the moisture content of the clay. She swept up his mess, brewed his tea, all that junior-rank crap. But he also kept her at his side in the studio, explaining each step of the process, from the selection of the clay, to the shaping of the vase, to the layers upon layers of glaze, and then firing the final product. What came out was truly special.

Laurel's internship would take five years. Dennis met her as she was wrapping up year two, just getting to the point where she was being allowed to fire a few small pots and bowls. Things progressed nicely over the next two years. She traveled with her master to Japan to select clay. She knew how to mix the glazes. She got to the point where the master turned her loose in the studio. She was making her own bowls, and they were starting to sell, though she wouldn't be making the big money until she was a certified master.

She was just starting her final year when she got sick. She tried to keep working, but within a few months she was too ill. She left the ceramicist's property and moved back to Santa Cruz, where Dennis took care of her. But during all that time, during the internship and right up until she got too sick to continue, she and Dennis were working on their master plan.

"She bought a piece of land near Big Basin, deep in the Santa Cruz mountains. The plan was to build a studio there. It was sort of complicated. The kiln has to be wood-fired, built out of this one kind of brick. You have to have a special storage room for the clay, moisture controlled. We didn't get too far, just buying and clearing this plot of land. We built a small cottage and an outhouse. It might surprise you to know that your little brother is now the sole proprietor of five acres of prime forest acreage, I shit you not."

"She left it to you?"

"That and a couple of sweet rental properties in Santa Cruz, two bungalows in Seabright."

I fell back in the sand, laughing. "You own two bungalows in the Seabright district but live in a trailer in Watsonville?"

"It's all tied up in the courts, man, a royal mess. Her parents are coming after me, big time. That's where Jimenez comes in. He says I have the law on my side. It's just a matter of time—and the legal expenses, which are going to soak me."

"She left all this to you."

"She died without a will or a trust. I've learned more about intestate succession laws and probate code than you would care to hear."

"Wait a minute," I said, sitting up. "That means you and Laurel…"

He nodded. "About six weeks before she passed. Just drove down to the county courthouse and did it! The custodian was my witness."

"Congratulations," I said. "How come you never told me?"

"We didn't tell anybody, which is one reason her parents are so pissed. Ours was not a traditional arrangement. Laurel was in pretty bad shape, physically, but we'd never been closer, emotionally. It was a business move, in a sense. She knew what would happen if her parents inherited her estate—everything she'd worked for, everything she'd planned, gone. Plus, you might say she was looking out for me, leaving me something to build on. I didn't know she owned title and deed on those two rental properties! Even in death, that sweet girl will surprise you."

A nearby eucalyptus grove perfumed the air with its intoxicating, minty scent. I tried to wrap my head around what Dennis had shared with me. One part of me felt hurt that he'd hidden this from me, his only living family member. He'd had a profound love, found a soulmate and even married her—all of it secret, all of it hidden.

But what should I have expected? In the ten years since our mother had passed my brother and I had rarely talked. There was no bad blood or anything. We'd just taken different paths. Neither of us understood why the other one lived his life the way he did. Add to that the fact that monastics are necessarily withdrawn from a lot of lay life. And Dennis, well, he just doesn't pick up the phone or send you an email.

Regardless, I had no room to criticize him for keeping secrets. I had plenty of my own, having told Dennis very little about my final year at Castle Rock. In truth, I wasn't ready to talk about any of it. It was all a little too fresh, too raw. Maybe it was the same for him.

The hiss and snap of Dennis opening a beer can called me back to the moment. "Last one," he said, handing it to me.

"You still haven't told me what Rafael meant," I said, taking a long sip. The beer was nearly warm now.

"The farmer has returned? That's up on the land. A pot farmer was up there, squatting a few months ago, putting in a grow. I had to run him off, threaten to call the sheriff. I guess he's back. Now I got that to deal with—again."

He railed on for a minute about how he hated confrontation. This whole thing was more of a headache than it was worth. He had half a mind to walk away and let the psycho parents win. Worried he was going to talk himself into a bad decision, I put a hand on his shoulder and he stopped, mid-sentence.

"I want to see it," I said. "I want to see this land."

4

It was in late spring, following a heavy winter, as I recall, that Rev. Eno began postponing and rescheduling our weekly tutorials. He urged me to keep up with my reading and we would eventually get to all of it, and for a while I did make an effort. I'd been assigned the Senjō chapter of Great Master Dōgen's *Shōbōgenzō*, a treatise on bathroom etiquette. Of course it's more than that. It's a humble reminder that, with every action we undertake, at every moment of the day, we have an opportunity to practice mindfulness and respect. No action is unworthy of our attention. I'd read and re-read the chapter several times, keeping the material fresh in my mind for my next meeting with Eno.

A month passed. I felt my training had stalled.

Finally, one afternoon Eno asked to meet, but it wasn't for instruction. We walked through a grove of trees to a small pet cemetery in a far corner of the monastery grounds. He apologized for the repeated cancellations. He was busy, he told me, working on a history of the monastery. It was taking up more and more of his time.

"I'm afraid that, for the time being, I'll be unable to continue our weekly tutorials." He smiled warmly, as if comforting me.

I looked away, down at a small headstone for Biffer, *canis fidelis fiduciam*, aged eleven years. "Master, what am I to do?"

He'd worked it all out, he assured me. I was to begin study with Rev. Chuso, one of the senior monks. In a few weeks or months, when Eno had finished his book project, he would reevaluate the question of directing my studies, but he was over-taxed in so many areas that the prospect of returning to the direct tutelage of a junior monk might simply be impossible.

An alpine wind gusted through the tall pine with a soft swish. Broken patches of sunlight dappled the forest floor. I understood then that our long sessions of study were permanently finished. I don't know any other way to say it: I felt I'd suffered a great defeat, that I'd somehow lost him. I knew, even then, I was too invested in the man, that I'd let his role, his example, his leadership over-shadow nearly everything. Perhaps he sensed this, too, and this was his way of forcing me to work past it.

Then he surprised me by asking how I felt about the upcoming changes in the bursar's office.

"I'm sorry, Master. What changes?"

"Reverend Keido hasn't spoken with you?"

I shook my head. The bursar and I rarely spoke. In addition to being a middling accountant, Keido was a grouch. I stayed out of his way as much as possible.

Eno frowned, shaking his head. "You should have been told by now." Keido was due for a medical leave to facilitate a series of surgeries. "You've been appointed interim bursar," Eno informed me.

My eyes widened. If I was saddened by the loss of Eno as my teacher, I was positively terrified of being put in charge of the books. "How long will Keido be absent?"

"Six months, maybe longer. He leaves in two weeks."

"Master, I must tell you—"

"—You're doing good work," he interrupted. "It's time to step up and assume more of the responsibility for the running of this monastery."

"I need help."

"We'll find you someone. Leave that to me." We walked a little further, then stopped at the base of a tall cedar. Eno brushed his fingers across the bark. "I realize this news must come as a surprise. I apologize for dropping it on you like that. I'm not sure why Keido hasn't spoken to you."

"He doesn't communicate well."

"I suppose not."

"Nor is he any kind of bookkeeper. Since I'm stepping in as bursar, I must tell you that the office has been mismanaged for some time." I detailed several cases that Keido had delayed, or overlooked, or simply ignored. A contractor who'd done some work for us last summer was threatening to sue.

Eno turned to face me. "Why am I just learning of this now?"

"Until now, it hasn't been my office."

Eno adjusted the sleeves of his robes. "We'll talk further, Kanshin. For the time being, please obey my requests. You will meet with Rev. Chuso to resume your studies, and you will assume your new role as bursar, serving until further notice."

"Yes, Master."

And then he left me, his stride long and urgent. I lingered in the cemetery for a few more minutes. The graves were littered with pine needles and dried leaves. I would mention it to the groundskeeper, who would send someone out. Every job in a monastery has its appointed worker.

REV. KEIDO NEVER DID INFORM ME of the changes in the bursar's office. A week before his medical leave began, he simply quit showing up. Nor did I see him in the meditation hall or the dining room. He was too ill and out of sorts, I was told. I fretted over the complaints I'd shared with Eno. Had I been unfair, criticizing a sick man?

Maybe. But I hadn't known.

Either way, his mess was now mine to clean up. The problems were real, and now that I had full access to the office, I realized the scope of things. It was worse than I'd anticipated.

Budgets were incomplete. Accounts hadn't been reconciled in months. Tax forms were missing. We'd hired numerous independent contractors, but no 1099s had been issued. And so on. It was a miracle we'd never been audited.

Overwhelmed, I demanded immediate assistance. That fell to one of our long-term lay residents, Alice Yu. She proved to be a wizard when it came to organizing. Within a couple of weeks, she had the files in order and all the outstanding bills and invoices lined up in neat rows, in chronological order. It made my ongoing job of sorting out who to pay and when that much easier.

Alice and I worked smoothly beside one another, mixing in a bit of friendly chat with the business. It was refreshing to speak with someone new, someone not so tangled up in the web of monastic life. (A monastery is like a family; you don't get to choose who lives beside you, your brothers and sisters in the practice. We're all there out of a shared sense of purpose, a calling, if you will. Take away that shared purpose, and there would be plenty of folks whom I wouldn't otherwise care to know.) I came to look forward to those hours with Alice, listening as she chatted with me about her background and her ambitions. She had a lot of questions about monastic life and Buddhist practice, which I tried to answer.

Alice was a writer. She'd earned her M.F.A. at a prestigious East Coast school and, not long after, published a book of short stories with a small press. She resisted the lure of teaching, preferring to eke out her existence as a writer by cobbling together various freelance jobs and, whenever she could, winning fellowships and residencies. When I asked, she rattled off a list of places she'd visited: Hedgebrook, MacDowell, Byrdcliffe. The life she described sounded rather appealing. She stayed for a month at a time, had her meals prepared for her, and spent her days writing and reading. In the evening, she dined communally with the other artists, followed by wine on the porch and fascinating discussions that often stretched into the night. Minus the wine and the staying up late, it didn't sound all that different from a monastery.

Most recently, she'd won a Fulbright award and had traveled to Taiwan for a year to study the White Terror and the legacy of the soldiers imprisoned or tortured by Chiang Kai-shek. It was her intention to write an historical novel from this material, but something had gone wrong; her project disintegrated. Whatever raw nerves or painful history she'd uncovered, it stopped her cold, and she left Taiwan empty-handed. She returned to Oakland and spent a restless year trying many things: yoga, wilderness camping, and finally meditation. That's how she discovered Rev. Eno and Castle Rock.

She liked it there—at that point, she'd already been at the monastery for three months—but she wanted me to know that this stay was merely an interlude. She needed to get her writing life back on track. She was in the process of lining up her next residency. It was nearing the time for her to move on.

"You'll try again to write your book?" I asked. I'd never known a writer.

She rifled through a stack of bills until she found what she was looking for, jerking it from the pile with an agile snap. "I'll write something, Rev. Kanshin."

"You know, Rev. Eno is working on a book. A history of the monastery." I explained that, until he'd undertaken that project, Eno had been my private teacher. "He's gotten so deeply into the writing, he's had to quit mentoring me."

"How do you feel about that?"

"I'm pissed," I said, before I could stop myself. Immediately I regretted my choice of words. "Sorry, that didn't sound very monastic."

I took a deep breath and started again. "It's a reminder of impermanence, that all things must change."

She looked up at me, narrowed her eyes, and then burst out laughing. "I like you, Rev. Kanshin. You're real. You remind me that monks are just human beings, struggling to get along like the rest of us. It's an important lesson for a lay person like me."

Embarrassed, I dropped my gaze to a stack of bills. "Glad to have helped you along the path," I grumbled.

ALICE AND I MADE MAJOR PROGRESS in the bursar's office. We bought new accounting software. I enrolled in an accounting class at the local junior college. I issued a round of checks to some of our creditors, with assurances that our debts would soon be cleared. After six rather demanding weeks, things quieted down. Much of this was due to Alice's assistance. Truly, I couldn't have done it without her. I considered her essential.

And so, when one of our novice monks showed up one afternoon, cheerfully announcing that the vice abbot, Rev. Nanshin, had tasked him with serving as my assistant, I was disappointed, but not necessarily surprised. It was June. I assumed Alice had secured her next writing residency and was preparing to leave. It just seemed odd that she hadn't mentioned anything to me.

A couple of days later, I passed her in the cloisters, and I stopped to ask about her plans.

"Actually, I'll be staying a little longer," she said. "Possibly through to December."

"Then you can help me with the accounting!"

Smiling, she shook her head. She had another assignment.

"With whom?"

"Rev. Eno," she replied. "I'm editing his book."

"Ah, his history of the monastery."

That's how it started out, Alice said, but the project was evolving, becoming something more like a spiritual memoir. It chronicled Eno's early years following Master Kanzu, and the founding of Castle Rock monastery, digging deep into Eno's development as a young monk, the challenges and the rewards. It was unlike anything he'd previously written.

"He's definitely got something," she said. "He knows how to pull a reader in."

"To teach them the dharma," I suggested.

"I suppose some readers will take it that way. I'm trying to draw out his voice. If he wants to reach a larger audience, which he says he does, he's going to have to write in a more relaxed, personable way. The reader has to get to know not just Reverend Master Eno; they have to get to know Timothy Vonn."

Hearing the Master's lay name on the tongue of a guest arrested me. "And you feel you know him?"

"I'm getting to know him," she said, "on the page. Today we were working on an essay about baseball. Did you know he was recruited to Berkeley on a scholarship? He was batting .325 and getting heavily scouted when he met Kanzu."

I plunged my hands into the sleeves of my robes. "I thought he was a philosophy major."

"He was. A second baseman and a philosophy major, until he dropped out. It's pretty amazing. When people read that, they're going to relate. That's, like, all-American stuff."

Here was a side of Eno I hadn't fully seen, a more personable man, more confidential. I'd studied at his side for years. In some ways, he knew me better than anyone. And I liked to believe that I knew him. Yet, in one conversation, Alice reminded me that I knew little of his personal life. Why was he was sharing intimate details with a stranger?

This conversation haunted me. I felt twisted up and blue. I'd been supplanted by an outsider—that's how I saw things.

It seemed colossally wrong. What was Eno writing? And why was Alice Yu the first to read any of it?

As a monk, I'd been warned about the many obstacles to one's practice, greed and delusion among them. One can't erase such feelings; they arise and dissipate. The practitioner learns to note each mood as it occurs, dispassionately sitting through the storm, watching it pass. Kōshō Uchiyama calls this "opening the hand of thought."

I did not open my hand. I clenched it, tightly, banging my fist against anything in my way.

As I look back upon it now, I see it clearly. It was not clear to me then. I wanted not merely to bruise, but to be bruised, to feel the tender ache of a deep wound, to wince and cry out in pain, to pity myself for all I would not allow myself to become, and to fail on my own terms, sweet monster of my own creation.

REVEREND ENO BECAME MARKEDLY less visible around the monastery that summer. His weekly dharma talks were handed off to other senior monks. He stopped attending ceremonies. He did not eat with us in the communal dining hall. And he began to travel, leaving the monastery sometimes for weeks at a time.

Of course, the monks were curious. (Monastics are terrible gossips.) He might be away on business, they said, visiting our various priories and meditation centers sprinkled up and down the West Coast. He might be at our remote hermitage site for an extended stay to rest, to study, to contemplate. He might be called back to Wales, visiting our sibling monastery there, the seat of our order.

I let them speculate and said nothing. They thought highly of him; he was their abbot.

I knew where he was, because I had purchased his air tickets and paid for his hotel rooms. He was in New York City with Alice. They were visiting editors and literary agents, selling his book project. Two round-trip tickets (coach). Two rooms at a mid-priced hotel in Manhattan. Dinners at various (vegetarian) restaurants around the city. A visit to MoMA. Then a nonfiction literary conference in Boston, where he hobnobbed with some big names. (I looked them up.)

It was around this time that the vice abbot of the monastery, a quiet and amiable female monk, was called to Wales to assume the abbotship of our sibling monastery, nestled in the steep, wooded hills of Gwydir Forest. We were all sad to see Rev. Nanshin leave. She was among that first group of monastics who'd studied under Master Kanzu, and had served dutifully as Eno's assistant for many years. That left the immediate question of who would be appointed as her replacement.

There were a few very senior monks from that founding group, but one, my old pal Keido, was quite ill; two were running the priories in Portland and San Francisco (sizeable jobs); and the last was healthy but among the surliest of the monks. Rev. Hojun had been tenzo, or head cook, for ten years, and we all dreaded kitchen duty because it meant being snapped at constantly. It's been said that the tenzo is the single most important job in a monastery. They're not wrong. More than once, I've sat down at table with my fellow monks after a long day and found myself transported by the simple grace and elegance of the evening ritual—a room full of monks sitting in noble silence, passing dishes to one another, blessing our food, and then eating in a quiet and efficient manner. If the food is good, your day gets that much better. And if the food is great—which it often is with Rev. Hojun in charge—then your day improves tenfold. Oh, her crispy eggplant is a jewel in the crown of the Buddha! Quite possibly the closest I've ever come, gustatorily speaking, to nirvana. (That's actually a joke we used to make, a monk joke. That's a thing.)

Rev. Hojun might be some kind of magician in the kitchen, but the thought of her being in charge of the entire monastery sent shivers down everyone's spine. That left Eno with a difficult decision: either pull a monk away from one of the priories, or pick from the handful of slightly less senior monks—Ansui, Toön, or Gyoki, all of whom occupied important leadership roles in the monastery—or step out of the line of seniority to pick from among the next group of monks. There were several to choose from, but many of them had less experience with administration.

Weeks passed. Eno said nothing. Gossip swirled. Factions formed. Certain monks were not on speaking terms. I swear it felt like middle school at times. I didn't know whether to be shocked or entertained.

No one knew what Eno was thinking, but at least I knew where he was. His trips to L.A. or New York, attending writing conferences and meeting with agents and editors, continued. He did a fourteen-day residency at an artist's colony in Wyoming. These were not inexpensive ventures. And Alice was his companion for nearly all of it. They were remarkably discrete. They were almost never seen together outside of his chambers. No rumors about them circulated. I kept what I knew to myself.

What did I know? Looking back, I want to say I did know. That I was not surprised. But memory is unfixed, unstable, cloudy. Who do I want Rev. Eno to have been? Who do I need him to be now, as I write this memoir with a poison pen? For even the hints and innuendo I am layering into this narrative seem calculated and malicious.

The truth is, I loved Eno. He was much more than a teacher to me. He was a spiritual guide, a leader, an example. I suppose he was like a father to me. Certainly, he became more like a father to me than my own father ever had been, having walked out of our family when I was eight, and Dennis six. Our father was a violent, argumentative man, and his absence in our lives was an improvement. My father and I were never close, and when he died during my senior year of college, I spent more time grieving over what might have been rather than mourning the stranger who'd passed.

I suppose Eno filled that gap, to some extent. Whatever Eno was for me, I found him and for seven lovely years I had him. I treasured him and loved him and learned from him. I had him, and then I lost him. And when I lost him, I lost myself.

5

Dennis and Laurel's parcel was west of Boulder Creek, tucked under the chin of Big Basin Redwood State Park. Gorgeous land, a lightly wooded pasture, partially cleared, on a sloping hillside. Lush forest surrounded the property. A small cabin stood near the gate, overlooking the pasture. A tiny outhouse stood behind it. Inside, the cabin was snug and cozy, with a sink and a counter, a small table and chairs, and a queen-sized bed in a small bedroom. A pot-bellied stove stood in one corner, a box of firewood at the ready.

Dennis rummaged around in the cabinets, cataloging what he had. Some plates and mugs. A jar of tea, long gone stale, and a bottle of rye whiskey. He took two glasses from the cupboard and poured us each a finger. I thought I might want to rinse my glass first, but Dennis told me there was no running water, just a well and a standpipe a few yards up the hill.

He held his glass up before me and we toasted.

"What are we drinking to?" I asked.

"To Laurel, and all this beautiful land." Dennis knocked back his entire shot in one gulp, wincing.

I sipped mine judiciously, enjoying its sweet bite on my tongue. "What are you going to do with it?"

"That's the million-dollar question." He poured himself another splash of whiskey. "Actually, this land was appraised at closer to four mil."

"She made you a millionaire!" I laughed.

"On paper. Like I said, it's all tied up in the courts. Probate—it's a bitch!"

Laurel's parents were suing him for everything, Dennis explained. Rafael Jimenez said he had nothing to worry about, though it could take months or even years to settle in court. "The irony is, I'm willing to share. They can come up here, build a little cottage or something. Keep it simple. Honor Laurel's wishes. No 'development.' No condos or McMansions. And they can't pressure me to sell."

We walked around the upper portion of the property, which had been cleared. Dennis showed me where things were to go: the kiln over there, a climate-controlled building for the clay over here. They were going to put in a vegetable garden. Goats would control weeds and undergrowth.

As he spoke, I listened carefully to his cadences. Often boyish and boisterous, Dennis now sounded reverential and measured. He was in earnest. And it struck me that his love for Laurel had transformed him. It gave him a focus, a reason to be. And now she was gone.

I asked him what he planned to do with the land. He couldn't do exactly what Laurel wanted, he told me. He couldn't build the kiln and import the clay. Even if he did know what to do, which he didn't, how many people could use it as Laurel intended? Not many.

"So, I don't know. But I feel like I need to do this as a way to honor her and complete the grief cycle, or whatever." He kicked at a rock, sending it tumbling down the sloping hillside. "I need to think of something."

"Not just leave it for the pot farmers," I said, trying to lighten the mood.

"Exactly. If it's the same dude as before, not a major problem. He talks tough, but once I get the sheriff involved, he'll skedaddle."

I followed Dennis across the pasture, covered in low grass and wildflowers, a spattering of lavender and yellow. Slender seedlings, their trunks scrawny and thin, young limbs reaching out like curious fingers, punctuated the pasture. In the distance, a stately line of Douglas fir, big leaf maple, and California live oak. Dennis stopped and took a pair of binoculars from his backpack. He quietly studied his land, sweeping the glasses first this way, then that.

"Not the same dude," he said, lowering the binoculars. "Looks like a smaller grow. But he's been here a while."

I'd heard enough stories about pot farmers banging up the locals. "Maybe we should call the sheriff."

"Maybe we should," Dennis said, "but not before I get a closer look. Come on."

I held his arm. "What if they've got guns?"

Dennis smiled. "Don't worry, Clint. This is strictly recon. We're Peeping Toms. Can you do stealth?"

I shuddered at the question. It was a sensitive topic for me, but this wasn't the time to go into it. I gave a reluctant nod.

We crossed the pasture, zigzagging between trees. A chain-link fence had been erected, covered in black netting. We stood at one corner, peeking through. It was a small grow. A couple dozen mature plants stood in plastic bags of potting soil, or some in old tires. Even I could tell it was haphazard, seemingly thrown together. More like a hobby garden than a full-fledged operation. It almost didn't seem worth the effort.

We skirted the perimeter, following the fence along the south side. Farther down the hillside, in a copse of birch, I saw a blue dome tent, near which stood a folding table, a couple of camp chairs, and a propane tank. Garbage was strewn everywhere: empty tin cans, plastic water bottles, beer cans.

Dennis kept moving forward. I whispered, "That's enough," but he ignored me. Moving forward seemed reckless. We approached the campsite, which appeared empty. Bottle caps littered the ground like shell casings. Damp, half-torn boxes of mac and cheese ground into the earth. Cigarette butts. Being there seemed stupid and dangerous. My hands trembled; my shoulders twitched with anxiety. What more did Dennis need to see? I'd seen enough. There definitely was a pot farmer on his land! A feckless president has been impeached, the coronavirus threatens every inhabited continent, and here we are, trying to evict a pot farmer? It was time to call in the experts.

The zipper on the tent moved, slowly at first, then in one long, quick motion. A scraggly headed, bearded young man stuck his head out. When he saw us, his eyes widened.

"Get the fuck out of here!" he barked.

"That's my line," Dennis said.

The man sprang from the tent, a pistol in hand. "I'm giving you two seconds to turn around."

"You're on my land," Dennis said, his voice surprisingly level and firm. "Not that you know it or care, but it belonged to my wife, who's dead now. She owned this land and she wanted to make art up here. I'm going to make sure that happens. That's the most important thing in my life right now. And that means you're leaving."

The man chuckled, staring at the ground. Bare-chested and scrawny, he wore dirty blue jeans and worn hiking boots. The pistol, thank goodness, dangled at the end of a loose, limp arm. I realized then he was exhausted. Dirty. He certainly didn't look well fed. I imagined he might be high, too.

"We're all pirates up here," the man said, then bolted into the grow in long, loping strides.

Dennis lumbered after him. Overweight and out of shape, my brother had no business chasing anyone. I didn't care where the pot farmer went or what he did, but I feared for my brother, who might be stupid enough to get shot and killed. I took off after them.

Somehow they'd found each other and were rolling around on the ground, hands flying. In no time at all, the farmer had my brother pinned to the ground, a knee on his chest and the nose of the pistol stuck under his chin.

"I'm-a blow your head off, you dumb, fat fuck!"

The farmer had his back to me and couldn't see me coming. I sprang forward, lowering my head and driving straight into his ribs, knocking him off balance and into the dirt. The pistol went tumbling. I quickly got my left arm locked around his neck, slid my right leg under his left, and rolled him onto his back, one leg and arm each locked. He was pinned, down for the count—the Superstar Cradle Finish, one of my best wrestling moves.

Dennis rolled over, kicked the gun out of reach, and moments later we had the guy's wrists and ankles zip tied. Writhing on the ground, hissing and snarling, he warned us his crew would be back any minute now. Dennis handed me the pistol and went up the hill, where he could get cell service, to call 911. I sat on a plastic bucket, several yards away from the farmer, who eventually quit flipping and flopping. He lay there in the dirt, sweaty and covered in soil. It surprised me when he started weeping.

By the time the sheriff's deputy arrived, over an hour later, Tony Gomez and I had covered a lot of ground. I knew he was a community college dropout who'd been homeless for a couple of years and got into growing sort of by accident. There was no crew. He was a lone operator, and this grow was all he had. We were about to destroy it, which would leave him with exactly nothing—right where he'd been two years ago when he got into all of this.

"That's what life is like for me," Tony said. "I start a thing and then it goes to shit. I can't never seem to get nowhere. I guess I'm just a fuckup."

I told him that, in a lot of ways, I could relate. We weren't too different. I'd had a couple of careers that, for different reasons, hadn't worked out. He asked what I did and I told him: I'd just left a Buddhist monastery, where I'd been a monk for seven years.

Tony asked me why I'd left.

Without thinking too much about it, I launched into my tale. I told him about Reverend Eno and Alice Yu, about my growing unease with their relationship. And then, for the first time since it had happened, I told someone how it all ended—a story I'd hardly had the courage to articulate even for myself. But I told him, this stranger, this interloper, this suffering fool. I told him and, as I finished my tale, I felt afresh the hurt and suffering, and also shame. Shame for what I'd done, and shame that I hadn't told anyone but Tony Gomez. Shame that I hadn't told my brother, who'd already told me so much.

Gomez received this stoically. He'd seen much, much worse from his fellow humans. "So, what are you going to do now, padre?"

I told him I was waiting tables in Santa Cruz and trying to figure out the next step. I too faced a new beginning.

"But you're not going to jail."

"No, I'm not."

"Pinned to the ground by a Buddhist monk," he said, laughing. "That just about caps it."

When the sheriff arrived, I asked the deputy if I could shake Tony's hand once they cut off the zip lines. They allowed me this small grace. I thanked Tony for the conversation and wished him good luck.

"Don't worry about me," he said. "I'm going to jail for a mistake that never should have happened. But you, you got all sorts of possibilities. Don't fuck it up!"

My brother and I watched as the deputy handcuffed Tony and then ushered him into the back of the cruiser, gently guiding his head so it didn't knock it against the chassis.

"You two seemed to hit it off," Dennis said. "What in hell did you talk about?"

I watched as the cruiser rolled slowly off the property, brake lights flashing in staccato pulses. "I need to tell you something," I said, "but not today."

6

My meetings with Rev. Chuso were irregular. Mostly this was due to our work schedules. Chuso was head of Guest Services. That's a big job. The monastery holds one or two retreats a month, open to the public. For an introductory retreat, we might get two or three dozen newbies up from the Bay, who need everything from introductory meditation instruction, to spiritual counseling, to adjustments for their dietary restrictions and preferences. Chuso was drowning in the workload; like me, he needed a full-time assistant. The monastery simply didn't have the resources.

By mutual agreement, Chuso and I postponed my study sessions to the point where, I am ashamed to say it, I put the books down and waited to be told when to pick them up again. I had a hunch it wouldn't be until the vice abbot question was settled and we could all go back to some semblance of normal.

Meanwhile, Eno was hidden away in his chambers, immersed in his writing. He made no public appearances, took his meals in private, and was essentially living in isolation.

Well, not exactly in isolation.

The more I thought on this, the more agitated I became. I decided I must do something. I must insert myself into the equation in some new way.

I told myself it was about business, plain and simple. I had a sizeable stack of financial paperwork on my desk, awaiting the abbot's attention. A draft of the next fiscal year's budget had not been reviewed. We had various debts we either had to honor or write off. The San Francisco and Portland priories were both asking for budget increases and additional personnel, as their sanghas were growing. In short, decisions must be made and dollars committed. Only Eno could make these calls.

I emailed the Master, requesting he visit the bursar's office at his earliest convenience. I received a response not from Eno, but from Alice. Eno was busy and would see me as soon as his schedule allowed. She signed her email "Alice Yu, Personal Assistant to Rev. Master Eno."

It's not hard to describe how I felt when I received this email. Enraged comes to mind. Irate. Seething. I could go on.

I couldn't go on. This could not go on. It just couldn't.

I marched down the cloisters, briefcase in hand. If Eno would not come to me, I would take the paperwork to him. I chose the hour that we had customarily met to study scripture, guessing that he might keep his personal schedule regardless of whether or not he'd ignored his public schedule. I found him in his chambers, sitting before a laptop, with a neat stack of manuscript pages on his table. I begged his pardon; did he have a moment for a few urgent questions?

He cocked his head and asked if we had an appointment. We did not.

"Then I am busy."

"I'm afraid these questions cannot wait any longer."

He asked me to come back in a couple of days. He trusted me to make whatever financial decisions needed to be made. I could update him later.

"We're well past all of that," I said more urgently. "I made those decisions weeks ago. These are the things that only you, the abbot, can decide. I have several pressing documents you must sign. Here are two that are now delinquent." I thrust the papers toward him.

He closed his eyes and sat still for a moment. Then he snapped shut the lid of his laptop and invited me in. For the better part of the next hour, I had his full attention—exclusively—and managed to get him to review and sign various documents. He apologized for his tardiness. He knew he'd delayed a great many things in the last few weeks, but he had been unusually busy.

"Working on your book," I said, nodding to the manuscript.

"You wouldn't believe what this project has become, Kanshin." He'd secured a contract, he told me. He had a deadline to get the first draft to an editor in New York, a date that was rapidly approaching. He was, quite literally, doing nothing but writing.

Yes, we know, I almost snapped, but held my tongue.

I sat pondering my next question, my head aswirl, partly consumed by the remaining business questions, and partly by my great curiosity regarding the book—and his ongoing work with Alice. She too had all but vanished on the monastery grounds, rarely showing up for meals in the dining hall. Upon request, an ally in the kitchen had informed me that she often took her meals with Eno in his chambers. Rev. Chuso had assured me (again upon my inquiry) that Alice still occupied her single room in the women's quarters and was in her chambers every night by the final gong.

But it was Eno who asked the next question. "How are your studies proceeding with Rev. Chuso?"

They were not, I replied. We were too busy with work.

Eno lifted his gaze from the table, fixing those penetrating eyes on me. "At the expense of dharma study?"

"Master, I'm not sure you fully understand the situation that we junior monks find ourselves in." I hastily recounted my trials in the bursar's office. I was desperately in need of a competent assistant. (The novice monk they'd sent in place of Alice lasted only two weeks before being called off to some other office.) The same was true for Rev. Chuso, in Guest Services. Like me, he was directing his full attention to that office. The hours appointed for study and contemplation were, lamentably, spent working.

Eno interrupted me with a loud slap of the hand on the table. "Blaming workload for lack of study is not going to advance your practice!"

I held my tongue for a long moment, staring at that stack of manuscript pages, before stating, "Master, with all due respect, I think that's unfair."

"Look at yourself! You've inverted your priorities. You're a monastic, not an accountant."

"Precisely. Please remove me if I am unsatisfactory."

He waved a hand dismissively. "Who else have I got?"

"I'm not in a position to counsel you."

He slumped back in his chair. "No one is, it seems."

I folded my hands in my lap. "We need a vice abbot."

"Of course I know that!" he barked.

"Then why haven't you appointed one?"

"It's not as easy as you think," he replied. "And, like you, I have been preoccupied." He nodded to his manuscript.

"Alice is helping you edit your book."

"It's more than that, Kanshin. It's safe to say that this book would not be written at all if it weren't for Alice's input and inspiration."

An expensive-looking fountain pen lay on the desk, uncapped. Its nib was gold and silver, with elaborate decorative etching. The kind of pen one receives as a gift.

"What does she do, exactly?" I asked.

He smiled. "Editing, offering feedback and encouragement. She's quite brilliant. Gifted with words. And she knows people in the industry. She helped me land this book contract, but now I am under the weight of a deadline, and I am a slow writer."

"You spend an awful lot of time with her," I said, cautiously.

"This is a very particular circumstance."

"It seems unorthodox," I continued, "an abbot spending so many hours alone with a lay person."

"What I'm engaged in requires an enormous amount of time and singular attention."

"Then take a leave of absence," I suggested, "or at least designate a vice abbot. You've all but abdicated your position. The monastery is in disarray. And for what? A lay person and a book."

I'd crossed a line. A junior monk does not criticize a senior monk, unless invited.

Eno poured himself a mug of tea from the squat, white pot. "You know what your problem is, Kanshin?"

I knew what came next. This was an old dance between us, a set of choreographed questions and answers, the pupil and his master. And if I wasn't exactly sure what he'd say, I knew at least this much: I had to ask for it.

"Master, how have I failed?"

"You never see the object before you with the necessary clarity." Eno lifted his teacup to his lips and took a sip. "You're a mediocre accountant. I trusted you to clean up the books without making too much fuss. I trusted you to be self-motivated enough to continue your studies without my constant oversight. You're entering your eighth year in those robes, yet you continually struggle to master the simplest aspects of monastic life. You're lazy and under-committed, and now, it would seem, you've let jealousy and envy cloud your vision."

He set the teacup on the table, pushing it away. "You've become a great disappointment." Then he stood and walked into the back room of his chambers, closing the door.

I pushed my papers into my briefcase, tears welling in my eyes. I hurried along the cloisters, chin lowered. It was late autumn and a chill hung in the air; the skies were dark with clouds promising rain. I sat for several minutes alone in the bursar's office, staring at the wall, my heart blasted and empty. I knew only to wait for the next ring of the bell, for then I would know what to do.

I SPENT THE NEXT FEW DAYS IN A FUNK. I was quite sure Eno was correct: I'd failed as a monk in every important way. That was the first time I contemplated leaving the order—a serious decision, as monks customarily take the vows as a life-long commitment, although there had been monks over the years who disrobed. Quite a few, actually. It was far from unheard of. But I could not, at that time, conceive of leaving Castle Rock.

A few days later, I found a handwritten note in my mailbox. I recognized the script instantly: Eno. *Ordinary people and sages dwell together; dragons and snakes intermingle.* This puzzled me. It was a quote from something, some text Eno and I had studied, though I couldn't place it. More to the point, what was he trying to tell me?

I tucked the note in the sleeve of my robe and carried it around with me for the next few days. It took me a while, a nice little bit of digging, but eventually I found it. The Thirty-Fifth Case of *The Blue Cliff Record,* a revered collection of koans. In it, a monk named Wu Cho encounters Manjusri, the bodhisattva of wisdom, who asks Wu Cho about the state of Buddhism in his region. Wu Cho's response is discouraging: "Monks of the Last Age have little regard for the rules of discipline." Wu Cho, who appears not to recognize Manjusri, then asks about the state of Buddhism in Manjusri's region, and the reply is what Eno scribbled on the note. It is cryptic and elusive, like a good Zen koan should be. A koan doesn't point the way directly, but works subtly via innuendo, suggestion, and ambiguity.

I puzzled anew over whatever message this note conveyed, presumably in light of our recent conversation. Eno wanted to be oblique and indirect; I resolved to let him be so. I thought then I could accept it.

7

Two men living in a cramped trailer was never going to work, especially when one of them craved peace and quiet, a clean bathroom, and a kitchen sink that was for something other than stacking dirty dishes dating somewhere into the prior month. The piles of pizza boxes, the empty beer cans, and the mountains of dirty laundry didn't bother Dennis. That was Dennis.

I should have kept my mouth shut and simply been grateful. I don't know if it was the stress of being pretty much flat broke with no real prospects, or feeling depressed, or even if it was just my little brother and I was still his big brother, but I couldn't keep my damn mouth shut. After getting woken up one too many times at two in the morning when he was hooting at the television, or opening the trailer door and breathing in the rank stench, or simply fearing sitting on the toilet seat, I unloaded on Dennis, shouting that he was a damn slob and he needed to get his act together.

"You know," he said, calmly, "I think I'm giving you a break here. As I recall, you asked to move in. You're welcome to stay until you're ready to leave, but you've got to quit hassling me, man. I'm not your college roommate."

"But it's simple human cleanliness." I pointed to the kitchen garbage, literally overflowing with dirty paper plates, burger wrappers, and god knows what else. "Take the fucking garbage out!"

"You take it out."

"I took it out last time, and the time before that. I'm the only one that ever takes it out."

"Chill. I'll get to it."

"You'll get to it? When will you get to it? When do you ever get to anything?"

Shaking his head, he said, "Who pissed in your Cheerios?"

"It just blows me away, how you can postpone your life like this. Push everything off to tomorrow."

He threw the TV remote onto the dirty coffee table and stood from his chair. "I'm not postponing my life. I'm living my life. And it's none of your fucking business how I do it!"

"So, you're happy living like this? Like a pig? Did Laurel like it, too?"

He cocked his head and gave me the cut-eye. "What do you have to bring her into it for? You never even met her, bro. Keep her name out of your slanderous mouth." He stormed over to the garbage can, bent down, and picked it up. Pizza boxes and burger wrappers fell to the floor at his feet. "You want to take out the garbage? Here it is. Come and get it." And he tossed the bucket at me, garbage flying out. I side-stepped it, watching it fall and vomit its contents onto the tile floor.

"You want clean counters?" With a swipe of the arm, empty margarita mix bottles, beer cans, and soda cups clattered to the floor. "There you go! You want clean dishes?" He grabbed a dirty plastic bowl out of the sink and threw it against the wall. It fell to the floor, spinning and tumbling askew.

"You think I live like a pig? Fuck you! I live how I like. You have no idea the hell I've been through in the last year, losing Laurel and going through all of that, then having her parents biting my ass, trying to take away everything she gave me. I hardly have anything, and she gave me everything she could. She loved me! She loved me!"

He bent his head down, as if studying the floor. He brought a hand to his forehead, obscuring his face. He stood, frozen, for a long moment. Then a great, heaving sob wracked his body, followed by a wet gasp of air.

It startled and surprised me. Immediately, I felt like a cur. "Dennis, I'm sorry."

"The only damn person in this world who actually loved me! The only one!"

"I love you."

"You're just a nagging motherfucker with a chip on his shoulder about some shit I don't have anything to do with." He barged past me, ran into his bedroom, and slammed the door. I heard the mattress springs squeak as he threw himself onto his bed, shouting expletives at the walls, or more likely at me.

I stood in the kitchen, the smell of spilt spaghetti sauce and greasy burger wrappers wafting up, a swirling aroma of filth. I felt terrible. I didn't want to upset my brother that way. I meant to inspire some kind of reaction, I suppose, but he was right. Who was I to barge into his home and start ordering him how to live in it?

I knelt and began collecting the stray bits of garbage. When the bin was full, I took it out to the dumpster and emptied it. Then I came back into the trailer and began collecting every stray bit of trash I could find. Junk mail tucked in behind empty beer bottles. Soda cans left half-empty on the coffee table. Empty mac and cheese boxes left piled up by the stove. I threw it all in the bin, filling and emptying it several times. I washed the dishes and wiped down the counters. I gave the stovetop a once-over. I found the bucket and the mop, and a bottle of Pine-sol, and I swabbed the kitchen floor. By the time I was done, the living room and kitchen weren't looking half-bad.

Dennis still hadn't come out. I wasn't sure what I would say if he did.

I washed up and grabbed my coat. It was ten o'clock, usually my bedtime, but I felt uneasy. I decided to go out for a walk.

It was a cool, quiet evening. The air smelled mildly sour; the farmers must have been fertilizing their fields, perfuming the air with eau de pig shit. Outside the trailer park, a few blocks south on the boulevard, was Eduardo's, a sit-down Mexican joint. I sat at the bar, ordered a tall beer and a plate of nachos, and got to thinking.

I had to move out. But the last time I ran the numbers, I was still months away from having the money for a deposit on a single apartment. And I was quite sure I wanted a single apartment. I also needed a car. And health insurance.

The morning newspaper lay folded on the counter, smudged with taco sauce. The headline read "Victims of the Downturn." Oh crap, this country is so screwed up! A poor person is made to feel ashamed and stupid and hopeless, as if there's nothing to be done. This, the wreckage of our empire.

I thought of the mornings I awoke at Castle Rock to find a brilliant white blanket of snow covering everything. It always made me feel optimistic, like the world was full of limitless possibility. Where, where could I find that again?

Watsonville, Watsonville, where is thy song?

It seemed like I only knew one way to get back into the game, and that was by returning to social work. Even if I wanted to do it, I needed to get recertified, which meant taking classes and filling out paperwork and paying the fees. It was the only thing I knew how to do, professionally, but I also knew, in my heart, it wasn't what I wanted. And that was the bigger problem: I didn't know what to do. The only thing I had going was a jar full of cash tips that was slowly but steadily amounting to something. It was hard, in my head, not to see all of this as aimless drifting. I may have had my reasons for leaving the monastery and re-entering lay life, but it wasn't for this.

DUE TO MY SPLIT SHIFT AT THE CAFÉ, I had three hours off in the middle of the day. I typically spent this time at the public library, or at the Santa Cruz Bookshop, or simply strolling around town. I was beginning to recognize some of the staff at the coffee shops I frequented, as well as some of the drifters and street people. I gave directions and recommendations to tourists. (I always sent them to my café; when they showed, they tipped generously.) It made me feel like I was becoming a local.

I told this to a fellow waiter who laughed and told me I wasn't a local until I'd ordered the Ortega burger at Caspar's, a local dive bar. There was no Ortega burger on the menu at Caspar's, he told me. You had to ask. The chilis are grown by the owner's abuela, sun ripened and harvested by hand, the old way. Then fire-roasted just before they lay it on your burger. Out of this world, he assured me, and only available by request. A local legend.

Burgers weren't usually high on my list, but I was intrigued enough to hop on my Honda motorbike and roll over there. From the outside, it looked like a nondescript white box with a green awning and the name CASPAR'S BAR spelled out in crude block letters. A group of twenty-somethings hovered around the door, smoking cigarettes and checking out each other's new tattoos. Inside, it was dim and cramped, with a few cocktail tables and some battered chairs, and a flat screen TV in the corner flashing sports highlights. And there at the bar, nursing a Bloody Mary, was my brother.

I sat down on the stool next to him. "I'm sorry about last night."

"Hey, turns out you're right," he said. "It looks a lot better clean. I'll do the bathroom tomorrow."

The bartender asked me what I wanted. I ordered the Ortega burger with fries, and an iced tea. He smiled and shouted the order into the back.

"Damn, look at you," Dennis said, smiling. "Now you're a local."

I asked what he was doing drinking in the middle of the workday. He gave me a look like I'd just asked him to explain quantum mechanics.

"I'm taking a temporary break from where I know I belong. The real question is why you're here. Why is a former Buddhist monk waiting tables on a split shift and getting lunch at a dump like Caspar's?"

"Hey," the bartender growled.

"No offense, Armando." Dennis pushed his drink glass forward on the bar. "Hit me with another."

Then he turned to me. "Where do you belong, Clint?"

It was precisely the question I'd been wrestling with since leaving the monastery, and in the hours since Dennis and I had argued, it felt even more urgent. I'd worn out my welcome in Watsonville. I was the gear with no cog, idle for far too long.

I feared I'd made a great mistake. Not in leaving the monastery—I had no doubts that leaving Castle Rock was necessary—but in not having a clear next step. At the monastery, I'd had a role, a focus, a purpose, and a job. I knew what I was doing 24/7, even if it ultimately didn't seem like the right fit. Stepping away hadn't exactly brought peace or a new sense of purpose.

Who was I? I was a man sitting next to his brother at a bar. We'd had a fight about garbage—only it wasn't really about the garbage. I knew part of what it was about for Dennis. But he knew nothing of my side of it, because I hadn't shared that with him. It was time to fix that.

I turned to Dennis. "I haven't told you why I came here."

"To get an Ortega burger. They're pretty damn good, you'll see."

"I mean why I left the monastery."

"It wasn't a girl, you already told me that."

"There was a woman involved," I said, turning my tea around in my hand, "but not with me. Not that way."

"Now I'm intrigued. Do tell."

And that is when I told my brother why I left Castle Rock. I was glad I'd told the story first to Tony Gomez, because in retelling it I could correct certain errors or over-simplifications. But Tony Gomez didn't know me. He didn't really care what I did. Dennis knew me and cared. Telling him meant something. It brought us closer. And it freed me, in a way. I'd kept this terrible, twisted thing inside me, trying to bury it, when really all I needed to do was let it out into the open, to let it go.

After I finished my tale, we sat quietly. The burger had come and gone (it was indeed excellent). My empty iced tea stood before me on the bar. I think Dennis was on his third Bloody Mary.

"That's a hard road, my brother," he said. "Some seriously fucked up shit."

"You think I'm a creep."

"No," he said, quickly. "I'm not sure what I think just yet, but I don't think that."

"Thank you."

He plucked an asparagus spear from of his drink glass and nibbled at its tip. "Listen. Regardless of what went down, only one thing matters now. That monastery game is over. It's all behind you, for better or for worse."

"Lately it seems for worse," I muttered.

"Don't look at it that way." He picked up his drink, draining the last, long sip with a noisy slurp. Then he wiped a bar napkin across his mouth. "When Laurel was dying, well, you can imagine. I had a hard time accepting it. The suddenness of it. The inescapability of it. The unfairness of it. A whole list of things. At one point, I was ranting in her hospital room, and she just cut me off. Literally told me to stop talking. She didn't want to hear the negativity. We couldn't change the fact of her death, she said, but we could change how we approached it.

"So I asked her, 'How am I supposed to feel about my wife dying?' And Clint? I wish you could have seen her face. She gave this sweet, ever-loving smile, and she said, 'Let's make it a thing of beauty.'"

I wished then, more than ever, that I'd met Laurel, so I could better share this part of my brother's life. "And was it like that?" I asked. "Did it become a thing of beauty?"

"It truly did. It's hard to describe. Someday maybe I'll tell you what that last month together was like. Every day was a gift, man, a blessed thing."

"That's amazing."

"She was amazing," he said, wiping an eye. "So, I learned something from her that day. Beauty doesn't just pop up. It's something you make out of all the shit life tosses at you."

"That's why you want to make that property into something," I said, "not let it go to waste."

He nodded. "I want to make it a thing of beauty, for Laurel, if I can just figure out how."

"Maybe I can help you with that," I said. "In the meantime, I won't hassle you again about the trailer. I'll be moving out by the end of the month."

"Where to?"

"I'll figure something out," I said.

It was time for me to get back to work. I paid for my lunch and my brother's bar tab, a small way of thanking him for listening to my story, and for sharing another part of his.

In the days that followed, I thought a lot about what Dennis told me, about making good out of the bad. I knew he was right. The question was where to start. I had to look for new angles, and be open to possibilities. The old leap of faith. I'd done it before.

I recall one afternoon at Castle Rock during an intensive retreat. For ten days, we sat in meditation from five in the morning until nine at night. There were breaks for meals and a long working meditation in the afternoon, but the rest of the day was spent sitting on the cushion. It was grueling, both physically and mentally challenging. I hadn't yet decided to become a monastic. I was still a lay person, though the thought of shaving my head and donning the robes had become a steady refrain. I went into this retreat thinking I would settle my mind on this point. I would know, by the end of those ten days, which direction to head.

Three days in, I was ready to call it quits. My knees and back screamed in agony. I spent several meditation sessions simply counting my breath, waiting for the bells to ring so I could stand and walk. (Walking meditation, which filled many of the periods between sitting meditation, is incredibly slow, but at least you're up and moving, if only a little.) Sitting down for each new meditation session seemed like its own special challenge, yet I kept sitting down. This, despite knowing I could, at any moment, simply get up and walk away. My car sat in the visitor's parking lot, at the ready. No one would stop me.

Nevertheless, I remained, resolute on enduring. I think I was searching for that line, the spot that would either be my breaking point or my salvation. I no longer knew which one I wanted.

Somewhere in the middle of a long afternoon sitting, five days into the retreat, I heard thunder. It sounded far away, a gentle rumbling like timpani. Gradually, the storm moved closer. The natural light in the meditation hall dimmed. The thunder grew louder as the storm approached. And then it started to shower: gradually at first, then escalating to a full-fledged downpour, a great wash of rain and booming thunder that lasted for a good twenty minutes. The sound encompassed me, wrapping around me like a blanket. I listened intently to everything: the water overflowing the gutters, cascading onto concrete; sheets of rain lashing at the sides of the meditation hall; great cracking peals of thunder that shook the walls.

Gradually, the storm weakened in intensity. The rain slowed to a drizzle, then stopped. The light began to rise. By the time the bells were rung, signaling the end of the meditation period, the sun was shining. I stepped outside during the break, nursing my aching knees, to find the court-yard bedazzled with crystal raindrops, sparkling beautifully, a world washed and renewed, all things singing out in replen-ishment and wonder. I felt an intense awareness of everything around me, an intimate connection to all things. For the rest of that day—for the rest of the meditation retreat—I felt ensconced in joy, an acceptance of my true circumstance.

I'm not saying any of this right. There aren't words, exactly, for what I'm talking about.

There was no trick, no magic secret. I wasn't blissed out or high. I understood that my body still ached and pained me. It just didn't bother me anymore. All my concerns and complaints fell away, peeling off me like so much dead skin. I'd simply done what the teachers had repeated a thousand times: be wholly present, in the moment, acutely aware of your actual circumstance. Let go of all the rest.

Later, when I described this to Rev. Eno, he told me I'd experienced kensho, a moment of enlightenment. When I expressed doubt that that is what had happened, he smiled. "Do not expect that you will be aware of your own enlightenment."

Those words stuck with me; I have never forgotten them.

8

Eno had made no move toward filling the vice abbot role. It had become clear that no big changes were imminent, and so the gossip and rumors quieted. For my fellow monks, this sufficed. But for me it was another matter. I quietly fretted over what I saw as my Master's inaction, which seemed to me an abnegation of responsibility. But I'm not being completely honest. What really bothered me was what, or who, was distracting him.

One moment lingers in memory. On a Sunday in late autumn, after Rev. Eno had delivered the dharma talk—his first in several weeks—the sangha gathered outside in the picnic area, enjoying a brilliant, mild morning. This tea is but an hour, which Eno usually spends drifting from party to party, being sure to greet as many people as possible. That is appropriate for the abbot on such an occasion. On this day, however, Eno almost immediately nestled into a sunny corner of the yard with Alice, and there they sat for the entire hour, in matching Adirondack chairs, sipping tea and chatting. Whatever they were talking about, it engaged them wholeheartedly. They smiled and laughed, a world unto themselves.

There were other members of the sangha milling about, waiting politely for a chance to step in and speak with Rev. Eno, but he gave no indication that he noticed them. Wholly focused on Alice, he ignored everyone else.

It seemed outrageous, given that they spent so many hours together during the regular week. What more could they possibly have to discuss?

Yet there they sat, even as sangha members dispersed, even as we began to put away the chairs, even as the kitchen crew collected the dirty teacups and empty cookie trays. They lingered, the two of them, absorbed in one another, talking as fervently as they had for the entire hour, until they finally stood and, after Alice made her formal bow to the Master, Eno took her hand.

He took her hand!

He took her hand, clasping it between his two palms, and bowed to her. I distinctly heard him thank her. The smile on her face was radiant. And, as she pulled her hand from his, I swear she gave his hand a knowing little squeeze.

I had rarely seen Eno clasp anyone's hand. He almost always bowed to everyone, usually with his hands tucked away in the sleeves of his robes, or more formally in gassho, with his palms pressed together. It seemed to be part of his power, to be just that little bit removed and formal, a little icy, perhaps.

I could not wipe this image from my mind: her slender hand, sandwiched between his two palms, the beatific smile on her face, and the master bowing before her, thanking her. And that little squeeze: Alice giving Eno that extra bit of acknowledgment, encouragement, and affection.

It was nothing; it was everything. In my tangled mind, I couldn't tell the difference. That doesn't excuse what I did next, but it might explain why I couldn't stop myself from doing it.

IN THE FIRST PHASE OF THE THING, I simply made it my business to know where Alice and Rev. Eno were at any given time. It wasn't hard. A monastery is, after all, a closed environment, and the patterns of its residents are regulated by a common schedule of work periods, meal times, meditation sessions, and so on. Eno and Alice were a bit removed from all of that, but in so doing were even more predictable: squirreled away in Eno's chambers, presumably working on his manuscript. I made it my business to know when meal trays were delivered to his chambers, and how many. I made it my business to know when Alice left or returned to the lay residence hall. I collected this information from a few key sources, but much of it I gathered on my own. Being bursar naturally meant I had business with nearly every office, from the kitchen to the physical plant and the guest services. I made my way across the grounds, crisscrossing as I collected my information under the guise of business. I was sly, yes. But as I say, there really wasn't much to report. Only hunches to confirm.

Autumn unfolded in this way, like a stream following its urgings, and I its dutiful cartographer.

THEN, ONE MORNING IN EARLY December, Eno startled me, appearing in the bursar's office clutching an invoice. I received it. It was for a fully furnished guest cottage in Mendocino. Ordinarily it rented for several hundred dollars a day, but a lay member of the sangha had offered it to Eno at a deep discount.

It must be paid immediately, he said, to secure the reservation.

"I'll put it in the queue," I said, tucking it into my stack of bills.

"If we don't pay it within twenty-four hours, I lose the spot."

"We have any number of bills that need to be paid immediately, many of them requiring your signature." I pulled a file folder from my desk rack and dropped it on the desk. "Would you like to review them?"

He did. He spent the next twenty minutes signing paperwork. He signed indiscriminately, wherever I told him to. I confess I enjoyed having him there, subject to my commands. When he'd finished, I told him I'd send the down payment for the cottage that afternoon.

"Mendocino is a lovely town," I said.

"I suppose," Eno replied, with a shrug. "I need three weeks of absolute isolation and focus to complete my book project. It's very close, and my deadline looms."

"You must be excited."

He rubbed a hand across his brow. "I'm in agony. I've never done anything like this. I had no idea writing could be so torturous."

"But you have Alice to help you."

He stared at me dead on, icily. "She's a wonder, Kanshin. A gem. You have no idea."

Oh, but I did.

IN THE WEEKS LEADING UP TO Eno's planned December retreat, he once again withdrew from public ceremonies and daily rituals. He handed his Sunday dharma talks off to other speakers. He was rarely seen at our Sunday social teas. Rumor had it he'd cut back on his time counseling the senior monks. He'd long ago ceased private instruction with me, of course. I hadn't forgotten that.

It was now generally known that Eno was writing a book, and that he was devoting nearly all his time to it. This wasn't necessarily out of the ordinary. Other monks had written books. Master Kanzu, before passing, had published several books of spiritual essays and an autobiography. We had another monk, formerly a professor of Asian languages, who'd undertaken a translation of Dōgen's *Shōbōgenzō*, a monumental project that took twelve years to complete. That Eno, as abbot, might want to collect his teachings did not strike anyone as odd or unprecedented.

What did strike us as unexpected was the sudden appointment of Rev. Ansui as vice abbot. No one saw this coming, least of all Ansui. She'd served as prior of our Portland sangha for over ten years, building it into a robust, thriving community. She hardly had any time to plan for the transition; Eno demanded she drop her duties in Portland immediately and return to Castle Rock. He would appoint a prior for Portland in due course. We all knew what that meant.

With a forced urgency that could only seem awkward, Rev. Ansui was made acquainted with all aspects of running the monastery. Of course, having led a priory, she was not unfamiliar with the administrative side of things. She made it a quick tour, visiting each office for a day or two, getting a sense for how things worked at Castle Rock. A spell with Guest Services was followed by a visit to the kitchen; a tour of the sacristy preceded her visit to me in the bursar's office. (She asked innumerable questions and thoroughly reviewed our ledgers.) Finally, she spent time with Rev. Danzu in the physical plant (formally known as the external sacristy), following him and his crew as they de-iced walkways and driveways, repaired a frozen pipe, and shoveled snow. Ansui was in her sixties and not particularly suited to physical labor, yet she dutifully gave it a go.

Rev. Ansui was well-liked by her fellow monks, and she apologized repeatedly for the awkward intrusions, endearing herself to us.

Looking back, I think I understand: Eno was planning his next move. He wanted to finish his book and sell it to a publisher, hoping it would make a splash. He would remain abbot of Castle Rock, but his demands at spiritual retreats, book fairs, and conferences would increasingly pull him away. He wanted to become a spiritual celebrity, the next Pema Chödrön.

I might be wrong about that. I might be unfair and biased. I never got to read his book. No one did. To my knowledge, it has never been published. I'm not sure he finished it. That's because nothing worked out the way he wanted. What happened instead surprised all of us.

9

I typically spent my leave time visiting friends, or my cousin in Southern California. For a change, I decided to take a week in December and head for the coast. I told myself it was a scenic drive. Tourism. I told myself I hadn't been to Fort Bragg in ages. I strolled through Noyo Harbor, watching the busy fishing boats as they offloaded for the day. I sauntered around downtown, poking into shops. I took a long walk out at Point Cabrillo, savoring the sweeping view of the coast. I visited the old plug of a lighthouse, sturdy and stout. I sat on a picnic bench watching humpback whales breeching a half-mile offshore. And then, why, yes, when you're in the area you would naturally drive a little further south on Route 1 to the village of Mendocino, a charming, artsy enclave, with cafés and galleries and a wonderful bookshop overlooking a picturesque headland.

All that while, I had a certain address in mind, a cottage just a few blocks away, perched on a knoll overlooking the Pacific Ocean. Inside of which, at that very moment, my master was no doubt hard at work, composing his book.

I didn't know what I wanted to do with that information. I didn't know—or I could not admit to myself—why I was there.

In a backstreet café, I lingered over a latte and a left-behind copy of that day's *San Francisco Chronicle*. I strolled the long sidewalk along Main Street, facing the bay, thinking about driving back to Fort Bragg for an early dinner. I told myself it was time to let go of whatever I was clinging to, whatever had brought me to that town. Along the horizon, the first pink brushstrokes of sunset hovered in the late afternoon sky, so appealing. I thought I might walk out to the tip of the point to watch the sunset and—

A few yards ahead of me, a couple spilled out of a café, its golden lights aglow. She wore a long, white down jacket. He was bald and wore a navy peacoat. Laughing, they pulled each other close.

The door of the café flew open and a waiter stepped out onto the porch, waving something. "Tim! Your hat!" Tim turned to meet the waiter, who jogged down the sidewalk with the hat. Tim thanked him. With a graceful swoop of his arm, he placed the hat upon his head, a brown felt fedora. The hat of a gentleman.

Then he turned and rejoined the woman at his side. They walked down the sidewalk, arm in arm, perfectly alone with each other.

Not alone. We are never as alone as we think we are. We are never alone enough.

Stepping into the shadows between two buildings, I crouched behind a hedge, spying the couple as they strolled down Main Street, heading toward their rented cottage. They had no idea there was a witness to their outing. They could not feel my gaze, how it lingered, how it burned. At the corner of Main and Heeser they turned a corner and disappeared into the dusk.

I turned the other direction, hiking out past Portuguese Beach to the tip of the headlands. I stood in the stiff onshore breeze, reveling in the waves crashing against the shoreline. The spray exploded in a magnificent cascade, one massive swell after another. A blue-green breaker lifted up, like a giant from its knees, lurching toward the rocks, colliding in a crescendo, expending every ounce of energy in a magnificent explosion, the spray like an unfolded palm, fingers desperately grasping for purchase, and then collapsing, the remnants of this cacophony falling down, down, back into the ocean, returning to the churning cream bubble fizz of spume, a sloshing turbulent cauldron awaiting the next unstoppable swell.

Yes, I thought, yes!

I marched off the headlands, heading back into the village with a ferocious determination. It would start with a confrontation, a kind of unveiling. It was not hard to find them. I'd memorized the address, having looked it up multiple times on Google Maps. I strode resolutely down one lane and then another. In the dim, hazy glow of a winter dusk I found the cottage, blue and white, nestled amongst others, peppering a knoll with a fine sea view. The horizon was pink with the glow of a setting sun.

I marched up to the front door and pounded furiously, shouting Eno's name. A neighbor's dog barked, sharp and fierce.

A light flicked on inside the cottage. Then the porch light flared. The door opened. There stood not Eno, but Alice, wearing a black turtleneck sweater and white pants, looking very stylish.

A look of horror twisted across her face. "Kanshin!"

Out of the dark, behind her, emerged my master, wearing blue jeans and a heavy rag wool sweater. He gently moved Alice aside and stepped forward, filling the doorway. He fixed that penetrating gaze on me. For one excruciating moment, we stood exposed to each other.

"What are you doing here?" Eno asked.

"I came to see you."

"About what? Is everything all right at the monastery? You could have called."

"Not about that," I said. "May I come in?"

He turned to look behind him, briefly. "No, I don't think so. I'm not prepared for guests."

"The cottage is smaller than I expected."

Eno lifted his chin, a look I knew only too well. "I'm surprised by you, Kanshin."

I smiled. "Just one bed?"

"Don't talk to me like that. I'm still your master, and you're my disciple."

The words inflamed me. In a flash I raised my hand and slapped him across the jaw.

His chin trembled. He blinked rapidly, eyes brimming with tears.

"Thank you," he said.

Startled by my own boldness, in awe of this thing I'd just done, I was not prepared for that response. But I was not about to relent.

"You should know that I—"

He shut the door and retreated into the darkness of the cottage. In the divided glass window panes I saw my reflected face, fragmented and sectioned like puzzle pieces.

"Eno!"

I pulverized the door. The neighbor's dog resumed its insistent barking, sharp and fierce.

I stood on that porch long enough to feel my heart rate slow. When I stepped away, my mind was in a tangle. A chilly winter breeze swept in off the ocean, damp and sharp. I bundled my winter coat tightly against my robes as I walked down the lane, back into the heart of the village. My robes! My robes! These scraps of cloth designed to wrap me in the fields of the Buddha's teachings, limitless and everlasting. What had I become?

10

I returned to Castle Rock in a turbulent state. Eno had not arrived. He did not call or email. He'd left on a three-week writing trip, and he stayed away for the duration of that time. I had nothing to do but wait.

My days were steeped in misery. Of course, I'd witnessed something damning and outrageous. But what was there to do about it? One part of me thought I should confide in our vice abbot, Rev. Ansui. But that would mean owning up to my own misdeeds, and I wasn't prepared for that reckoning.

I thought I might wait for Eno's return and then speak privately with him. What we'd say to each other, I couldn't guess. After what I'd done in Mendocino, I wasn't even sure I had the courage to present myself to him.

During one of our first spiritual counseling sessions, Rev. Eno asked me what I wanted in becoming a monk. I didn't have a prepared answer to that question. I said the first thing that popped into my mind. I told him I wanted to bring meditation into everything I do.

He nodded and smiled. I knew then I'd said the right thing without over-thinking it, the perfect monastic gesture. Eno's confirmation set me glowing.

That seemed like a different world now. The world I lived in was not the world I had wanted to live in. That world was lost.

I was wrong. It was the same world.

A SIERRA NEVADA WINDSTORM CAN be an unnerving experience. The tallest Doug firs sway like drunken choirboys. The wind blows through their branches, swelling from a sigh to a roar and back again. Leaves and pine needles fly through the air, peppering windows and doorways. Shorn limbs tumble onto roofs or car trunks with a startling thwack. The wind gusts can snap a full-grown tree in half.

I have difficulty sleeping through these storms, troubled by the disquieting restlessness of the world around me. I might read or meditate. I might lay in bed, staring into the darkness, praying that a tree trunk doesn't crash through my bedroom (it happens). It's one thing I don't miss about living in the mountains.

A heavy windstorm blew through in January, in advance of a blizzard that would eventually dump a foot of snow on the region. We spent a long afternoon getting the shovels and salt crystals ready, and gassing up the blowers. The snow started at around three in the morning. (Unable to sleep, I kept checking.)

I rose at five with the bells and made my way, groggily, towards the mediation hall. The winds had started to die down, and snow had started to accumulate. The first round of shoveling would come during the morning work period. As one of the younger, able-bodied monks, I was always expected to pitch in. I didn't mind. Shoveling snow is a good workout, clearing the mind as well as the walkways.

Later that morning, after our meal, I grabbed a shovel from the work shed and made my way across the grounds to the Guest Hall. There on the front porch stood Alice, wearing her white down coat, with a fluffy black scarf coiled around her throat. A duffle bag sat at her feet. We were both surprised to see each other.

I slowly climbed the stairs to stand beside her. "You're back," I said.

She trained her fiery gaze on me, the unmistakable glare of contempt. "You've completely destroyed him."

I uttered a sharp laugh. "I destroyed him?"

Rev. Ando, one of our novice monks, stepped out of the door wearing a winter coat, a fob of keys in her hand. "Rev. Kanshin! I'm driving Alice to the bus station."

"If we could have a moment," I said.

Ando lowered her gaze. "Of course. I'll go start the engine. The car will be very cold." She trudged through the snow, leaving a trail of footprints I would soon erase.

"He can't write," Alice said. "He can hardly speak. He's having a spiritual meltdown."

"Don't blame me. The two of you made a choice."

"You're a snoop. A dirty spy."

I straightened my spine. "But that's not the real issue, is it? It doesn't matter if there was a witness or not."

"You have no right to judge him. Where is your compassion?"

"It's so easy for you. You get to walk away." I leaned in, closer. "What are you waiting for?"

Her eyes flared. "You're not a monk," she said, reaching for her bag. "You're a monster!"

She charged past me, crossing the yard and heading for the waiting car, exhaust hovering in the cold air. The brake lights flashed, the car rolled slowly out of the lot, and she was gone. I knew I'd never see her again.

I began shoveling the sidewalk, removing one scoop of snow at a time, clearing a path for others. Ironic, as I myself felt lost.

The front walk finished, I made my way around the corner, towards the back entrance. In one corner of the yard of the Guest House stood a small shrine. There sat the Buddha, cross-legged, hands in a mudra, eyes lowered, his head and shoulders covered in a light dusting of new snow. He sat in a stillness so graceful, so composed, so elegant. This amidst a world of endless suffering, a swirling cacophony of anger and shame and regret. He offers everyone this path, and the promise of the cessation of suffering if we can only follow him. Somehow, though it stood before me with open arms, I'd missed it. I miss it even now.

11

Ahab, in the early chapters of Melville's opus, remains hidden in the captain's quarters. Yet the crew feels the dread weight of his aura; his very silence and invisibility casts a spell over the entire ship. His absence becomes a powerful kind of presence. All the crew can do is carry on with their business, wondering when or if their leader will make an appearance.

It was like that.

All the monks were speculating. He'd taken ill. He'd experienced satori. His book had been completed. His book had fallen apart. He was a night owl, toiling away in the wee hours and sleeping during the day.

I said nothing, silently bearing the weight of what I knew, wearing it like a hair shirt. All my doubts and grievances, all my regrets and complaints, every stray thought and memory tumbled around in my head like pebbles in a tin can, with about as much import.

It went on like this for several days, maybe a week. One bleary day bled into the next. I only recall I was in agony, felt suspended in limbo, awaiting judgment—his or mine, I couldn't tell the difference.

In an effort to regain some sense of direction, I returned to my studies. I read a lengthy commentary on the Heart Sutra. I listened to old dharma talks. I read the poetry of Ikkyu and Ryōkan. And, perhaps inevitably, I reached for *The Blue Cliff Record*, the treasured collection of Zen koans that Eno and I had spent so many hours poring over. In the Eighth Case, the monk Ts'ui Yen concludes a meditation retreat by telling his fellow monks, "All summer long I've been talking to you, brothers; look and see if my eyebrows are still there." (By this he means to acknowledge the impossibility of describing the transcendent in mere words; in Ch'an Buddhism, there is a saying: if one speaks too much, one's eyebrows might fall out.)

Ts'ui Yen is answered in turn by three monks, who variously reply:

"The thief's heart is cowardly."

"Grown."

"A barrier."

That final line haunted me. I kept turning it over in my mind, thinking about all the different barriers we erect (or accept) in our lives, what they're for, and whether, finally, there's anything we can do to surmount them.

I moved to my cushion, where I meditated. When I stood up thirty minutes later, I re-read the Case in its entirety.

Then I went to my computer and fired off an email to Eno containing a line from the pointer section of the Case, a kind of preface to the koan: *When the great function appears, it does not keep to any fixed standards.*

That's all I wrote. I didn't even include a subject line.

Sometime later, Eno replied, asking me to meet him at the stupa at noon.

THE STUPA HONORING MASTER KANZU, the founder of our order, is a large, stout, stone pillar, inside of which the master's ashes rest. It's a quiet spot at one end of the public area of the monastery, around the corner from the Buddha hall, rather private and secluded. The afternoon was bright and still. A light snow had fallen overnight, blanketing everything in a pristine veil of crisp, white snow.

Eno sat on a bench, wearing a bulky brown winter great coat, in an open patch of sunlight. Though there was room on the bench beside him, I sat on a different bench, several feet away, in the shadow of the stupa. I did not look to him or meet his gaze. We did not greet one another. We sat silently, each in the presence of his master.

"Have I ever told you how Kanzu and I found this spot?" Eno finally began. "We'd looked all over. The redwoods on the coast. A farm in Sonoma County. Some urban sites in San Francisco and Oakland. Nothing seemed right. Kanzu wasn't sure, in advance, what he wanted. He kept saying he'd know it when he saw it."

Eno rubbed his hands across his lap, a warm smile on his face. "Someone told us about a disused lumber camp in the Sierra Nevada mountains. It was in shambles, let me tell you. Old equipment here and there. Piles of scrap. The Buddha Hall—one of the old saw houses—you wouldn't have believed it. Kanzu and I spent half a day looking around. I saw oil drums that needed to be removed; I saw bunkhouses teeming with mice; I saw overgrown weeds and bushes and broken sidewalks. It needed so much work, I figured it wasn't worth it.

"Kanzu saw something else. After we'd completed our tour, we sat down with the realtor. The owner was looking to sell and would negotiate on the price. It all looked good on paper. Finally, Kanzu excused himself. He needed to be alone. I don't know exactly where he went. He never told me. For an hour, I sat with the real estate agent, drinking cold coffee, while Kanzu sat and, I am sure, meditated deeply. When he returned, he looked radiant. I knew before he opened his mouth. He later told me that a very powerful sensation had washed over him while he sat in silence, a rich sense of this spot's spiritual rightness. He knew, on some deep level, that this was where he should build a monastery, and that if he built it, it would last."

He placed his hands on his knees, as if bracing himself. His voice trembled as he spoke. "It was his life's work, founding Castle Rock. It was here that he trained Ansui, Hojun, Nanshin, Keido, and me—the monks who founded this order. We've all been here since the beginning. And it has been my job to continue that work, to keep this monastery running, and to further my master's wise aims and goals."

He paused a moment before adding, "And I have failed completely."

I looked directly at him. The smile on his face was outrageous. He was beaming, radiant with unmistakable joy.

"Do you know why I came to Mendocino?" I asked.

"I believe I do."

"I'm not going to apologize."

"Perhaps you shouldn't. Disruption can be a fruitful teacher."

"Spare me your poetry."

"Very well." He pushed at a dab of snow with the toe of his boot. "I'm prepared to hear whatever it is I need to hear from you. You may speak frankly."

I turned the prayer beads on my wrist. This was the moment I'd waited for, the moment I'd yearned for. All the speeches I'd rehearsed in my mind, all the invective, all the rage—it bubbled like a stew in my head, an incoherent mess.

"You're a fraud," I blurted out.

"If I have failed, I have failed on my own terms. The same is true for you."

"I don't claim to be in any position of authority or power."

He furrowed his brow. "Anyone wearing those robes is in a position of authority."

I buried my face in my hands. Every accusation I wanted to hurl at him seemed true of me, too. What was I to do? I knew I must relinquish my anger, at least a little. That would be a start.

I sat up and squared the corner of my robe, neatening a fold. "I know Alice left."

He nodded. "Her absence is most keenly felt."

"Will you be able to finish your book?"

He looked away. "I am reminded that there are other priorities, seeing to the health of this monastery chief among them."

Far across the monastery grounds, a heavy bell was rung three times, slowly. The low, sonorous chime hovered in the air about us, as if part of the sunlight.

"What else do I need to hear from you?" Eno asked.

"For weeks I've been planning to assail you with a screed," I said. "I wanted to denounce you, to call you out. But now, as we sit here face to face, I find that I can't say much of anything."

"And why do you think that is?"

"How can I speak? I am only a hypocrite." Just saying it felt like unfolding a fist.

"Tell me something, Kanshin. You journeyed to Mendocino to find something, and you most certainly did. To what did you return?"

A dollop of snow fell from the stupa to the ground, where it spread like a pristine stain. There, in the direct sunlight, it would melt and vanish very, very slowly.

"A barrier," I replied.

The Master raised his hands in full gassho, bowing at the waist, an ancient gesture of gratitude.

Tears rose in my eyes, rolling down my cheeks one after another. I didn't wipe them away. I just let them come. Eno sat quietly, his patience its own kind of testimony.

When I'd finished, he stood and held out his hand. "You too are a man in the weeds," he said. "Let us come out together."

I rose and took his hand, and together we left the stupa.

A FEW DAYS LATER, ENO CALLED an assembly of the order. Only the sworn monastics were invited. No novices or lay people were allowed. He gave a long, intimate talk that evening, sharing with us how the book project had grown and evolved. Alice Yu had started out as a kind of editorial consultant, but had slowly become more essential, guiding him through the process of seeking out agents and interested editors. They challenged him to reconfigure the book as a memoir, something more intimate and personal. Alice encouraged him, reading and commenting on his work. Gradually, through that process, they began to develop feelings for one another. He acknowledged that he'd let these feelings cloud his judgment, that he'd violated his monastic vows, and that he no longer felt capable of serving as abbot of Castle Rock. He was resigning, effective immediately.

But it was what he said next that shocked many of us: he was also disrobing, revoking his monastic vows. He and Alice had agreed to part ways. He would not be with her. He would re-enter lay life as a single man, Timothy Vonn.

This news stunned the sangha. Only later did it occur to me that he never mentioned my name, or my role in any of it, a gesture I could only regard as supremely generous.

Rev. Ansui became the next abbot of Castle Rock, formally accepting the duties she had, for many weeks now, been charged with. In this respect, the monastery handled the shift rather gracefully. On the surface, it would be hard to say that anything much had changed at all.

But things had changed. It is hard to explain what Eno's departure meant to me. I'd spent months in a misdirected state of anxiety, jealousy, and bitterness. For Eno to resign and disrobe, for him to transform himself so suddenly and so completely—I confess, the sudden absence of my object of interest, the focus of my obsession, my center of gravity… it left me directionless. I know it sounds absurd, but without Eno, who was Kanshin?

The answer frightened and disturbed me.

I continued on, trying to rediscover my purpose at Castle Rock. I spoke with senior monks. I eventually took a short leave of absence in an attempt to clear my head, staying at the San Francisco priory with no responsibilities other than to think things through. Really, Rev. Ansui could not have been more kind.

But nothing seemed to work. I'd lost the plot. I didn't know why I wore the robes. I had no true conviction.

Let me be clear: I didn't have a crisis of faith. I am still a Buddhist. I still meditate and study the dharma. I try to live my life in accordance with those teachings. What happened, specifically, was that I no longer understood why I was a monastic. I did not feel like a monastic. I felt like someone trying to convince himself to continue as a monastic. In the end, I decided to drop the charade.

Six months after Timothy Vonn left Castle Rock, I made my choice. Early on a Saturday morning, without fanfare, I was driven to the local bus station and that was it. I left, just as Vonn had left, with a suitcase and a small amount of money to get resettled. I heard he headed back to Berkeley, perhaps to complete the degree he'd walked away from when he became Eno. I took the bus to the only place I could think of, to visit the only person I knew who would take me in.

When I left Castle Rock, I was a wounded person. I worried I was making a colossal mistake. I felt like a quitter, a failure, a fool. I left behind a whole identity, a place in the world. I was terrified, but that was only because I was abandoning the certainty of the thing I knew, walking towards the unknown, desperately seeking something, or someone. And I found him, thank god I found him, my brother.

12

The sheriff came and ripped out the grow on Dennis's property, hauling the plants off to a storage facility (it's evidence). The lead deputy noted that this was the second time they'd been called to the property. Growers are always looking for isolated plots of land without a tenant, he reminded us. Unless something changed, we could probably count on it happening again.

Dennis and I spent several afternoons cleaning up after the sheriff. They took a lot of the big stuff, but the site was far from pristine. Trash was everywhere. Half-used bags of sod and plant food. Broken hoses and beat-up camp chairs. Used tires, which Tony Gomez had used as plant beds. An unbelievable amount of crap, and it all had to be hauled up the hill so we could lug it to the county dump. Dennis borrowed a trailer from a friend of his. I think we made four dump runs.

Over the next few weeks, Dennis and I took turns visiting the property. We tried to make an appearance once a week. When I went, I walked the whole thing, making sure no one was squatting or moving in. I sometimes brought a weed whacker to fight back the tall grass. And I started cleaning up the cottage. It was a great space, small and cozy. Spartan, but I liked it that way. Clean and simple. It had electricity. It had a well and an outhouse. It had a queen-sized bed, a table and chairs.

When I suggested to Dennis that I stay up there, he slapped his forehead. "Dude, we should have thought of this months ago." But then he paused. "You sure? It's pretty damn isolated."

He had a point. Fifteen minutes on narrow, winding roads out to the nearest town on State Route 9. Another half-hour into Santa Cruz. Once you're up on the land, you're alone. Like, really alone.

But, yes, I was ready to try it. We both knew I'd overstayed my welcome in the trailer.

Dennis gave me the green light to make improvements. I put in a gravity tank and an electric pump. Soon I had running water in the kitchen sink. I built a shower house with a solar-powered water heater. I got a small propane range, and a fridge. I put in a small garden with lettuce, tomatoes, and beans. I gave the entire cottage a proper cleaning, floor to ceiling. Then I painted the interior, a simple off-white.

The isolation did not bother me at all. It felt restorative and healthy. Ikkyu perhaps puts it best.

A Hermit Monk in the Mountains

I like it best when no one comes,
Preferring fallen leaves and swirling flowers
      for company.
Just an old Zen monk living as he should,
A withered plum tree suddenly sprouting a
      hundred blossoms.

Dennis couldn't believe it when he visited me a few weeks later.

"I thought you were going to give it a try. Looks like you've flat-out moved in!"

"I like it up here. So far."

He was glad to hear it. There'd be no more pot farmers camping out, leaving a mountain of trash. "You're not planning to put in a grow, are you?"

Moving up there was the best thing. My mind quieted and settled. I began to feel like I knew where I was, and why. Life got easier. Dennis didn't charge me rent. He considered the improvements, and the fact that he had a caretaker on the land, more than a fair trade. This allowed me to save my money. I bought a used pickup truck, a big improvement over the motorbike. Eventually, I quit waiting tables and got a full-time job at a bookstore in Santa Cruz, health benefits and all.

Dennis won his court case, clearing the inheritance from Laurel. Not long after, he moved into one of the cottages he'd inherited in Seabright. He was still renting the other one out, but it was mine if I ever wanted to come down off the hill. Not a chance. I was content on the property. Something about stepping outside in the morning, hearing the intense, pure stillness of the forest surrounding me was very powerful. On some mornings an ethereal, silver mist hung in the air. It was damp and chilly up there, but I knew I'd found the right spot for the time being. Even the drive became its own sort of ritual, as I left the bustling city behind and slowly peeled everything back.

Dennis came up for dinner one night. I made a simple meal, a mushroom stroganoff and a salad made from my garden. He was impressed with everything I'd done to upgrade the cottage. The land looked great. But he was still thinking about why Laurel had purchased the property in the first place: to make a pottery studio. She wanted to make art there. He still needed to honor that in some way. But, as we'd discussed, setting up a ceramic studio was out of the question. He poured himself another finger of whiskey. "I want to do something. I'm just not sure what."

I had an idea, something I'd been contemplating for several weeks, just waiting for the right opportunity to present itself.

"An artist's retreat," I suggested. We'd build some small cabins, maybe a dozen or so spread around the pasture. Studio space for painters and writers. A shared kitchen and dining area. Artists could come and stay for brief residencies—a month at a time. They'd have a cottage to sleep in, and a studio to work in. They could pay a small fee, or it could be totally free and subsidized. It would be rustic and quaint, but it would appeal to a certain kind of artist.

When I'd finished, Dennis nodded. "Like your friend."

I was touched that he remembered that part of my story, as painful as it was. "Alice Yu. She was my friend, yes. Once." (BTW, if you ever read Alice's novel *There is Nothing in This World*, the Mr. Bones character is based on yours truly. Not exactly flattered, but certainly I recognize the tribute.)

Dennis thought for a minute. "That might be the ticket," he said, growing excited. "That might work. That's pretty much what Laurel wanted." We talked a little bit more about it. He had a sizeable amount of cash at his disposal now, after the settlement. He might even consider selling the rental cottage, if necessary. But he had one condition. I would need to stay on as the caretaker of the property, at least in the initial stages. Only then would he feel comfortable moving forward.

I said I would.

"Hot damn!" he shouted, and we poured another round of whiskey. "A toast to Laurel!"

The retreat would become a modest success, attracting mostly young artists early in their careers, ceramicists and painters and writers. Dennis has a small endowment from which we pay out various stipends and awards. We advertise. At the end of each residency we host a reading and exhibition. We've started to draw a good crowd—artists, patrons, and buyers from Santa Cruz, Monterey, and even the Bay Area. I enjoy the work. During the first two years of my tenure as Resident Director, I composed the first draft of this memoir.

I can say I am content, for the time being, and I know enough about this world to be grateful for that.

WHEN A MONK RESIGNS, HIS ROBES are gathered and stored in a special cabinet. They are not destroyed or reassigned. They are not repurposed. They await the possible return of their owner, who may one day make the decision, again, to shave his head and take the vows once spoken by the Buddha.

Acknowledgments

Thanks to Linda Rogers, always my first reader and the one closest to my heart. Thanks to Henry Hughes for asking me to write a fishing story and helping me get the details right. Hearty thanks to Fred Arroyo, my brother in spirit, for many shared years of support, encouragement, and generous feedback. I'd also like to thank Karissa Chen, Kent Rooney, Emily Wang, and Darren Haughn, author of the blog The Salty Egg (thesaltyegg.net), for sharing details about their experiences in Taiwan.

Thanks to the Department of English and the College of Humanities and Fine Arts at California State University, Chico for their support of my creative endeavors.

I am deeply grateful to everyone at Cornerstone Press for their hard work on this book, including Dr. Ross Tangedal, Paige Beiver, Sam Bjork, Chloe Cieszynski, Gwen Goetter, Sophie McPherson, Eva Nielsen, Holly White, and Ava Willett.

Some of these stories were initially published by literary journals, sometimes in different form. "Unfinished Business" was first published in print and online at *Dappled Things*. "Packing Out" appeared online in *Men's Matters Online Journal*. "The Photograph" appeared online in *ArLiJo*, the Arlington Literary Journal.

Homage has always been an important aspect of my work. I thank David Quammen for the stories in *Blood Line: Stories of Fathers and Sons* (Graywolf, 1988), which partly inspired "Packing Out." Gina Berriault gave me the spark for "Searching for Florence" (vide *Women in Their Beds: Thirty-Five Stories*, Counterpoint, 2017). Lines of verse quoted in the story are adapted from Malcolm Lowry, *Under the Volcano*, J. B. Lippincott, 1947.

I quote a few lines from "La Mort," music and French lyrics by Jacques Brel, English lyrics by Mort Shuman and Eric Blau, Warner Chappell France.

Quoted material in "Welcome Back to the World" is drawn from: *The Blue Cliff Record: Volume One.* Translated by Thomas and J.C. Cleary (Shambhala, 1977); *Dhammapada: The Sayings of the Buddha.* Translated by Thomas Byrom (Shambhala, 1993); Ikkyu, *Wild Ways: Zen Poems.* Translated by John Stevens (White Pine Press, 2003); Michel de Montaigne, "Of Books." *The Art of the Personal Essay: An Anthology from the Classical Era to the Present.* Ed. Phillip Lopate (Anchor, 1994).

Rob Davidson is the author of four previous fiction collections: *What Some Would Call Lies* (2018), *Spectators* (2017), *The Farther Shore* (2012), and *Field Observations* (2001). His work has appeared in *ZYZZYVA, Hayden's Ferry Review, Indiana Review, The Normal School, New Delta Review,* and elsewhere. He teaches creative writing and American literature at California State University, Chico.